Charlene,

Kentucky Miracles

Sagebrush Ranch Series, Book Three

by Marlene Worrall

Blessings & Love

Marlene Worrall

Published by Forget Me Not Romances, a division of
Winged Publications
Copyright 2018 Marlene Worrall

This book is a work of fiction. Names, characters,
places, and incidents are either products of the author's
imagination or used fictitiously. Any similarity to actual
people, organizations, and/or events is purely
coincidental.

ISBN-13: 978-1-947523-20-3
ISBN-10: 1-947523-20-1

Dedication

To the glory of God for the gift and joy of writing!
Praise His holy name!

Acknowledgements

For the brilliant, remarkable Cynthia Hickey. I'm not sure she ever sleeps!

May God rain down his richest blessings and joy upon her and her family.

.

Chapter One

Dana rose before the sun came up. Two months from now, on the first Saturday in May, the world-famous Kentucky Derby would take place. She could barely contain her excitement. She glanced over at Graham. He slept soundly. She took a quick shower, grabbing breakfast on the run. She'd prepared hard boiled eggs the night before to save time in the morning. It was 4:00 a.m.

She scrawled a note to Graham, leaving it on the kitchen table. Jumping into her white SUV, she drove to the track, where she would meet the exercise rider, which today was Jacob, the jockey for Firelight Fancy. Graham and the ranch hands would take good care of the horses in her absence.

Firelight Fancy had taken first place in the Preakness Race just three days ago. His health issues were behind them. It was full speed ahead. Jacob was poised and ready to excel and take the purse at the upcoming Derby. *God is on our side. We're bound to win.* He grinned savoring the triumph he prayed would soon be theirs. Daily, he was faithful to commit the colt, training and the upcoming race to the Lord. *With God all things are possible* was his mantra.

At the track, Jacob mounted the colt, doing a fast warm-up. In twenty minutes, he would race Firelight Fancy against another colt, prepping for the big day. He needed to make sure the colt was used to dirt flying in his face, as well as being accustomed to competing. Jacob practiced getting the colt out the gate when the starter called the start of the Kentucky Derby. That was a crucial aspect of prepping him for the big race. He sensed the colt was fast moving into a competitive racing spirit that would hopefully take them to the victory they'd been praying and dreaming about since acquiring the colt. The countdown was on. Fifty-seven days until the world-famous Kentucky Derby.

Jacob was in his glory. He was born for this. He believed victory was ahead. He was counting on it. He'd been enthralled with the equines ever since he could remember. Aunt Ginny had raised him on her farm and encouraged him to go for his dream. She'd been a remarkable woman, running the farm solo after his uncle had died. He'd lost both his folks in a freak highway accident and she'd raised him from when he was...as she was fond of saying "Knee high to a grasshopper." Blaze had been his favorite colt at her farm, but he'd ridden the other horses there as well. The old house still stood. During his years there, growing up, it looked as though a heavy gust of wind could blow it over...it still looked that way. But somehow, God had seen to it that the house remained intact. He'd never married. He took care of Aunt Ginny now, the way she'd looked after him in his youth. God was good, and he never ceased to marvel at the extra-ordinary ways he turned everything to the good for those who loved Him. Aunt Ginny had taught him to stay in the Word like she did. He'd been only four or five when she'd started saying things like: *"Seek Him while he may be found." "In all your ways acknowledge Him, and he shall direct your paths."* Because of her loving guidance, he was grounded in the Word.

The old tumbledown shack brimmed with paintings and plaques, depicting the simple, godly life of those ardent followers of the Lord. He'd always believed that he was destined to be the jockey for a Kentucky Derby winning colt. Then, he would fulfill his dream of building a new house for himself and Aunt Ginny. God's Word assured him that He would bestow blessing and prosperity upon his faithful followers.

He had long admired the famous portrait of the old man seated at a table, head bowed in prayer as he gave thanks to the Lord for the loaf of bread and butter sitting on the table; along with his open Bible. He, too, gave thanks in everything like Aunt Ginny had taught him.

The competing colt won the race this morning. Jacob was disappointed but he gave his head a shake. *If it was easy, everybody would be doing it. Training a colt and competing for the Derby is a formidable challenge. I'm equal to the task, Lord. And so is Dana.* He dismounted, soon shaking the hand of Tony Starr, his winning competitor. "Nice work, Tony. Thanks for the race." Jacob grinned. He loved the camaraderie that existed between the jockeys.

Tony grinned, pleased. Soon he remounted the colt and rode him back to the barn.

Dana wasn't feeling well today. Her tummy felt queasy and she wasn't nearly as focused on the training as she usually was. *Must have been that spicy, Mexican food we had last night.*

But the next morning, Dana threw up after breakfast. *Was she pregnant?* Instantly, some scriptures popped into her mind. They were about children being a blessing from the Lord. Stunned, she immediately phoned her doctor, requesting an appointment and tests.

Dr. Milla Sikonas confirmed positive test results. "Congratulations, Dana. You and Graham are going to have a baby."

Dana sat in the chair at the doctor's office in a state of shock. Her former doctor had told her she could never have children. She'd accepted that as gospel. But now she was pregnant. A deep well of joy bubbled up inside her. *Lord, you are so good. You are a great and mighty God. And there is none like you.* Joy bubbled up inside her.

"I'm...really...actually... pregnant." She jumped up from the chair, hugging Dr. Sikonas and twirling her around. "Yippy. It's been one of my ...secret dreams for ages...one of the desires of my heart." Her face was lit with a beaming smile. "I think I'll pick up a bottle of good champagne, put it on ice...and maybe ask Violet to make something special for dinner...and then I'll make the announcement to Graham." She was over the moon. This was really, really amazing. *God was amazing.* A scripture popped into her mind. *"Nothing is impossible with God."*

Graham sat in his den, his nose buried in paper work, when Dana burst into his private space. She felt like the cat that swallowed the canary. She peered at Graham, her heart bursting with joy.

"What's goin' on Dana? Something good just happen?"

She flashed him a huge smile, peering into his cobalt blue eyes. She paused for effect. She'd always used the dramatic pause to emphasize a point. Danielle had taken her to numerous theatre productions when she was a child. She'd always been fascinated by actors and the theatre, picking up a few tricks along the way.

"Yes, Dana?"

"Graham...Sweetheart..."

"Yes, Dana...what is it? Spit it out." He peered over at her from his chair across from his Louis .6th desk, a touch of irritation playing across his features.

"Honey, I'm pregnant." Smiling, she threw her arms around him in a display of jubilation.

"Come on..."It was several minutes before he was able to form words from his gaping mouth. "I...I thought you said you couldn't have children..."

"Well, ya...like that's what I thought. That's what my previous doctor told me. But Dr. Sikonas has just confirmed that I'm with child." She smirked. "I have champagne cooling on ice. Follow me, Da Da."

4

He did as instructed.

In the colossal country kitchen, Dana popped the champagne cork and poured the bubbly into three champagne flutes. She served Graham and Violet and then herself. "To our beautiful, new baby." Dana's eyes brimmed with tears of joy. "My heart can barely hold more joy."

"To you and Graham and the baby." Violet raised her flute, overjoyed. She beamed as the three of them clinked glasses. She took a healthy sip of the bubbly. "Very nice." Champagne had always been Violet's favorite wine.

Will showed up as though he had peripheral hearing. He saw the celebration. "Are y'all celebrating something?"

"Dana is going to have a baby." Graham's face beamed. "We're going to have a baby." He corrected himself.

Will was stunned and struck silent for a few beats. Soon, he found his voice. "Wow. Cool."

A sour expression changed his countenance. "Like…does this mean we have to baby-sit?"

Graham chuckled. "We'll cross that bridge when we come to it. Right now, we're just adjusting to the idea ourselves."

"Just as long as you don't fill *all* the upstairs bedrooms with kids." Violet loved to tease. Her eyes twinkled as she glanced from Graham to Dana, sipping her champagne.

"Ya, Dad. Like we're running a horse farm here... not a kid's farm." Will smirked.

Jay showed up in the kitchen. He headed toward the fridge but stopped when he saw the celebration. "Hey, what's goin' on?"

Graham smirked. "We're going to have a baby."

Jay was stunned speechless. "A baby? Really?" He said it like maybe she was going to have a cow.

"It's been known to happen, Jay." He winked at his son.

Jay was silent a few beats and then grinned. "Cool. Very cool." He paused. "What are you going to name the baby?"

Jay peered over at Dana and Graham, trying to adjust to the idea.

"I have no idea." Dana's smile was radiant. "I think maybe it will depend on whether it's a boy or a girl." She winked at him.

It was a cool, overcast day. Everyone lounged around the vast living room sipping champagne. Violet served caviar and crackers to go with it.

Dana glanced out the long bank of windows facing the veranda from the living room at the front of the house, rays of late afternoon sunshine flickered as though waiting in the wings for a signal to show up on the horizon to endorse the happy occasion. *"We'll have a lifetime to share...so many ways..."* Dana suddenly began to sing and dance around the house, overjoyed. "A child...a child...I'm about to have a child..." She could hardly believe the sea of emotions sweeping over her. She could not contain her joy.

Graham stood and twirled her around. Suddenly, they were dancing, the kids had gone off to their rooms or somewhere in the house and Violet had sneakily put on romantic music and tactfully vanished. It was their special, private moment of bliss; the celebration of one of one of God's greatest blessings in life — a baby.

That night Dana was overcome with emotion. She sobbed in Graham's arms. "Oh honey, I can hardly believe I'm...we're...going to have a baby."

Dana was surprised how quickly her body chemistry changed. Though it had only been a month, she was already rejecting some foods and craving others. Her doctor had said that would happen in a couple months, but it had happened sooner. She craved rare and exotic foods, along with ice cream, etc., etc. Her interest and focus in the upcoming Derby waned. She became plump. Overnight, it seemed.

Graham teased her when he found her sitting at the kitchen table in the middle of the night, gorging on chocolate ice cream and chocolate cookies.

Tears sprung to her eyes. "How can you be so cruel, Graham? A baby is growing inside me. I have no control over what she...or he...wants to eat. I can't help it. This thing is bigger than both of us...having a baby is the most incredible experience a woman ever goes through...other than the bliss of intimacy, of course." She smiled at Graham.

"Of course. Well, I'm just sayin' Dana... that you should try to...well...to take it easy. Slow down a little."

"Like I can control this, Graham? I wish I could."

"Of course you can, honey. Just take it easy. You don't have to give in to every craving, you know."

"Really? That's not how I heard it."

"How did you hear it?"

"Never mind."

Chapter Two

Danielle was incarcerated. She'd pleaded insanity but it hadn't washed. Despite the fact that the sheriff did not have concrete evidence of her role in Dana's kidnapping, the judge ruled that there was enough evidence against her to convict her of conspiracy. She was sentenced to four years at Kentucky Correctional Facility.

She felt wretched. *I was made for better things than this. I have a great capacity for learning and accomplishing things. Somehow, I have to get out of here...get my attorney to appeal the decision. Something.* But even as the thoughts crossed her mind, waves of sadness washed over her. *She was back in prison. Back to the exact hole she swore she would never again look upon.* "Lord, where are you?" It was a cry born from unspeakable desperation; a cry from the depths of her soul. She'd have to break out. There was no way she could survive four years in this dungeon.

The correctional officer, a tired, beefy, older woman with a nasty disposition led her down a long, dreary corridor with cells on either side.

Forlorn, lost women, holding the grey steel bars enclosing them, stared at them as they strode down the corridor. *No, God... I can't do this.*

The officer stopped at one of the tiny cells. She pulled out a key and opened the door.

Danielle peered around at the small cubicle with mounting horror. A beefy, hostile blond woman was lying on the upper bunk bed. She stared at Dana, a sullen expression on her face.

Oh nice. I've got a real charmer for a cell mate. I'd better make the best of it. If I'm going to be her roommate, I might as well make up my mind to get along with her. One glance told her that would be no easy task.

"Annie Jackson, say hello to your new cell mate, Danielle Lockhart."

Annie glared at her from the top bunk bed. A scowl formed on her plump lips. "Welcome to Paradise. You're gonna love it here."

The biting sarcasm wasn't what she had expected. *Never show fear. Never allow anyone to intimidate you.* She ignored the caustic remark and the overwhelming feeling of futility welling up inside her. Forelorn, she plopped down on the lower bunk.

She was quickly incorporated into a routine of working, cleaning, etc. *This is not a fun place to be. How soon can I get out of here?*

The correctional officer checked on her as she struggled through the drudgery she'd been assigned. Cleaning toilets was a rude awakening to the harsh realities that awaited her in this hole. The officer peered at her and checked on her progress. She was cold. Devoid of all feeling and humor it seemed to Danielle. There was not even a trace of sympathy. The matronly looking woman peered at her. "You'll get used to it here. First couple of weeks are the toughest...after that...piece of cake."

Wow. The warden is human after all.

At dinner, Danielle was seated at a long table with the other female inmates, slopping down tasteless hamburger, soggy vegetables and soft, cheap bread. *She had to get out of here. She felt like she couldn't breathe.*

"New here, ain't ya?" A giant woman looked her over and smirked.

"Yeah."A shiver ran through her. She scowled.

"I'm a lifer. Bin here seven years so far..." She stared at Danielle, an odd expression on her face. "I remember you from the last time you waz here." She nodded, a strange, knowing expression flashing over her features.

"So...why did ya come back to this God-forsaken hole?" Her eyes swept over Danielle. Then she stared at her, an odd, unreadable expression reflected on her features.

"What difference does it make? I'm here. That's it."

"No need to get snarky. Ah'm jest tryin' to make you feel okay about bein' here."

Danielle realized she'd better get off her high horse. A little humility might be in order ."I'll tell you later. Right now...I'm just adjusting to...everything."

"I bet yer bein' here has to with that daughter 'o yers...that horsewoman. Dana isn't it?" She smirked, showing several missing teeth.

Danielle saw red. She had the urge to slug the woman. She restrained herself, instead shooting her a look of disdain. She remained silent.

Two buxom female correctional officers stood nearby, watching the women like hawks. The heftier of the two stared at Danielle as though she could read her mind. She lumbered over to her. "Take it easy. It's gonna take some time to adjust to everything...and everyone around this place." Her eyes travelled over Danielle, assessing her. "Better finish dinner before it gets cold."

Danielle watched the hefty, uniformed women strut off after a little while. She leaned over to Norma, speaking almost in a whisper. "Well...isn't that something? A little niceness."

"Ya. Ever since Billie started here, riots and fights have decreased. She's one of them... Christian women, you know...preaches on Sundays. You should check it out. She's really somethin'.'"She raised her eyebrows, nodding. "Lot of hard-core woman been converted since she showed up here." She grinned. "Maybe yer gonna be next." Her eyes swept over Danielle, taking her in. She shot her an odd look.

"How long has she been here?" Danielle peered at the women.

"Like...maybe about a year... I guess." She shrugged, soon taking the last sip of her coffee and staring into the empty cup. "Don't know why they can't give us a second cup of that lousy coffee..." She shook her head in disgust.

"The lack of perks goes with the territory, I guess." Danielle shrugged. *Lord, how am I going to survive four years of this?*

Danielle lay awake the entire night. She could hear her roommate snoring and making other weird sounds, like a whistling noise. Her cot was thin and uncomfortable, no matter which way she turned, she couldn't get comfortable. The air was heavy and stale. *Lord, please let me get some sleep. Help me to adjust to this dreadful hole."* She knew she had to take one minute at a time, one hour, one day and one night at a time. If she did that, maybe somehow she would make it through the bleak days and lonely nights stretching ahead, and survive until the glorious day of her release.

The following evening, Danielle sat at the long table trying to eat the slop they were given, after waiting in a long line to receive it. It was a tasteless stew with that same, soft, cheap bread she despised. *Lord, I've got to get out of here. How can I get out of here?* She knew the correctional institute was surrounded by acreage, though she didn't know how many acres. She also knew it was about seven miles from Lexington.

It was Sunday morning. She decided to check out the worship service. The bulletin board said it started at 10:00 a.m. She showed up early, taking a seat in the front row. Sure enough, Barbara, the warden that had cut her some slack when she'd first arrived, stood in the front of the podium in the small chapel. Singing with great joy, she led the small group in old gospel tunes starting with *Amazing Grace.*

Danielle was touched by the beauty and simplicity of the service. "This is the day that the Lord has made. I will rejoice and be glad in it." *Lord, I see that you have purpose in the pain. Maybe this whole exercise is about causing me to be totally dependent on you. Is that what this is about, Lord?*

The message was simple and profound. Accept your circumstances. Worship God with your whole heart. Seek Him, and you will find a purpose in your pain. That purpose for starters, Barbara said, was to draw close to Him and rest in Him.

When Danielle walked out of the service with the other inmates, she was inspired to spend time reading the Bible. She went directly to the library and began scouring the shelves for inspirational books. Bibles were free and available. She took one. *Lord, how did I get it so wrong? How did I go down the wrong road?* How had she sunk so low that she'd wound up in this vile place?

Back in her cage, she prayed silently, asking God for forgiveness and mercy. Only He knew her heart. Only He understood her sorrow and what had driven her to behave as she had. Dana had been her whole life and she hadn't wanted to lose her — not even to marriage. They 'd been confidants, best buddies. But she'd allowed her jealousy to propel her into wicked deeds. Now, they were estranged, and Graham was protecting Dana from her. She was alone. She regretted giving up so much to help Dana achieve her equestrian goals. Though at the time, it had seemed like the right decision. And that's why she'd felt justified in kidnapping her for the ransom money. Because she had poured her whole life and the money she had, into grooming Dana for jumping and then training horses. And suddenly, she was left out in the cold. And her finances had taken a tumble.

She'd been convicted of a lesser charge because there had not been concrete evidence that she had masterminded Dana's kidnapping. Still, she knew that the word on the street was that she had set it all up. She'd been convicted of the lesser charge, conspiracy to commit a crime, in the absence of solid evidence. She'd underestimated the sheriff. Still, the evidence had been thin at best. The judge had sentenced her to four years with the possibility of parole in three years.

SIX MONTHS LATER

Danielle had grudgingly settled into the wretched routine of incarceration. At night, tossing restlessly on her cot, she replayed the events that had culminated in her winding up here.

She awakened suddenly, in the wee hours of the morning, struck with a brilliant idea to escape. She sat bolt upright in bed as the idea soared through her brain. She would need to go solo, of course. She couldn't trust anyone here.

She knew the service trucks showed up once a week. Of course they were carefully watched with guards, but that was still her best shot. If she could use her beauty and sex appeal to distract one of the drivers, maybe she could hop in the back of the truck and simply jump out first chance she got. But how would she know where the driver was going? And, more importantly, how would she have the chance to access the truck? Also, they would spot her when they unloaded the truck. It was a lame idea.

Then it struck her. She would buddy up to Barbara and get into the church thing, keep her nose in the Bible, continue to sit in the front pew of the chapel and somehow come up with a better plan. The warden had mentioned that a couple of guest musicians were scheduled to visit the jail a couple weeks from now. Maybe she could sneak out with them somehow.

Nah. That wouldn't fly. It was going to take time to cook up a plan that would be solid. And that's one thing she had.

Time. The clock seemed to tick in slow motion, the days dragging by, one blurring into the next. *She didn't belong here. She had to get out. Each day the obsession to break out accelerated.*

Chapter Three

Dana couldn't believe the bad timing. She had
to deal with morning sickness just when the intense part of
training the colt was accelerating; and the Derby was just
over a month away. Still, God was in control and she relied
on him. If they were destined to win the purse, it would
happen. She had to have faith and believe that all things
worked together for good for those who loved the Lord,
according to scripture.

Dana had read about her Mom's incarceration, of course.
Graham had forbidden her to visit her. They'd both heard
rumblings about Danielle's possible involvement with her
kidnapping. No concrete evidence had been amassed.
Though she'd heard rumors about the conspiracy theory,
Dana chose to believe they were vicious rumors. Graham
thought otherwise. She acknowledged, though, that her Mom
knew some shady characters. She'd chalked it up to poor
character judgement on Danielle's part.

She pulled herself together and drove to the track.
Having called Jacob earlier, she knew he was already there,
working the colt. Another race was scheduled for 2:00 today.
She prayed that their colt, Firelight Fancy, would win. If he
could get enough wins under his belt before the derby, he
would start to feel invincible and hopefully soar to the head
of the pack on the big day.

AT THE TRACK

Jacob soared down the track goading Firelight Fancy to accelerate. Horse and rider were one. The connection was that powerful. Jacob felt the power under him. *This colt is a winner. I just know it.*

Dana looked on, praying fervently and watching them closely, looking for any weakness, any flaw that could be improved upon before the Kentucky Derby took place.

THE ESCAPE

Danielle couldn't stand being locked up a minute longer. She would go bonkers if she stayed here. She felt claustrophobic, depressed, enraged. Like a cougar locked in a cage. Cougars didn't belong there and neither did she.

She hatched a plan. She'd wait until the outdoor activities were well underway tomorrow. Since she was in a minimum security women's correctional institution, rather than a regular prison, there was a relative amount of freedom when the women played basketball and other outdoor sports. She despised all the sports, mostly because she was forced to participate. She made a valiant effort to become involved, though, knowing that pleased the warden.

Danielle was a lousy basketball player but she gave it her best shot, determined to participate, regardless. She waited until near the end of one of the games, when most participants were tired and keen to get back inside where they could at least relax. Most of the women were overweight and out of breath. Some sat on benches, catching their breath after participating in sports.

She saw her opportunity. "I'm going to use the Ladies' room," she told the warden," as she began walking in that direction.

"Okay. I'll go with you." The warden gazed at her, catching up with her.

Darn She headed for the Ladies room, picked a stall and went inside. Soon, she flushed the toilet and came back out. She would have to carefully research the movements of the warden and her associates, before making her move. Walking off the low security grounds should be a cinch. But she would have to do it when the group disbursed, heading back inside. She'd move to the end of the line forming to go inside, duck behind the small clump of shrubs at the edge of the property and then race off to freedom. She'd have to keep her wits about her and move with lightening speed once she got off the property. She might be caught on tape. Still, she would chance it. She wasn't sure if security cameras were in place or not. She hadn't heard of anyone successfully escaping. She'd overhead a couple of inmates at dinner one night. They were speaking in hushed tones, but somehow she caught the gist of it. Security cameras here were not comprehensive. Rumor had it that they would soon be updated. That's when she knew she had to make her move. Now.

Once she got on the outside, she knew she'd have to jog up to the highway and continue for the seven miles to Lexington, unless she got lucky hitch-hiking. The thought of that unnerved her, but it was the lesser of the evils. Having the sheriff pick her up and haul her back here was a frightening thought. She knew there was dense forest for miles on either side of the institution. She'd seen it when they'd driven her here. She could duck into the forest when a car approached; or try thumbing a ride.

If she could get to Lexington without being picked up by the sheriff, she'd have a good shot at surviving on the outside. If she made it, perhaps she would board a plane to Mexico City, change her name and get lost in the crowd. When the heat was off, she could work in an orphanage. She would need cash right away. That was the first problem.

A month later

Danielle observed the warden and her associate very carefully. She watched where they stood, walked, everything they did. It was all computed. She also carefully observed the inmates, watched their every move, being careful to fit in and follow the rules.

Breaking out of a minimum security prison was a challenge, and she thrived on challenges. . While the other inmates went along with the regiment, she scrutinized everybody, especially the warden and her associates. Most of the inmates took whatever was handed to them. Not her. She was a fighter, a survivor. No way was she going to rot in a cage for the trumped-up charges that put her here. That stupid attorney she'd hired had goofed. He should have gotten her off. Now it was up to her to snatch her freedom back. That was a status she deserved. Maybe being incarcerated was the best thing to happen to her. At least now she would have to end her obsession with trying to win Graham's affections. And maybe that was a Godsend.

She waited until the warden was chatting with one of the inmates. She observed the warden's eyes peering around, checking that everything was in order. The conversation became intense. *Now. Go. Go. Go.* One last glance around as roughly fifty or sixty women mingled on the fields, engrossed in a variety of sports, including Bocce Ball and Basketball.

She made her move.

Slipping behind a small cluster of trees nearby, she believed she was undetected. She took a deep breath. The first step was done. Next, she quickly opened the low gate and vanished. She had her alibi ready, in case she was caught in action. "I wasn't feeling well. I felt like throwing up. I didn't think I could make it to the bathroom...so I moved away from the others..." She doubted she'd be believed if it came to that, but she'd try anyway.

God was on her side, she hoped. Even if what she was doing was wrong. Somehow, she'd slipped past a cluster of women, muttering about feeling sick and having to throw up. A few of them scattered because of it. Soon, she'd vanished off their radar.

Freedom. Sweet, glorious freedom. It never tasted better. The wind on her face was cool. It mirrored the cool, desolate feeling that swept through her soul. *Please God, don't let me get caught.* She knew she had no right to ask Him for any favors, but that didn't stop her. Nothing and no one ever stopped her, once she'd made up her mind to take a particular action. She ran as fast as she could and kept running, praying fervently she would not be detected. She knew they did a head count after the women were herded inside, after the outdoor sports period; though she'd noticed it wasn't always thorough.

Time was of the essence. Once she was discovered missing, authorities would of course notify the sheriff. She wasn't sure how fast road blocks could be implemented or how fast a police car could pick her up. She had to move like lightening if she was to avert being hauled back by prison authorities.

She knew the highway was seven miles up the road. It was heavily treed on either side of the road. *If a car approaches, I'll duck into the woods, until it passes. She was glad she was fit and strong. She could power walk or run for miles.* Hitchhiking was dangerous but it was the only option available. *Lord, please send your angels to watch over me.*

She would likely be discovered missing once the women were inside and the head count implemented. Or someone might have seen her, or the lookout tower might have spotted her. The sheriff could already be on her trail. She had to get off their radar. Fast.

Hitch hiking was her best chance of survival. It was dangerous, of course, but jogging down the road, not knowing when the police might catch up with her was crazy. She calculated the worst-case scenario: If her disappearance was noticed right away and the sheriff was dispatched, they would easily be able to figure how far she would likely have gotten on foot. If she hid in the forest and spent the night there, the prison officials might figure that out and show up with their bloodhounds, tracking her down. Hitching a ride with a trucker was her best option.

Pray. That's all she could do. *Lord, I don't know if you're still talking to me, but...if you are, I just want to say that...I'm sorry. I'm sorry for my past sins and I want to start again. I know I don't deserve a fresh start or my freedom; but Lord, I feel desperate to be free again. I have a passion for life. And...Lord, there's something I want to do, something I need to do. I want to contribute to society and work in an orphanage. I need to find my passion and follow it.* Tears streamed down her faced. *"I've wasted so many years."*

"My precious, precious child, I love you so very much. More than you could ever possibly imagine. I created you. I know your life from beginning to end..."

God *was* still talking to her. He knew what her hidden passion was. She'd wanted to open an orphanage ever since she could remember, but she'd been bitten by the greed bug and had opened up a couple of businesses, instead. They'd thrived for a while, but ultimately had failed. As much as she hated to admit it, her ex nailed it when he'd labelled her a failed businesswoman. In retrospect, she knew why that was. It was because her god had been money. So God had to allow her to go through the exercise. But she had not been blessed in business. That was not her assignment. She knew he wanted her to get that and seek the One who loved her and could help her fulfill her assignment on planet earth. She'd sought money and success with the fervency that should have been used to seek God Almighty. She'd had to file for bankruptcy. She took solace in the fact that when God closed one door, he opened another. *Was He about to open a new door now?* She was counting on it.

She kept glancing back, looking for vehicles, while praying fervently for a good guy to pick her up. A long-distance truck driver in a massive truck slowed down and pulled over to the curb. A rugged, big guy with a weathered face and stern countenance leaned toward her. "Hop in, lady. Hurry up."

Here goes, Lord.

He kept his eyes on the road, barely acknowledging her. After he'd driven a few miles, he glanced over at her. "Where you headed?"

Good question. I wish I knew. "I'm ah...I'm headed to Lexington."

"Okay."

"You can drop me off downtown Lexington, if you would. I'm going into a church to pray."

He flashed a quick glance her way, but remained silent. He just kept on driving. Neither of them spoke. He stopped in front of an old church downtown. "Good luck, lady. It must have taken a lot of courage to walk out of that women's prison." His eyes glimmered, a cheeky grin playing across his lips.

He knew this whole time and never said a word. Surely you sent him to me, Lord. "That's one thing I've never been lacking."

"You better take this." He handed her a couple of twenty-dollar bills.

"God bless you. Thank-you so much." She leaned across lightning quick and kissed his cheek before jumping out. *So far, so good.*

She hurried up the old stone steps to the quaint church in downtown Lexington. Forgive me, *Lord. You are a great and mighty God. If you'll help me survive this escape and not get caught, I will serve you the rest of my days.*

She shivered at the thought of getting caught and hauled back to prison. They would doubtless add more time onto her sentence, if that occurred. She had to remain free. She knew it would mean watching her back and doing as much as she could under cover of darkness. *How quickly God forgave sins. Did she forgive others as quickly? She would make sure of it in the future.*

On her knees, she sought the Lord for comfort, praising him for allowing her to escape the sordid life at the women's correctional facility. He had great and awesome things in store for her. She was sure of it. She would walk into her destiny. Maybe in the future, if she did enough charity work, and contributed enough to society, she would receive a pardon from the president. She knew it was rare; but nothing was impossible with God.

She prayed fervently for some time. Soon, she sensed the Holy Spirit chastising her for breaking rules and escaping. But she also felt God showing her that he knew she had learned her lesson about the pursuit of money and putting it before God. Silently, she prayed. *Lord, I'm sorry about my obsession to attract Graham. I repent of that and my jealousy toward my step-daughter, Dana. I am deeply sorry, Lord. Please give me another chance with them. I'm sorry...I stooped so low and masterminded Dana's kidnapping. Please forgive me and give me another chance with them and everything else.*

She wept bitterly. The terror and shock of being on the run was a formidable challenge, but if God was on her side, she would make it. She felt the gentle whisper of God. *You are about to move into the purpose for which I created you.*

"Lord, you are a great and mighty God. I will devote myself to serving you and helping others. I know what I did was wrong, but please have mercy on me." She wept, but soon rose. She needed to move to a safer place. She glanced around the small church. A smattering of folks knelt, praying.

Chapter Four

Dana and Graham watched the evening news in the family room. An all-points bulletin had been issued. An escaped women prisoner..."

Suddenly, Dana was on high alert. Horrified, she listened, as the newscaster described her mother and the prison break. "Police are on the lookout for a woman who escaped the minimum-security correctional institution in Lexington, late this afternoon. The escapee is identified as Danielle Lockhart..."

"The Women's Correctional Institution in Lexington reported that she was first noticed missing shortly after outside recreational activities took place late this afternoon. The escapee is approximately five feet, six inches and weighs about one hundred and thirty pounds. She has short blonde hair and was last seen wearing a grey uniform. It is uncertain what the escapee is wearing at this time. Authorities believe she may be in the vicinity, possibly in the downtown area. She is considered not dangerous. And it is believed she is not armed. However, if the suspect is approached or apprehended, authorities are uncertain as to how she might react. She was undergoing a rehabilitation process at the time of her disappearance, and previously spent a brief stint in the psyche ward at Lexington University hospital before her recent incarceration. Authorities say she has a flair for donning wigs and costumes and is known to be theatrical and speak with foreign or Southern accents. She might have significantly altered her appearance and personality, making it difficult to spot her."

Graham and Dana looked at each other in horror. "What is she up to now? She bought that little cottage...I really thought she was going to settle down, go to church, maybe eventually meet a nice man..."

"Dana. I don't know who you're talking about; but it's not Danielle. Surely you've figured out by now that the woman is a chameleon. She moves from one charade to another. I don't have her all figured out, either. We need to commit her to the Lord and get on with our lives. That's all we can do, really."

Dana burst into tears. She'd become incredibly emotional since becoming pregnant. So much had happened. "Graham, I'm headed out to the track, tomorrow morning. Firelight Fancy has another race. And I want to work with him as much as I can. I think we've got a winner this time."

"So do I, honey." He thrust comforting arms around her. "That's my girl. We need to move forward."

Out at the track the next morning, Dana liked what she saw. Jacob soared down the track, egging the colt on. He finished second. The competing colt was only a head in front, but their colt hadn't won. *Lord, let him win tomorrow.*

"You know, for the first time since we started working with Firelight Fancy, I think we've got a really good chance at winning the roses...honestly, I think we're going to do it this time. I think we're going to take the purse, Jacob." Tears of joy welled up in her eyes. "It may have been a blessing in disguise. We don't want the colt to think he's invincible. He needs to keep competing hard."

"We'll make it." Jacob smiled at Dana.

"We'll keep on keeping on. We'll keep praying, working hard...and pressing forward; and maybe...just maybe, God will step in and we will have the victory."

Danielle couldn't believe her luck. They were having a sale in the church basement. In a flash, she snapped up a pair of jeans and a ragged black sweater. She slipped into the ladies' room and put on the jeans and sweater. She wanted to blend in with folks as much as possible. She hurried out of the church and down the street, peering nervously around. She was headed for the movie theatre. It would be a great place to hang out while she plotted her next move. She'd bought a blue baseball cap at the sale for a dollar, also. That would hide her hair and mask her face somewhat.

She'd been happily surprised when the truck driver pressed the bills into her hand. "You're gonna need this, darlin'" He grinned. "I didn't see nothin' if anybody asks. Good luck, honey. You're a nice lookin' woman." She'd smiled at him. *Thanks Mister.* Her ID was still in the prison. It would take time for her to get fake ID and embark on the journey she had in mind. *If I can just stay off the radar of the authorities for a few days, I can cook up a way of getting some cash to buy fake ID and a plane ticket. Then she could slip onto a flight heading for Mexico. She intended to work in an orphanage, with the goal of running one. She'd had that dream since she was young. But it had been stuck on the back burner when she'd become a horse enthusiast, helping her late son Stephan and Dana become equestrians. Now it was her turn to fulfill her own destiny. She could hardly wait.*

She hurried to the nearest bus stop in hopes of borrowing a cell phone. She couldn't hang around for long. A young guy with long hair sat on the bench, smoking a joint. "I'll give you two bucks if I can borrow your cell for one quick call?"

He looked her over. Then put his hand out for cash. "Yeah, okay. Make it short."

She gave him the two bucks. Thanks to her photographic memory, Pete's phone number flashed into her mind. He picked up on the third ring. "Hey Pete. It's me, your old buddy…"

"Danielle?"

"One and the same. How about picking me up…" She told him to meet her at the theatre. Once there, she could maybe borrow another cell phone and tell him exactly where she was.

She blended in with the street crowd. She didn't totally trust Pete, but he was the only person she knew that might give her some cash, since he owed her some and had a soft spot for her. She was fairly certain he wouldn't squeal. That was unspoken street code. They had some history. He wouldn't want to be in her bad books, either. She watched for his car, saw it and hurried over to it.

She jumped into his old black Mercedes, breathing a sigh of relief. "You sure get around, Danielle. They should write a movie about you. You're full of surprises."

"On my epitaph I want it to read *She made a lot of mistakes, but she lived life to the fullest. Never gave two hoots about what other people thought or said and fulfilled her God-given destiny.*"

"Pete… will you help me? I need fake ID. I'll be travelling as soon as I can."

He didn't answer right away. He drove around town. She prayed silently.

"Yeah, okay I'll help you. This one time. You get in trouble again. Don't call me."

"Fair enough. You get in trouble, you can call me. I'll call you with my cell number as soon as I get one."

Danielle was ready to embark on her mission. With her new passport and new name, which was Letita Lopez, she boarded a jet bound for Mexico City. She'd been there once before when she was in her twenties. She'd been haunted by the extreme poverty, street urchins, child beggars and small, makeshift huts where entire families lived. She'd also seen opulent villas on a cruise around Acapulco. Fluent in

Spanish, she figured she could survive there. She'd booked a room in a small hotel, using her new cell phone.

She wore her new black, curly wig and fake lashes, plus a cute cheap outfit she picked up at the airport. She packed the jeans and black sweater in her Tote bag. It was nobody's business that she travelled without luggage. Once aboard the jet bound for Mexico City, she spent her time in prayer.

Sunday morning found her in a large, thriving church, filled with people praising and worshipping the Lord. The Charismatic Church was on fire for God. She met Selma, who ran a large orphanage near Mexico City. "I'd like to volunteer or work there." Letita made her request quickly known. She joined a group of folks socializing in a large room off the main sanctuary, where coffee and cookies were being served following the service.

"We are trying to get more funding. Right now, we wouldn't be able to pay you, Danielle. But we sure could use your help." Selma smiled, warmly.

"That's okay. I want to work there. The thing is, though, I'm looking for a place to stay, I just arrived here from... "She wasn't about to reveal that she came from Lexington. Instead, she chuckled. "I've lived in so many states in America I don't know which one I could call home." That got her off the hook.

"You could have one of the rooms above the garage. Bettina left recently to get married. I've been saving the room for an emergency. The church sometimes asks me to help out, since I have such a large house."

"How much?" Danielle had to secure the place as quickly as possible.

"You can stay there gratis for now, because you're going to be working without a wage for a while. We'll just take it one day at a time and see how it goes."

Lord, you have miraculously answered my prayer. "I hope I can catch a ride there with you. I don't know my way around here and I haven't bought a car yet."

"Of course. My old jalopy works just fine. The mechanic I use is a member of the church. He takes good care of my car."

"Sounds like one big, happy family."

"It is."

Danielle got settled into her room above the garage. She was happy to be in Mexico, starting a new life. She'd always loved the tropical climate in Mexico City. Her new friend unwittingly helped her forge a new reality and begin the process of carving out a totally new existence. She felt that God was about to use her mightily.

But that night, a silly incident unsettled her, and she hoped it wasn't a portent of thing to come. It was about the middle of the night when she was startled awake by a shrill, wailing sound. The noise was a cross between an ambulance siren and a shrill scream.

A seagull screeched, soaring through her open window and freaking her out. Stunned, she jumped up out of bed and chased him around the room, finally managing to shoo him out the door. Weird. Really weird. She was in a foreign country and she guessed it was just the beginning of surprises and twists coming her way. Maybe it was a warning to be wary.

The next day, Danielle joined Selma at the orphanage. Selma was well into her seventies, but her spirit was remarkably youthful, her mind as sharp as a razor. "There are eighty beds in this place. We also have a waiting list." She smiled at Danielle. "Come...let me introduce you to some of my friends." She took Danielle by her hand, leading her into the first room. A quick, cursory count told Danielle there were twenty beds in the room. Plus there were six cribs. One sweet little girl, perhaps about four, kept saying "Mommy, Mommy...where is Mommy?" Tears cascaded down her sad, puffy cheeks. She looked so sad Danielle felt like crying with her. "Mommy, Mommy. Come home. I miss you. I'll be good. I promise." The tears streamed down the forlorn child's face.

Danielle couldn't stand it a minute longer. She rushed over to the crib and without requesting permission, picked the child up and held her close to her breast. "Oh darling, it's okay. We're going to look after you. Mommy will be back soon." Danielle just said whatever seemed logical to calm the child down. Soon, she wiped away her tears. "We'll take good care you, honey. Are you hungry?"

She nodded. Then hiccupped and sniffled. Gradually, the tears subsided.

The poor child. The poor, sweet little darling. After a while, she set her back down into her crib. The child seemed a little more settled.

Selma took Danielle down the hallway, showing her other rooms. When the tour was complete, Selma took her into the Employee's Room where she told Danielle to help herself to a cup of coffee. Danielle poured herself a cup and topped Selma's coffee up.

"Si. Gracious. We're short staffed. Trying to get more government funding. We have a long waiting list. Every child here is needy. If you can help and want to volunteer until a position opens up, that would be wonderful. Right now, I can't promise you anything. But that could change any time. The younger women here sometimes get married and move away...well, you never know..."

Lord, I know I belong here. **But how will I eat? What little cash I have won't last long.**

Trust me.

Selma had taken her to a popular outdoor Mexican restaurant. The happy, festive sound of Mariachis resounded throughout the place. Colorful hats, vases and decor in vivid pinks, corals, turquoises and other bright hues cheered her up, making her forget her troubles.

They had just finished their spicy tamales and guacamole, when a nice looking mature man approached them. He grinned at Selma. "Good evening, Selma. Nice to see you. I would still like to have that meeting we talked about."

"What part of *No* don't you get?" Selma spoke dismissively to the handsome gentleman.

Danielle couldn't believe her eyes or ears. Her sweet but dumpy, new friend was snubbing a rather handsome, older gentleman. She smiled over at him.

He didn't return the smile. Instead, he glanced at Selma and motioned that they would talk by phone. Then he turned, walking out of the place.

"Who was *that?"*

"Him? Oh, that's Eddie Shaw. A local businessman. He wants to buy the land the orphanage sits on...wants to develop it into a High Rise. I've told him no a hundred times. He doesn't get it. He won't take *no* for an answer."

"Wait a minute. If you can get a hefty price for the place, why not sell it? You can always build another orphanage."

Selma shook her head. Negative. "No. There's no land available. That's why he keeps bugging us. We need to hold onto it. The Lord has shown me that we will make even more money in the future for the property."

"Entirely possible of course. You don't think the market has peaked out? I don't know. But I'm going to find out." She shrugged. "I'll do some research on your behalf."

"Don't bother. You don't listen. I just told you that the *Lord* showed me that we will get even more in the future."

"I'm sorry, Selma. I...I just got so excited about the offer."

"Forget about it. There will be more offers; and they will be even better."

She couldn't get Eddie Shaw out of her mind. He was tall, with dark hair, greying at the temples. And very handsome. He had a wide jaw line and tiger eyes which flashed yellow flecks in chocolate brown ."Is he American or a local Mexican?"

"Actually he's an American Jew…from New York…moved here some time ago. His wife died. Doesn't seem to date much. He's always alone."

I can remedy that. Lord, don't forget me. She had certain scriptures emblazoned on her mind and heart. *"You have not because you ask not."* Then she remembered she was on a mission. She had a purpose and needed to fulfill it. She couldn't afford to get side tracked.

Volunteering at the orphanage was going really well. Danielle knew she was where God wanted her to be. Finally she understood why nothing in the past had worked out for her. It was because she had not been in the centre of God's will. She had wasted her time with the beauty salon and Ladies' clothing boutique, plus her brief foray into the criminal world. She hoped that she was about to come into what God had planned for her. She would throw her heart, mind and soul into the orphanage. God had been nudging her for years about pursuing that avenue, but she had ignored the promptings of the Holy Spirit to her peril; travelling down dead-end streets. Now, by the grace of God, she was moving on to a new and glorious life. A life led by Almighty God, creator of heaven and earth. *Lord…again I ask you to please forgive me for escaping incarceration. But I really think I can help the children emotionally. I have so much love I can pour into their lives. You know it's what I've always wanted to do. I lost my way. But you've never left me, and now I've found my purpose.*

Eddie Shaw was a distinguished gentleman. He kept dropping around for coffee unannounced. Danielle spoke to him, while Selma ignored him. "I would like to hear more about your interest in buying the orphanage. Maybe I can help." Danielle smiled at him.

Eddie admitted he wanted to buy the land and build a high-rise on it. But by the time she was through with him, he was in tears and promised instead to help Selma with the design and building project for a new, modern orphanage. "Maybe I've been missing what God has in store for me. Maybe this is what I'm supposed to be doing."

"Many of us tend to run ahead of God. But it never works out. We must be led by the Spirit or our life will have way too many problems and complications. There will always be challenges and problems, of course. We face them every day; but when we are on the right track, there is a certain, unshakeable peace and harmony in our lives." Selma smiled. "You know...it's funny. You already look more peaceful than when you showed up here."

Eddie bought the property. True to his word, they bulldozed down the dilapidated orphanage. Construction began immediately on a large, ultra-modern orphanage. He was there every morning when daylight broke. He worked with the foreman, project manager and construction workers.

Selma and Letita knew that because they drove by the site early every morning to check out what was happening. And they met Eddie daily to chat about the magnificent new orphanage being built.

Chapter Four

It was as though Danielle had dropped off the planet. News of her low-key escape from the Women's correctional center had faded. Still, Graham and Dana wondered what happened to her.

6:00 a.m. Monday morning. Jacob and Dana were at the track putting Firelight Fancy through his paces. Soon, colt and rider took a break. Dana had brought a couple cups of coffee for them. She handed one to Jacob. He grinned, took it, and waited for her input. "I don't have much this morning. Just stay the course, Jacob. Don't do anything different. He's lookin' real good right now, don't you think?"

"I sure do, Dana. I'm continually praying that God's favor will be upon us." He grinned. "It would be so amazing to win the Derby and bask in the glory of the roses." He chuckled. "I can just see us raising that trophy high in the air, smiling for the cameras, reveling in the lavish display of roses…" He hesitated for a moment. "Can I share something with you, real quick, Dana?"

"You don't need to ask. Go."

"I want to lay hands on the colt, and ask for God's protection, favor and for God to cause him to soar ahead of his competitors…"

"I'll do it with you, Jacob. Horses are one of God's most remarkable creations. I mean when you think about it...when the rapture occurs, Jesus will descend from heaven riding a white horse as he sounds the trumpet. So...I think he loves the equines, too. Let's pray over him right now, Jacob. That's a wonderful idea." As they prayed over the colt, his ears suddenly perked up. He became more alert. She sensed that the colt's determination had increased. "Okay. Back to work."

The morning work-out was over. *She wondered idly if Danielle had gotten fake ID and moved to another country. Knowing that Danielle spoke Spanish and that Mexico was a cheap place to live, the thought crossed her mind that she might have relocated there. Maybe Danielle would get involved with an orphanage like she'd always talked about. They'd always shared a kind of mental telepathy, sensing what was happening with each other. But Dana, of course, didn't know if this was actually where Danielle had disappeared to. What did it matter? Graham had forbidden her to contact Danielle. He'd repeatedly said that he didn't trust her.*

Firelight Fancy was performing magnificently well. This morning they worked on getting him out of the gate. The starting gate was one of the keys to winning the derby and crucial to the colt's success.

The clock ticked rapidly toward the first Saturday in May when the Kentucky Derby race would capture the world and announce the champion winner. *Lord, please let Firelight Fancy take the purse. The colt she and Graham had bought proved a wise choice. She really believed he could win, and they would walk away with the coveted purse. Would that happen? They were about to find out.* Soon, it would be time for the big race. Dana could hardly wait. *Of all times to become pregnant. She felt like throwing up then and wasn't sure if it was the bad timing of her pregnancy and resultant pressures and conflict of adjusting to motherhood and carrying a child while doggedly pursuing the purse.*

Graham had joined Dana and Jacob this morning. She loved it when he came to the track. His emotional support and input, along with God, gave her the strength to keep on keeping on. She waved to him from the track. The colt continued to perform well, exceeding expectations.

Dana and Graham finished dinner and proceeded to the family room to catch up on the news. There was lots of hype about the upcoming race. Dana scrolled mindlessly through the TV channels, stopping at a documentary on orphanages in Mexico. She just had this crazy hunch that that was where her Mom was. She didn't expect to see her on TV of course, but she was curious to learn more. "Honey, the documentary starts in a couple of minutes. I'm going to watch it. Do you want to join me?"

"Nah. You can let me know later tonight how it was. I'm going into the family room to see what sports are on."

The documentary was enlightening. It struck at the core of Dana's soul because she had been an orphan languishing in an orphanage when Danielle had rescued her. She would never forget her for that. Though she'd only been five at the time, she remembered it as clearly as though it had been yesterday. No matter how many bizarre or questionable things she did, Dana would always love her and never stop praying for her. Sometimes at night, when Graham wasn't around, she prayed that God would do a miracle in Danielle's life. And if money had been her god, she prayed fervently that it would change.

Dana believed in synchronicity.

Violet picked up the ground line. "Hello Sheriff. One minute, I'll get Graham." She hurried over to the family room. "Sheriff's on the line for you, Graham."

Graham picked up the phone. "What's up, Sheriff?"

"We've heard rumblings that Danielle is in Mexico volunteering at an orphanage. Do you know anything about that?"

"First we've heard of it. Weird, though. We're just watching a documentary on it."

"Synchronous. Happens all the time. Well, as far as we

know she's not dangerous. And she was never convicted of being part of Dana's kidnapping. But she did break the law. She escaped from a women's correctional institution. If she contacts you, let us know. She's not a high priority for us right now; and she's not considered dangerous. But she *has* broken the law. "

"Thanks for the heads up. We'll contact you immediately if we hear from her, Sheriff." Graham turned to Dana. "Wonder what she's up to now?" He shook his head. "I'm glad I'm here to protect you. Dana."

"Thanks honey." She smiled though her heart was breaking. *Mother, what's going on with you? I still love you. I'll always love you, no matter what you do.* "If the authorities are on to her, it will just be a matter of time before she's picked up and deported, I guess." Dana frowned. "A part of me wants to contact her and warn her to lay low until the heat is off." She rolled her eyes, like...dumb... dumb.

"Honey, she's a survivor. We'll leave it up to God as to whether or not she'll wind up back in prison serving a longer sentence; either way, she's not really free, because she's on the run from the law." Graham leaned over, taking Dana in his arms. He held her tight, kissing her fervently. "I know this is hard for you, honey. I'm sorry. The best thing we can do is just lift her up in prayer and leave it with the Lord. He is in control."

Dana fought back tears threatening to overwhelm her. "Lord...please protect Mom."

"It's going to be okay, honey. Something good will come out of this. I don't know what. But I just have hunch about that."

"I hope you're right."

One glance at the local Mexican newspapers and an investigative reporter's findings about money corruption in the orphanage system, and Danielle knew it was time to flee.

If those types started snooping around, it would just be a matter of time before her real identity surfaced. She would do a moonlight flit. If authorities had been tipped off and were looking for her in Mexico City, she would grab a bus and go to another city or town in Mexico. Maybe work as a dishwasher, so she could hide in the back of the restaurant. She'd changed her name to Letita Perez, and had been fortunate to find a black, Cleopatra style wig. She wore it constantly.

Danielle's Spanish was improving in leaps and bounds. Also, she'd quickly become entrenched in the way of life here. She enjoyed the laid back, low key life style. It gave her plenty of down time to enjoy the warm, sultry days. Most of the folks she met were friendly and vibrant, though of course there were shady characters and snarky folks here like everywhere. She would stay in Mexico, at least for now. Maybe she had some Spanish blood. Who knew? There were lots of fair-skinned Spaniards as well as swarthy ones.

She took a bus to Zacatecas, and hoped to find a job and a place to live there. It got her out of Mexico City where reports were snooping around. The town was quaint, charming and delightful. Ornate, pink limestone buildings peppered the area. The captivating little village was set in a valley surrounded by mountains. She spent a couple of nights here by a miraculous and unexpected invitation from Fina, an old, hunched over Spanish woman she'd met at church the first Sunday after showing up here. She was reminded of the wonderful character in the Tennessee Williams play, *La Madrecita de los Perdidos* which translated from Spanish meant "Little mother of the lost." Secretly, she wanted to be that character.

She'd hooked up with Fina in the social room after the church service. They'd bonded instantly. It was as if she'd known the woman all her life. She marveled at how her new friend brimmed to overflowing with love, joy and compassion. "Don't spend money on a hotel. I have a guest room. You'll stay with me." *Lord, you are a great and mighty God. There is none like you. Your mercy and compassion are new every morning.*

Fina drove an old jalopy. Letita thought it might fall apart before they reached their destination. Yet, somehow...Glory to God, despite the old jalopy sputtering and coughing up weird noises as she drove, they made it to an ancient, tumbledown villa.

The quaint villa, perched on top of a hill, was surrounded by flourishing, colorful gardens, was a treasure. Nestled among other older villas, her home was pale pink stucco and had a red tile roof. A pair of Palm trees flanked the entrance.

Over Quesadillas and local wine, Fina filled her in on the town. "You'll be my house guest for as long as you need to. All I ask from you is that you help someone in need if the opportunity arises. We are all put on this earth to help one another." She smiled, showing crooked and missing teeth. "And it is in blessing others that we receive joy and blessing." Fina rose from her armchair and headed toward the kitchen. "I'll make some tea."

Danielle remained in the kitchen, sipping tea from the small, circular table there. Fina sipped her tea while making Mexican food consisting of Quesadillas, Guacamole and Mexican chips"

"What can I do to help?" Letita was anxious to be a good guest, of course.

"You're good company. I hate being alone."

"I never want to leave Mexico. I've found my new home." Danielle watched her hostess expertly prepare the Mexican food. "I hope I will be a blessing to you, just as you've been to me."

"Relax. You already are. I hope you like my cooking. It's hot and spicy."

They sat together enjoying lunch.

The old woman was wizened and bent over but her

enormous, dark eyes spoke volumes. Her hair was pulled back in a chignon which suited her well. *She must have been a real beauty in her day. She still has traces of classic beauty despite her advanced age.*

"You tell me where the nearest grocery store is, and I'll go shopping later today or tomorrow...whatever suits you. I'd love to try cooking some Mexican dishes."

"We should use up what is here. I have a container of black bean soup in the fridge. We'll have that for dinner. I keep a good stock of dried beans and other staples. Depending on what you want to cook, I probably already have it in the pantry."

"Whatever you say. *Thank-you, Lord. I don't have to spend what little money I have.*

"Who knows...maybe you'll make Mexico your permanent home. A lot of Americans come to visit and never go back to America. Maybe that's what you'll do."

"Maybe I will." *This might be an answer to prayer. If I can stay here until I figure out exactly what I'm going to do, things might just work out really well.* "How long have you lived in the villa?"

"My husband died twelve years ago. We were married in our twenties. He inherited some money from his family, and we bought the villa. I guess I've lived here...well over sixty years."

Danielle communicated easily in Spanish. When she got to heaven she would make sure to thank God for her photographic memory. She thrived in the tropical weather, mingling with the locals and adapting to their culture. "I'm going to try to get a job as a cook in a restaurant. Failing that, I'll work as a server or dishwasher."

"I want to work at one of the orphanages, but until I get a paying job there, I'll volunteer while making a living in the restaurant business." She had to lay low until the heat was off. Still, she had to work, so she'd have to take a chance. If she could make herself indispensable by cooking and cleaning for the older woman; in addition to being a companion, maybe things would work out great.

She kept a spare wig in her Tote bag. It was auburn and curly. If for any reason, she wanted to change her look again, she could do it as fast as a quick visit to the Ladies' room. Her favorite was the Cleopatra-style wig, though. It was remarkable how much it masked her look. She would lay low until time had passed, and hopefully the heat was off, then she would prayerfully consider when or if she would return to Mexico City.

Both wigs had served as an excellent camouflage, allowing her to evade the snoopy investigative reporter. If they hadn't shown up, asking a lot of probing questions, she'd still be there. But given how nosey he was, she knew it was wise to disappear. She didn't want to be around while they filmed the documentary. She was tempted to fake an emergency, but she didn't want to add lying and deception to her long list of sins. She packed up her sizable Tote bag, leaving a note for her hostess. She said something had come up that needed her attention. She had to travel but hoped to return as soon as she could.

Danielle spent every spare minute listening to Spanish tapes and reading books on how to speak Spanish, determined to become as fluent as possible as quickly as possible. Between living in Mexico and possessing a photographic memory, plus the Spanish she'd studied at University, she easily conversed with everyone here.

She'd hopped on a bus marked Ecatepec to get here. She felt that she'd been led by the spirit, because the chances of meeting a woman like Fina, who subsequently invited her to be her house guest, were slim and none. Still, it had happened. So she knew God wanted her here.

The woman at the Mexico City orphanage had sensed her desperation just before she left. A couple of them slipped her some pesos. "Don't worry about it. Just pay me back when you can," one of the women said. She'd smiled, her dark eyes twinkling. "The Lord told me to do it. You're in a foreign country. I don't know why you're leaving the orphanage; but I hope you'll be back. You take care of yourself. Estare' orando por ti. She knew that meant I'll be praying for you." It was a wonderful send-off and a tearful good-bye. It was amazing how much they had bonded in the short span of time they'd been working together. "Hasta luego." Danielle said. "Mucho gracious."

She considered heading to Oaxaca City. It was reputed to be the culinary and cultural capital of Mexico. Getting a job as a server there would likely be a cinch. She started rehearsing a conversation in Spanish that would be typical if she worked as a server. Even if she had to run a dishwasher, it would be good; because at least then she'd be out of the line of fire.

Ensconced in the villa, she began to feel safe again. She needed to make some money. Fast. And she wanted to bless her hostess by giving her pesos as well as spoiling her with fabulous meals. They bonded.

Donning her "Cleopatra" wig and flashing a bright smile, she nailed a server job at the second restaurant she applied at. One of the servers had left the night before. Her timing had been superb. *Lord, you are so faithful. You are a great and mighty God. There is none like you. I will praise and worship you all the days of my life.*

THREE MONTHS LATER

Letita continued to thrive, working as a server, in one of the city's top restaurants. As she prepared to close down for the night, she heard her real name being called.

"Danielle"

She froze.

A tall, broad shouldered man with swarthy skin, piercing eyes and a curly head of hair with a receding hairline, grinned at her, gaping.

Go away. Please go away.

He grinned again. "Danielle. What are you doing here?" He was in her face.

Where did she know him from? She decided to pretend it was a case of mistaken identity. She knew just enough Spanish to maybe make it stick. "Senor, my name is Letita. Do I look like someone you know?" The man peered at her very closely, hesitating for a few beats.

Danielle pressed into service every bit of acting talent she possessed, ignoring him as she approached the table of a latecomer, to take their order. *Praise God. He's buying it.*

The man peered at her again. Then, apparently satisfied that it was a case of mistaken identity, resumed eating his dinner.

Sweat poured down Letita's face. *Could she continue to live this way? What were the chances of someone she didn't know recognizing her from...where? The businesses she owned? The horse world? Who knew?* She couldn't figure out the connection.

She forgot about the incident until the next morning when she went out for coffee at one of the dozens of outdoor restaurants. She'd picked one at random. She'd just ordered a mug of coffee and was sipping it, while studying the menu options for breakfast, when a stranger plunked himself down on the bar stool next to hers.

"Danielle...what are you doing here?" He leaned in closer to her, whispering and grinning. "I know you escaped from prison. How long do you think you can run? Why don't you be a good girl and turn yourself in?"

Danielle was dumbfounded. *How in heaven's name did this man find her? And why is he speaking as though he knew her; knew everything about her?* "What do you want, senor?" She spoke in Spanish. "Senor, mi nombre es Letita."

He flashed his badge. He was an undercover cop. "Nice try, Danielle." He smirked.

Lord, no. I just got here. I want to work at an orphanage. I want to make a difference. You know how much

I love children. Please God. It's a waste of my assignment to be behind bars. Please God, give me wisdom. Danielle threw some pesos on the table and hurried to the Ladies' room. When she came out, he was waiting for her at the door of the ladies' room.

He flashed his badge again. "Game's up, Danielle. Time to return to America and finish your sentence."

"Lord, help me. Cause a miracle to happen. Please God." It was a silent, desperate plea and prayer born of desperation.

Just then, one of the most stunning women she'd ever seen sashayed into the restaurant, smiling at the handsome hunk determined to ruin her life.

In that split second, Danielle raced from the restaurant, as her red blooded male stalker turned his attention momentarily to the curvaceous, exotic beauty sashaying into the eatery. That was his undoing. Danielle fled, managing to mingle in with the busy street crowd, losing him. *That was close. Too close.*

Three hours later, Danielle checked herself into a tawdry hotel. She'd phone her hostess and tell her that she wouldn't be home tonight. She didn't want to be followed by the undercover cop. She would hole up in the crappy hotel room and flee in the wee hours of the morning. She hoped to grab a taxi and head back to the safety of the villa. Seeking work at a restaurant was a bad idea. She'd have to figure out an alternate was of making a living.

How would the police have tracked her down so fast? Still she knew the Federales were resourceful. Did she have an enemy among her small group of Mexican friends? Someone had to have tipped them off. But who? She hadn't told any of them about her past, and she'd gone by the name of *Letita Perez* since her arrival in Mexico. It was the name on her fake passport.

Dana was sick every morning now. She didn't know

how she could continue training the colt with any precision. Still, she had to do it. Training was in her blood. And winning the Derby was a goal she was determined to achieve. And with God's help, she would.

This morning she didn't get to the track until 6:00 a.m., though she usually arrived between before 5:00. The track was brightly lit, and the exercise riders, trainers and jockeys showed up then. She'd told Jacob she would be late, asking him to warm the colt up with some runs and record what the colt was picking up. They both knew it varied from day-to-day.

She finally showed up. And then threw up. *Oh Lord, now what? Do we have to scrap this whole Kentucky Derby race because I'm pregnant? I couldn't bear that. I must soldier on.*

She heard the Lord's voice in her spirit. *"My precious daughter, there are countless women that would be thrilled to be carrying a love child like you are. Do not be overwhelmed. Take one day at a time. But remain in me. I am the vine; you are the branches. Without Me you have no life. Abide in Me. And I will abide in you."* "Okay, Lord. Then please give me the strength and focus to keep training the colt while I'm carrying this baby."

My precious, precious child, it is I who gave you the desire to want to win the Derby. I have planted this great love and passion for horses inside you. I am watching over you. Trust me. Trust me with all your heart and lean not on your own understanding."

"In all your ways acknowledge me, and I will direct your paths." She finished the scripture.

Training went brilliantly. She felt fabulous. But that night when she got home, Graham hit her with bad news. "Dana, this information can't wait. Danielle has been picked up in Mexico and is being held in a prison there waiting extradition. How does she get herself into so much trouble?"

Dana's heart sank. The sheriff had warned her that the

charges against Danielle were serious, despite the fact that she was not convicted on all counts against her at her trail. "So I guess they're making an example of her. Because, I suppose, theoretically, if she escaped the low security prison with no consequences, she would set a bad example for the other women prisoners. And they might become copy cats."

"As a matter of fact, Dana, you've hit the nail on the head. Maury Penner, one of the best undercover cops around vied for the job. Turns out he loves Mexico and was fascinated by Danielle's profile. He volunteered for the job."

"Where did they find her? How did they pick her up?"

"She was hopping into a taxi in front of a seedy hotel. She was in some small town in Mexico."

Danielle was readmitted to Lexington Women's prison. She was fuming. She'd thought she could outsmart the system; yet they'd found her in Mexico only weeks after she'd fled there. Now they would be watching her like a hawk. She'd be stuck here. She knew they would slap a few more years onto her sentence. Doubtless, they would want to make an example of her. They'd have to be tough on her, to dissuade other prisoners from attempting to escape. She realized now, that was probably why she'd become a priority; a female escapee from a low security institution. They had to make sure no one else would try running.

Graham and Dana read the newspaper article with mounting horror. The headlines jumped off the page. "Local ex businesswoman, Danielle Lockhart, who was serving a prison sentence, recently escaped from Lexington Women's low security correctional institution. She was picked up in a small town in Mexico by an undercover cop. She is now serving six years instead of three."

Dana started sobbing uncontrollably. "My whole life is falling apart. I don't know what to do or say. Mom's in prison. The training is going well, but I'm not thrilled with it, you know. It's...well, it's just always that gut feeling, when you wonder if you're really on the right track...if you actually have a serious shot at the purse."

"I thought you said the colt was performing well, Dana. So...which is it?" They'd finished dinner and they were relaxing in the family room.

The boys had finished dessert, and they raced toward the games room. "I'm gonna beat you this time. You think you're unbeatable at chess? I don't think so." Will hurried after Jay toward the games room.

"I guess we'll find out." He grinned, mischievously. "Let's go play chess. You're my student, don't foget." Jay ribbed his brother and got it back in spades from Will. They loved each other deeply, but were very competitive, sparring constantly.

"Firelight Fancy is an amazing colt. He's doing great, honey. I guess I'm just...nervous. I want him to…win every race he enters...and he will. We're going to win. We're going to do it, honey."

Violet served tea in the family room. She raised her eyebrows addressing them both. "How much you wanna bet Danielle tries escaping again?" Violet smirked, glancing from Dana to Graham.

Graham raised his eyebrows. "No way. She'd not stupid. If she was caught once; she'd be caught twice. They'd add even more years onto her sentence."

"Not necessarily, Graham. Danielle is very smart...and very determined. She learns fast. She blew it the first time...but I'd be willing to bet that she isn't going to roll over and play dead."

"Well, let's not talk about her anymore. It's a sad situation. We'll pray for her, though, during our evening devotions...which maybe I should begin right now."

After the prayers, Graham and Dana retired early to their room to catch the news and see if anything of interest was on.

Violet brought in some light snacks. She set a tray of gourmet crackers with white cheddar cheese, along with chocolate cookies on a tray. She'd started bringing in snacks at night ever since Dana had announced her pregnancy.

That night, Dana was restless. Her heart broke for her Mom. No matter how bizarre she was, Dana loved her with all her heart. She sobbed bitterly. *"Make it better, Lord. Please. You said in your word that all things work together for good for those who love the Lord. Father, please cause a miracle to happen. Turn this whole thing with Danielle around...somehow, God....somehow."* She couldn't sleep. She tossed and turned, inadvertently awakening Graham. She'd tried unsuccessfully to muffle her sobs.

He folded her into strong, protective arms. "Dana, my darling... my sweet princess...you must not worry, you must not fret. The Lord holds her in the palm of his hand. He will see to it that it all turns out right..."

She sobbed bitterly. "I...guess...you're...right...honey." *What happened to you Danielle? What happened to you that turned you into a criminal?* Her heart was broken. They'd been so close. Like sisters. She'd thought she understood Danielle. She'd forgiven her for her obsession with Graham. She'd doggedly refused to entertain the idea that Danielle might have had a hand in her kidnapping. Now she was incarcerated again. How had she slipped so far off the rails?

The next morning, Dana threw up. She was violently ill. She cancelled the training session. First time she'd ever done that in all her many years of training. "Jacob, please exercise the colt and do the best you can. I won't be there today."

He never said a word. Doubtless, he'd read the newspaper and guessed what a devastating effect it had on her. "Of course. And don't worry about it. One day off won't change anything. Just relax. You'll feel better tomorrow."

His words rang with the joy and hope of comfort spoken from a devout man of God. He was a prince of a man. She was blessed to have him as the jockey for her colt.

But Dana didn't feel better. She felt worse in every way. Finally, she called her doctor and went in for an early ultrasound. She hadn't wanted to know the sex of the child, but now, suddenly, she'd changed her mind. The doctor confirmed that she was going to give birth to twin boys.

Dana was dumbfounded. Over the moon in one way but frightened in another. *She would be giving birth to two boys. No wonder she'd been feeling so queasy and was out of control with her cravings.*

Graham had gone into the city on business. When he came home later that afternoon, he found Dana lounging in the family room, a flute of champagne in her hand, and what looked like exotic food on a nibble tray. She flashed him a cheeky smile.

"Well...you look like the cat that swallowed the canary."

Dana smiled. "Pretty close. We're going to have twin boys."

Graham was dumbfounded. "Twin boys." He rushed over to her, throwing his arms around her. "I'm ecstatic. I've always wanted twin boys. Twins run in our family..."

"Now you tell me." She glared at him, still smiling. "Well...I'm scared but thrilled...I'm excited...elated...and terrified, honey."

"Oh darling, I'll be with you every step of the way. You can count on me. Always. Forever." He swung her around then, filled with joy and heady anticipation. "I'll join you in a glass of champagne." He headed into the kitchen to pour himself a glass of it.

Tears streamed down her cheeks. She was blessed to be married to this incredible, wonderful man. *Thank-you, Lord, for the blessing of a wonderful, devoted husband. Thank-you, thank-you, thank-you."*

Chapter Five

Danielle was fit to be tied. Livid. Fuming. Irate. There were no words to describe her state of mind accurately. She seethed. She spoke to the system as though it were a singular, evil entity. *You think you're going to keep me down. Think again. I'll break out of this hole and this time I'll be smarter. Better prepared. I'm going to begin my new plan for escape today. This time it's going to stick. Hawaii. That's where she'd go. She would die her hair black, grow it real long. Maybe get a job as a Hula dancer. Yes, that's exactly what she would do. She was a survivor. Nothing and no one would keep her down. She was an eagle soaring through the skies. Some folks just didn't get that.*

There were certainly challenges she'd have to overcome. She'd need cash for a new fake passport, plus money for air fare and hotel until she got set up. Maybe it would be cheaper and easier to just head down to Florida. She suddenly remembered an old GF she'd known since high school, who'd received a scholarship, gone to the University of Florida, and stayed there marrying into high society and great wealth.

They'd hooked up on Facebook some time ago. Her friend looked fabulous, was now a rich widow and lived in an opulent mansion in Palm Beach, Florida, overlooking the ocean. Maybe she could stay with her until she got a job and an apartment. She would contact her as soon as she could. Just like that, she remembered her phone number and address. It flashed into her mind. Her photographic memory came in handy more than once. There were major hurdles to surmount, of course; but she thrived on challenges. She'd have to get her hands on some cash to get another fake passport. And figure out the safest mode of transportation.

Just like that. She knew what to do.

The warden slipped soggy eggs and a piece of wilted toast in the slot at the bottom of her cell door. She also received one cup of lousy coffee. Hallelujah for that. The food did not look appetizing. It never did. But she would eat it, of course.

That night Danielle read her Bible far into the night. She heard the still, small voice of God speaking. *Do what is right. Pay your debt to society. You're here because of the poor choices you made. There are lessons you need to learn."*

"Lord...aren't you on my side? I can't stay here. I don't belong here. I have a life to lead." She whispered the words to the Almighty. "I'm sorry, Lord. But I can't stay here. Don't ask me to. I need to carry on despite the risk and cost." She whispered her thoughts to God Almighty.

All through the night she wrestled with the idea of slipping out of the minimum-security prison. Again. But how would she do it? They would be watching her like a hawk. It had been amazing that she'd slipped past the exterior video cameras the first time, though she had no way of knowing if they actually existed.

She decided she would bide her time for six months, becoming a model prisoner. Then, when she sensed the warden had stopped watching her too closely; she'd make a break for it. She would escape alone. It had to be that way. She couldn't trust anyone here.

Six Months Later

This is the day I get my freedom back. She heard the warning from God in her spirit. But she did not heed it. *Do not break the law. You must be a law-abiding citizen. It will not go well with you if try to escape. Instead, be a model prisoner and I will cause you to get time off for good behaviour. You can lead others to me while you are here. She was alone in the cell for a few days, her roommate was in hospital.* On her knees in her cell, she pleaded with God. "Don't ask me to stay, Lord. I can't. I just can't." She whispered the words hoarsely as tears of conflict and sorrow trickled down her cheeks.

Though she wrestled with it, she decided to disobey the voice of the Lord. Headstrong, she would make another break for freedom. This time, no one would stop her. Her destination was Palm Beach where Suzie, her old school chum lived. She had to get her hands on a new passport and cash. Neither would be easy to come by. How would she do it?

She wrestled with God all night. She knew disaster would follow if she disobeyed the voice of the Lord. But she had free will. *Lord, I don't want to disobey you. But I just can't face staying her for six long years. Even if my sentence was reduced to five if I became a model prisoner, I just can't cut it, Lord. Please understand. I'm sorry.*

That night she had never felt more alone in her life. It was as if God had left her to her own devices. A black, hollow, creepy feeling enveloped her. She had decided to deliberately disobey the voice of God and she knew she would pay a terrible price for that. Still, as though pushed by an evil entity, she was determined to make a break for freedom. The absence of the closeness of the Hoy Spirit caused her emotionally to continue on a downward spiral. *Soon.* She had to make the break soon, or she would go off the rails.

In the wee hours of the morning, Jacob tacked up Firelight Fancy at the track, preparing to put him through his paces.

Dana and Jacob worked him diligently at the track, pleased with his progress. Next, he would be racing against another colt. "I wish we could somehow convey to the colt the importance of the Derby, monetarily." Dana sighed.

"I think he gets it. Horses are highly instinctive creatures, as you know." Jacob grinned.

The competing colt won the race by a hair. Dana could see it irked Firelight Fancy. *Good.* As long as he had a feisty spirit and was driven to compete and win, they had a great shot at the big prize. They had worked hard to instill the competitive spirit in him. She allowed herself the luxury of imagining Jacob and Firelight Fancy up front and centre, basking in the adulation of a wildly cheering crowd, along with TV cameras and reporters.

In the barn at the track, Dana and Jacob rewarded Firelight Fancy with a variety of choice treats. They stood by observing him as he devoured them gleefully. Then, Dana and Jacob took turns murmuring positive prayers to him and stroking him on his neck and body.

At the house, Dana took a whiff of the Goulash that Violet was stirring in a large pot on the stove for dinner. "Bet it's going to be delicious."

Graham hovered over the dish, also. He gave thumbs up to Violet.

Together, Dana and Graham headed to the family room to see what the boys were up to. "You boys seem in rare form tonight. Did you have a good day at school?" Dana hugged for Will and then Jay.

After she'd hugged Jay, she realized he was downcast. "No. I got a "B" on my report card. I'm not happy about that. I'm a straight "A" student. I gotta figure out how this happened." He was sulking.

"What subject garnered the B?" Graham peered over at Jay.

"Math, Dad. Algebra."

"You're good at Math, son. I'm surprised you got a "B" also."

"Well, I guess I just have to accept it."

"Actually, you don't. I'll have a meeting with your teacher and find out why you got a "B" and how we can remedy it. We need to get to the bottom of this. Fast. You've been a straight "A" student for as long as I can remember." Graham was irked.

Mrs. Dahlstrom defended her position rigorously. "Jay is certainly one of my best students; but...he hasn't been...excelling in math. I expect more from him. I wanted to wake him up to challenge him to do better work."

"Can you be more specific? Would you mind showing me the algebra tests that he did not excel in? I need to know how to help him to get back on top again."

"I appreciate your interest in Jay's work, Mr. Van Rensellier. But I do *not* appreciate your challenging my decision to give him a "B." Quite frankly, that is *my* decision; not yours."

"May I see the test, Mrs. Dahlstrom? Surely you don't want me requesting a meeting with the principal for this small matter."

Annoyance spread over her face. She resumed her composure before speaking, however. "Very well. I shall show you the test. I have them here in my briefcase." She flicked through some files in her briefcase and then peered over at him. "Actually, I'm sorry, Mr. Van Rensellier, but I don't have them with me. They must be at home."

"I see. May I make an appointment with you right after school tomorrow? Please bring the test, and Jay and I will be here, so we can review his work." He smiled, knowingly. "I must warn you in advance, Mrs. Dahlstrom, if I disagree with your assessment of the grading after studying the algebra question, I will immediately request an appointment with the principal and expect you to be present at the meeting, of course.

"Certainly, Mr. Rensellier." Her countenance reflected a twinge of nervousness and annoyance.

That night, back at the house, Jay worked diligently on his algebra, with Graham sitting next to him, coaching him. It was almost midnight when they turned the lights out and went their separate ways to their bedrooms.

Two days later, Jay and Graham met Mrs. Dahlstrom at the school. She did a complete turnaround. She smiled at both of them. "I think I can safely revise the grade I gave him and give him an A. When I'm wrong, I admit my error." She smiled. "He's actually the best student I've ever had. If I've inspired him to work even harder, then maybe this was a good thing." She smiled, shaking both their hands. "I'm sorry, I must have been overtired...or overworked...or something... when I gave him the B."

Jay had learned a valuable lesson that day and Graham knew it.

When Danielle called Suzie, her old school chum in Florida, she got a recording. "I am in New York at my other home. I'm doing a series of lectures on theology at the New York University. Please check my website for details if you are interested in attending.

Perfect. All she had to do was vanish from the dungeon, undetected and contact her old buddy Pete who owed her some money and she'd be all set. A new passport, a new state and a new identity.

SIX MONTHS LATER

Danielle had spent the allocated time outdoors, while pretending to be involved with sports; plotting the details of her next escape.

The big day finally arrived. It was Friday afternoon, unseasonably warm and muggy for the first Saturday in May. The warden was in good spirits. She knew her shift ended at 5:00.p.m. With any luck, she'd be able to watch the Kentucky Derby on T.V. somewhere and see if Dana and her new colt won.

Danielle glanced furtively around, her heart in her throat. She could feel her heartbeat accelerating. She couldn't get caught. She had to make a clean break of it and race off into the free world outside of the daunting prison walls.

She went to the Ladies' room and when she returned, many of the inmates were disbursing toward the entrance/exit doors. *Now.*

She stayed at the tail end of the group of women again. The warden didn't seem to be anywhere around; though she was likely near the front somewhere.

She sent up a silent prayer, despite wondering if it would be heard, and then walked swiftly to the outer edge of the grassy field, just like she'd done the first time. If the warden or one of the snoopy inmates didn't turn around while playing basketball, and other sports, she would be able to make a clean break. If they did: she was toast.

Miraculously, she made it to the edge of the property without an issue. Just as she was about to flee, she heard a loud whistle and a sound like a blaring burglar alarm. *Oh no. I'm caught.* Her only chance of escape was to outrun her pursuers, which would bide her time until the inevitable police siren signaled that the Big Boys were after her.

Somehow Danielle made it to the edge of the forest and ran into the dense woods before she heard the inevitable siren. *Did she want to be caught? "God is not mocked. Whatsoever you sow, that you shall also reap."* It was too late to turn back; besides, she might make it.

Was she like Paul's friends in the Bible? *They'd wanted to take a boat out into the sea, but he'd warned them not to depart from the place where they were. He warned them that a fierce storm was on the horizon and the ship would be lost if they set sail.*

Headstrong, the men ignored his advice and set sail. Soon, a fierce, unrelenting storm approached, accelerating and becoming more violent by the minute. It raged, with no letup day or night. The men cowered on the boat fearing for their lives. Paul told them not one of them would be lost; but the ship would be destroyed. And so it was.

She was on the run.

Her old school chum Suzie Allen had led a blessed life, so different from hers. Miraculously marrying one of Palm Beach's wealthiest bachelors just out of University, she'd thrived in the marriage until his recent death. He'd been her professor and was significantly older than she was. She knew Suzie wouldn't remain a widow for long. She was the kind of woman that really needed a man and attracted them like a moth to the light. She was glad they had stayed in touch on Face Book; plus they'd chatted on the phone a few times Suzie had invited her to visit hr in Palm Beach. But given that she was on the run, she guessed Suzie might shun her. Still, she'd always had a big heart, and they'd been very close for many years. She wasn't expecting a positive response. But there seemed to be no other option. She could only imagine how Suzie would react when she learned it was her second prison break.

The road stretched ahead of her long, lonely and bleak. Deep forest lined both sides of the road. It was roughly seven miles to Lexington. She'd run until she was exhausted. If a vehicle approached, unless it was a long-distance trucker, she'd hide in the bushes. She knew of course that once she was discovered missing…which would be when the women were counted after the sports event. Then the sheriff and his boys would be on her trail. They could probably calculate how far she would get. They might think she had an accomplice and had a getaway car picking her up. She would need luck on her side. She had no assurance God was smiling down on her. Other than a massive truck, any other car could be an unmarked police vehicle. She shivered. She had to make it.

Truck drivers were usually solid, hardworking guys just doing their job for the pay. If she could flag down a trucker headed to Florida, she would have it made. Darkness had fallen, and Danielle was famished. She had to get a ride soon, or she'd be too weak to run. She considered the possibility of hiding in the forest until early morning. *No. She had to get out of the area and to another state. Fast.*

Chapter Six

Another truck approached. Sticking her thumb out, Danielle prayed it would stop. The massive vehicle slowed, pulling over to the curb and stopping a few feet from where she stood. It was pitch black outside. Her heart rate accelerated. She shivered. *Please God, let him be a good guy.* She couldn't see the driver very well, but he looked like an okay guy, though who knew. He was probably in his sixties with ruddy skin. He leaned toward her. "Hop in. Hurry up."

She Jumped in and buckled up.

The truck sped along the road. She waited for him to say something.

"Where you headed?"

"Florida. Palm Beach."

"No kiddin'." He raised his eyebrows. "You got friends there?"

"Yeah." She smiled. "I got friends there."

"Good for you." He kept his eyes on the road ahead. "What's a good-lookin' broad like you doin' hitch-hikin'?" He flashed a knowing grin. "DIdn't break outta that's women's prison, did ya?"He smirked, flashing her a knowing glance. "It's okay. ...Just relax... I ain't gonna turn you in." He grinned, keeping his eyes on the road ahead. "Hear no evil. See no evil."

He knows. Her heart stopped. *Oh Lord. Don't let him be a monster. A heckler is okay, though.* Of course, he'd be listening to the news and would have learned there was an escapee; a woman on the run.

"Don't worry. I ain't gonna turn you in. Did some time myself once…long time ago. Every day I thought about breakin' out. Never did, though. Didn't have the guts for it. I admire you, lady. And I'll tell you what else…" He grinned over at her. 'This is your lucky day. I'm headed to Florida…on my way to pick up a load of citrus fruit. "

Lord, you heard my prayer. There must be something you have for me to do in Florida. Something worthwhile. Have you already forgiven me? Oh, I do hope so.

She laid low at the truck stops. At the first one, he went in to the café and returned with chicken and chips and cokes for both of them. *Thank you, Lord.* She peered over at her new buddy." I really appreciate this."

"Hey, no problem. Glad to be of help."

"Just do the same for someone else when you can."

She nodded. "Yeah. I sure will." She reached over and gave him a hug. "Thanks a bunch."

They had just entered the state of Florida. A thrill raced up and down her spine. *I'll make a new life here. Reinvent myself. Maybe work at an orphanage.*

"Any chance of using your cell, Frank? I want to touch base with my girlfriend."

He reached in a pocket in his jeans and handed it to her. "I guess you know her number, do you?"

"Yeah. I…uh…I have a photographic memory."

"No kiddin' " He whistled, impressed. He gave her his number. "In case you need to leave a message. I won't tell anybody if you want to write it down." He smirked.

"I'll remember it. It's safer for you if I don't have it written on my person."

"You know…you're right."

She got through right away. "Suzie. It's your old friend from high school, Danielle Lockhart."

Silence. "The same Danielle that escaped prison and is on the run?"

This is not going well. "Aren't you going to say hello? You always said to look you up if I ever got to Florida. Well...here I am."

A full minute passed. "Okay, Danielle. Have your driver come up to 2777 Heaven High drive. I'll be on the porch watching for you. About how long will you be?"

Danielle took a very deep breath. *Was her friend going to have the sheriff waiting outside as well? She had no other viable option. She'd have to chance it.* She turned to her driver. She lives in North Palm Beach by the ocean. About how long until you drop me off? I can grab a taxi if you can get me to downtown Palm Beach."

"It's maybe an hour from where we are now."

Danielle told Suzie the estimated time of arrival.

The taxi driver dropped her off at the designated address. She hopped out and Suzie hurried to the cabbie." She insisted on paying despite Danielle's objections. She hugged her old friend, stood apart from her and peered at her. "Come on in. You must be starved."

Danielle was impressed by how fabulous Suzie looked. Regal. Slender. Almost as stately as queen.

"Come in, darling. You look exhausted. Your room is ready."T he floral caftan she wore was fabulous.

Danielle took a deep breath, hugging her old friend. She glanced around the spectacular house.

"I welcome the company, darling. I've been so lonely... I could die." She launched into song. "So lonely...I could die."

"Oh come on. Knowing you, you've probably already met someone."

"Actually, I have."

"Come on. Really?"

"Yeah. And he's a good one." She smiled. "But let's talk about you. What's goin' on?"

"There's no easy way to say this. I need a place to stay.

I'm on the run. I broke out of prison."

"I knew that, of course. And you expect me to harbor a prisoner?"

"Just for tonight. Tomorrow I'll figure out where I can go. I was doing time in a low security Women's correctional. I had an inept attorney. I shouldn't have been there. I had to take matters into my own hands. I couldn't waste my life there..."

"Your *life?* How long was your sentence?"

"Six years. That's a long time when you're holed up in an airless cell."

"I bet." She grinned. "Where are my manners? How about a very *good* glass of wine?"

"I won't say no to that."

"I put in a roast. Travelers are always hungry. We'll have potatoes, carrots and a salad. Let me show you to your room." She grinned, mischievously. "I see you travel light."

"You get a kick out of hiding an escapee, don't you?"

"Brings some excitement into my life, I guess."

"I thought you had a new man."

"Not exciting. Just nice...available and very rich. We'll see how he shapes up."

"What kind of business is he in?"

"Stock market mogul. ..and property investor...he's local. *He* was married to one of Palm Beach's wealthiest society dames."

"What happened in that marriage?"

"Nobody seems to know. Not even him."

Danielle burst out laughing. It all just seemed so bizarre. She was amazed that her friend asked so few questions about her incarceration and escape...amazed and very grateful.

She poured a California cabernet into two fine crystal glasses. They raised their glasses in a toast. "You know what? I have to be honest with you. I had a couple of break-ins...I've got a good burglar alarm system, monitored by a reputable security company. ..but I'll sleep a lot better knowing I'm not alone in this big house. And you're a tough broad. ..a perfect roommate for me. You're timing couldn't be better."

"You're not worried about harboring an escapee and all that?"

"Not really. I know all the Who's Who in this town. Anything happens...I'll just play dumb. Call in markers if I need them."

"Nice to have affluent, powerful friends." Danielle smiled, feeling more relaxed than she had in ages. She'd gone from the dregs of society to the pinnacle of high society in a very short span of time. *God must have a good plan for me, despite my failings.* A scripture popped into her mind. *"For I know the plans I have for you. Plans to prosper you and not to harm you..."*

There was a loud knock on the door.

"Expecting anyone?" Danielle peered over at Suzie, petrified.

"No. But maybe you'd better...duck out of sight. I've got just the spot. Quick, follow me." She hurried into a massive library located off the formal living room. Danielle followed her, moving quickly. Suzie opened the fake bookcase and Danielle slipped in.

Suzie put the wall bookcase back in place and headed for the front door. She peered through the keyhole. It was the sheriff. *No flies on them.* She hadn't had this much excitement in ages. She opened the door, smiling warmly. "Good evening, Sheriff. What can I do for you?"

"A little birdie told us you might be harboring a fugitive."

"*What?* What are you talking about? I don't know any jailbirds."

"We think you do."

She laughed. "Is this your idea of a joke? Take a look around yourself if it amuses you. You won't find anyone here, I assure you."

Twenty-five minutes later. "Okay, Suzie. Sorry to have bothered you. Have a nice evening."

"Thanks. You, too."

She didn't tell Danielle to come out of her hiding place. She never trusted the cops. She walked into the library and spoke through the bookcase. "Stay in there. I have a hunch they might be back."

"It's dusty in here and there seems to be very little air...but I guess I'll be okay." She spoke in a muffled voice.

"I'll put some Beethoven on to relax you, and I'll sit here reading a book to keep you company."

Twenty minutes later.

Danielle was not only bored being holed up here, but she felt like there was very little air here. "I need to come out and get some air."

"No. I told you...I have a hunch they'll be back."

The doorbell rang. "See what I mean?" She wasn't sure if Danielle could hear the door bell, or if the sound was muffled. She hurried back to the bookcase. "Don't move a muscle. I'll try to get rid of them as soon as possible."

She took a deep breath, got ready to smile and opened the front door. "Come on in guys...you want to do another sweep? Be my guest." Suzie raised her voice a few decibels, hoping Danielle would hear her and not try coming out.

Danielle felt like she had no air. She had trouble breathing...plus she had an overwhelming urge to sneeze. Her nose was tickling from the dust in here. But, thank God, she'd heard the warning in Suzie's words.

Suzie imagined how claustrophobic it must feel, being holed up behind the bookcase. She had to get rid of the officers quickly.

The two officers glanced at each other. "I guess it's probably a waste of time." They started to leave. The sheriff turned to the deputy sheriff. "Let's do another sweep, just to be on the safe side."

"Okay." The deputy sheriff nodded.

Suzie took a deep breath.

They started the grand tour again. Suzie raised her voice as much as she dared, in order to warn Danielle that the sheriff and deputy sheriff were determined to do another sweep of the house. "Whatever you like, sheriff."

Danielle couldn't stand it another second. There was no air in here. She didn't break out of prison to be locked up in this airless, stuffy pocket. She opened the bookcase a crack and spotted two officers stepping into the living room. Quickly and noiselessly she shut it. Her heart beat so fast she wondered if maybe they could hear it. *Better no air and no prison.*

They stood in the library as though they knew about the fake wall. The deputy sheriff glanced at the sheriff. "Thought I saw something move... in my peripheral vision." He glanced over at his partner. "Guess not. It's been a long day."

Suzie smiled, turning on the charm. "I've made fresh coffee if you'd like some." *Please say no. Please leave.*

Danielle felt like she couldn't breathe, her lungs were bursting. *Gee, thanks a lot. Lord, let me get through this. Then she remembered the Lord had warned her not to slip out of the prison. Did she really expect a life of blessing and joy after disobeying the clear leading of God?*

The officers took a few sips of the coffee and then got back to business. "We won't take up much of your time. Crazy...but I just have a hunch there's something here..." The sheriff looked tired.

"Suit yourself." Suzie showed the officers through the house again. She was ready to breathe a sigh of relief, standing on her doorstep as they were about to depart, when she heard a sneeze. Instantly, she started coughing to cover up what must have been Danielle sneezing from dust particles in the closed space. She smiled at the guys. "If I hear anything, I'll let you know."

The men exchanged glances. "I thought I heard

something…maybe not." The sheriff said.

"Sorry about my sneezing. My allergies are acting up again."

The sheriff glanced at the deputy sheriff." Let's go."

Danielle opened the bookcase and slipped out from the secret enclosure, gasping for air. "That was close. Maybe I should move on."

"To where?"

"That's the problem. I don't know."

"You're staying here. We just have to be super careful."

"How can I ever thank you, Suzie?"

"You can be my body guard, until I have a man in the house."

"Piece of cake." A few survival ideas flashed through her mind. "Got a gun or pepper spray?"

"Yeah. I've got an extra Colt 22. Know how to use it?"

"Of course."

Suzie headed for her home office, returning with the firearm and pepper spray. "I also keep some cash in the house…a $1,000.00. If somebody breaks into the house, I'll hand them the cash and tell them to flee. I don't know if it will work, but it's worth a shot."

Suzie served Crab Louie for lunch and chatted gaily about the new man in her life. "If you can completely alter your look and get new ID, I can probably hook you up with a wealthy bachelor. I know a few of them."

Danielle peered over at her, thrilled. "I can get a fake passport easily enough…soon as I get my hands on five to ten grand."

"That's nothing. I'll go the bank first thing in the morning. I'll loan you the cash. You'll repay me when you can." She thought better of it. "If they're watching us...that might not be wise. I'll start taking out cash today but not too much." She thought for a minute. "You know what? I have some stocks I've been meaning to sell. I'll do that today and get twenty grand for you. Then, neither of us has to worry."

"I am deeply grateful, Suzie. Meanwhile, I'll be your slave."

"I won't say no to that. I'll buy the food. You cook it and put the dishes in the dishwasher. Fair enough?"

"Very fair. And just let me know what else I can do."

"We need to change your look. Fast. I'll pick up a wig when I'm out and sunglasses." She looked Danielle over. "We're about the same size...though of course, I'm taller. I've got tons of clothes. Just borrow whatever you like for now. Oh...and I'll loan you some good jewelry. We don't want you looking like a pauper when we're trying to hook you up with one of Palm Beach's premier catches."

"Sounds exciting. Also, I want to hear more about *your* guy."

"He's a semi-retired attorney. Not great looking. But he's got a good heart and a great smile. I like him. Not sure why. I've never cared much about looks. I look at the heart...the inner man. And there...he's a giant."

"Great. And the guy you're going to introduce me to? What's his scenario?"

"Robert Bellagio. Italian. Much too old for you. He's in his eighties. He lost his second wife to cancer about a year ago. We run in the same circles…high society. Quite a few women I know have made a play for him. So far, he hasn't expressed much interest in any of them. You're younger than most of the women in my circles…plus you have a lot of pizzazz. I have a hunch he might like you. If you could get him to marry you, you'd have his name and you'd have a good life... you'd have it made."

"Is he spiritual?"

"I don't know. Ask him. Invite him to church. See what he says."

Three Weeks Later

Danielle, armed with a new passport and new identity is

ready to be launched into Palm Beach's high society. With Suzie's coaching, they came up with a fabulous new name: Sondra Silvers. And thanks to technological advances, she has changed her blue eye color to brown, as well as dying her hair a vibrant chestnut brown, despite usually donning her black wig. She started working out and eating half of everything, in order to take off a few pounds in a further attempt to alter her look. She reinvented herself totally, changing aspects of her personality as much as she could and concocting a new persona. Over a Spanish omelette she'd whipped up, she smiled. "I've never had so much fun in my life. I have a complete new identity."

"You do, indeed. It's no different than someone going on the witness protection program. When someone's life is in danger, the government sometimes awards a million dollars and a new identity to an individual. We're just borrowing their concept." She smiled.

Suzie was pleased with herself having had a big hand in the reinvention of Danielle. In the evenings she usually lounged around in a hostess gown. She had oodles of them. They were all in vivid, tropical colors. She told Danielle why that was. "I'm a financial planner as you know. During office hours, I usually wear black. As a financial planner, my office is in a separate building from the private hospital facility I represent. Part of my job description is to encourage wealthy patrons to invest in our facility. I help them organize their finances in such a way as to leave much of their vast wealth to the private hospital I represent. And, as vice president of the company, I often attend funerals. This way I don't have to drive home and change. I'm already wearing black."

"Makes sense to me." Danielle shrugged.

"That's why when I get home, I can't wait to change into something exotic and colorful. "She smiled. "Now that you have your new identity intact, I'll start introducing you to folks as an old friend from New York. We'd better get our stories straight. Where did we meet? How did we become friends?"

"You're the mastermind. *You* tell me."

"Well, it certainly can't be Lexington, Kentucky at high school. "I don't like to fib. So I'll keep it as close to the truth as I can. We took that one-week trip to New York together to a writing conference; back when we thought we were going to take the world by storm as New York Times Best Selling authors." She chuckled. "We're both bookworms. And though we didn't actually *meet in New York,* we did go there together and attend a book fair there, as well. We're both voracious readers. That's the connection."

"So you're saying we met in New York at the writing conference. And we actually did. Oh, that's rich. You were staying at your aunt's house in Palm Beach and we "met" in New York at the writing conference. None of that is a lie." She laughed. "If we want to be honest, I think God helps us do that, in spite of our failings." She smiled. "It's ironic that I started out wanting to be a writer...didn't wind up pursuing it...but married a famous author, instead. And I do have an impressive library, don't you think?"

"You do. I want to read some of those books. Meanwhile we can review the titles on Amazon and Goodreads, and check book reviews. I'll go on the internet and print out a list of best sellers and a list of popular authors. Maybe we'll have a contest to see who can read more books. I've discovered in life, that even when you love doing something; like reading novels, you need goals to become a high achiever. I mean...unless one is very rich and can afford full-time help, there are mundane chores and things we need to do, which demand our time. Everybody needs a push...even to pursue what they enjoy. A famous author once told me, "You don't grow, unless you're pushed." I think there's a great deal of truth in that statement."

"I think the key is that when questions arise, we answer one or two quickly and then change the subject...or maybe move around the room and hobnob with other folks. We circulate. What we want to avoid is getting into a long, in-depth conversation with any one individual. That could be a problem."

Suzie and Sondra, feeling more like sisters than best pals, like they'd been all through high school and university, hobnob with society's elite at a fancy cocktail party taking place at a grand, old mansion in the area. Danielle, AKA Sondra Silvers and Suzie mingle with the society matrons and younger, popular hostesses breaking into the coveted inner circle. The setting was a grand waterfront estate in Palm Beach.

"Sondra Silvers" is a big hit. Suzie easily manages to introduce her into the coveted, high society circles. "There must be sixty or seventy people here," Sondra whispered to Suzie.A twinge of nervousness raced through her. *But Suzie is right. I have to fully entrench myself in my new identity and take on the new persona. No one will ever figure it out.*

Not so fast. As "Sondra" mingled among the crowd, fighting a few fears trying to niggle their way to the surface, she noticed a large, mannish looking matron checking her out. A fast impression told her the woman was an undercover cop. She had a serious, focused air about her. She was out of place here. Since everyone else was clearly the *Who's Who in Palm Beach Society* and having an absolutely fabulous time...something about the woman sent up red signals. She had the distinct sense that the odd woman was on a mission. It disturbed her.

Suzie, who was brilliant and had masterminded her new identity and persona had schooled her on how to conduct herself at the parties. "If someone confronts you or otherwise attempts to intimidate you, smile, be gracious and move out of their sphere as fast as possible and hobnob with other folks." But when "Sondra" attempted to do that, she was thwarted. The matron followed her and planted herself smack in front of her, despite the welcoming smiles of a handsome, older couple who were happy to meet Sondra. "Have we met? The matron flashed her a knowing look, as she elbowed her way into the small cluster of folks chatting gaily. "I don't believe I've seen you around Palm Beach before." Her eyes narrowed. A suspicious look etched on her features.

"Possibly. I travel a great deal. Excuse me." "Sondra" flashed the gauche creature a smile, quickly circulating among the cocktail guests and losing her. *Looks like I'm right about her being an undercover cop. She can't prove anything. I am my new identity. And...I'm a fine actress, if I say so myself. Sondra Silvers, New York and Palm Beach high society dame and voracious reader. Old friend of local socialite, Suzie Allen.*

Danielle was hardly surprised when the suspected undercover female cop caught up with her as she chatted with two gentlemen. "Robert...how nice to see you." She invited herself into the small group.

"Have you met Sondra Silvers?" Robert peered oddly at the strange woman.

"No. She seems to be avoiding me. I wonder why that it?" The matron scowled.

"Must be your imagination, dear. I find Sondra very social." Robert Thornhill grinned.

Sondra rather liked him. He wasn't Suzie's choice for her. But it would be even better if she found her own man. Suzie would be good with it, of course. She was only trying to help, after all.

Chapter Seven

Sondra breathed a sigh of relief when she returned to Suzie's beach house. She parked her leased car in the garage and opened the door to the house. She was glad Suzie's Lamborghini was already there.

As she glimpsed the beauty and grandeur of Suzie's opulent home, she sensed that God had something special here for her in Palm Beach. He wasn't through with her yet. In fact, he was known for redeeming the downtrodden; picking them up from the ash heap and morphing them into stars. *Had he already forgiven her? She had certainly asked.*

Suzie milled around in the state-of-the-art kitchen, whipping up a fruit compote in her blender. She poured the mixture into tall, fronted glasses. "Try it." She handed Sondra a glass of it and joined her on the adjacent white faux leather bar stool.

The pals moved into the spacious family after the compote. A televangelist was on T.V. "You know, Suzie…that really *was* the best thing that could have happened. Everybody knows you have a long-term house guest. The wine rep job is a perfect cover. As it happens, I'm fairly knowledgeable about wine. And guess what? I've met a new man."

"Come on." Suzie raised her eyebrows.

"I have. I really have."

"Did he ask for your phone number?"

"He did. We're having dinner tomorrow night."

"No kidding. I'm thrilled for you." Suzie flashed a big grin.

Sondra smiled.

Dinner with the new man did not go well. He didn't come right out and say it; but she knew in her heart that he was up to no good. She got the distinct feeling that he was trying to determine her net worth before they went any further.

She had immersed herself in her new persona. As Sondra Silvers, wine rep from New York, she had no intention of pretending to be wealthy. Connected, yes; but not one of Palm Beach's super rich. So, if that's what he was looking for, it was just as well that she found out right at the start.

When Danielle had worked in amateur theatre, she had enjoyed making up a detailed profile of the character she was portraying and their idiosyncrasies. This was corroborated with wardrobe, hair style and various specific mannerisms. Blessed with a gift for inventing a rich, inner life of the characters she'd portrayed in the past, she found it easy to portray a realistic character.

Edward Turnbull asked way too many questions. *Was he an undercover cop? Surely not.* "Why did you decide to leave Manhattan and move to Florida?" He took a sip of the aged Cabernet from the elegant crystal glass.

"Are you kidding? Moving from the dirty, hectic, mad rush of the big city to tropical paradise? Do you really have to ask? When you get an invitation to come to Palm Beach from someone whose company you enjoy, you grab it." She smiled. "Let's cut to the chase. You want to know my net worth. Isn't that right? Well, let me just say, that if hooking up with a filthy rich society dame is your goal, you're barking up the wrong tree."

Her date was struck speechless. He'd reacted as she'd intended. She threw the ball back to him. "So you were a commodities broker. That's a very exciting business. You have to be very sharp and on your toes to survive in that world, I would think."

"Honey, I was the sharpest. Now I'm one of the richest men in Palm Beach."

Okay. Problem is, honey. I don't much like you. Too bad, really. But then again...I don't think you're particularly interested in me, now that you've determined I'm not super rich.

The server put the bill in a tray and her escort slapped down his credit card.

"Thank-you for dinner." Sondra smiled. *She was no longer Danielle. She had to think like her new imaginary character would.*

He grinned and seemed almost human for a few minutes. "Food is great here, isn't it?"

"Fabulous. Dinner was amazing."

"My pleasure."

I know he had a hidden agenda. Is he merely a gold digger, or is it something else?

They said good-night and roared off in their separate cars. Sondra knew he wouldn't be calling. That was just as well, because she did not want to date him again.

She drove back to Suzie's house feeling kind of sad. *Was she losing her charm? Was he an undercover cop? The guy was really, really strange.* "Maybe I'll fly back to Manhattan, if things don't work out here." She chuckled, fully immersed in her character.

Two days later.

As Danielle walked out of the supermarket wheeling groceries in a shopping cart, she saw the man again. *Strange I should run into him. Or maybe not so strange...m*aybe it's deliberate.

She didn't believe in coincidences. The man was stalking her. She was sure of it. Either he was an undercover cop; or he had a hidden agenda of some sort. *Was he a fortune hunter? A lot of beautiful women showed up here with the goal of finding rich hubbies. And some guys showed up hoping to hook up with wealthy society matrons. She was hoping she'd get lucky herself.*

"Party time." Suzie was always in a good mood. No matter what happened, she rarely veered from her upbeat, cheerful mindset. "Charlie Woodcroft has invited us to a sit-down dinner for sixteen. Just got the invitation in the mail."

"Good heavens. Do hostesses still send hand-written invitations for sit-down dinners?" Danielle was truly amazed.

"In Palm Beach they do. And one is either in the inner circle and invited to the right parties; or one is not. You can't bribe, cajole or con your way in." She chuckled. "The hostesses here either like you and invite you into their coveted inner circle; or they don't. If they decide they don't like you, you can't buy your way in with a truckload of cash."

Sondra chuckled. "Well, I'm glad you're an insider; and so far, so good, where I'm concerned."

Suzie was clad in yet another glamorous, floral caftan, this one was had a lime green tropical, floral theme. Rather tall and slender with high cheekbones, she could have been a model. Sondra wondered if she'd had cheek implants. Her full, high cheekbones were very becoming. Palm Beach plastic surgeons were among the best in the world. Maybe she'd have some work done herself down the road.

This morning, Suzie whipped up some scrambled eggs with red peppers and jalapenos. She served it to them on the patio table overlooking the ocean. "God has been good to me. One rich husband...suddenly, I'm a widow and I own the rights to all his books. I'm working on a movie deal for one of them, by the way."

"That's exciting...about the movie deal, I mean. Which one of his books is it based on?"

"A Sunny day in May."

"Come on. That's the title?"

"I'll get it for you. You should read it." She rose from

her Wingback chair in the living room, strode to the library and quickly located the book in the charming, built-in bookcase. Masses of books lined the shelves. She brought it over to "Sondra", handing it to her. "You should read it. It's absolutely brilliant."

"I will." Danielle loved her new life and invented persona. Sondra Silvers, wealthy divorcee from New York City. It had a certain ring to it. She loved her new identity so much that she felt that no matter what happened, she would never return to her former name and the bad memories accompanying it.

"Thanks. What's the novel about?" Danielle took it from Suzie's hand, and started leafing through it.

"I don't want to spoil it for you. Read it. You won't be able to put it down."

"I'll start tonight. I can hardly wait." She smiled. "You sure know how to get people to become bookworms in a hurry."

"Yes. The primary reason for that is because books are a bargain. They're the best, cheap entertainment available. Educational, if you want that... and...well… personally, I enjoy escaping into the imaginary world the author has created. And I simply adore biographies...."

"How close are you to making a movie deal?" Danielle's as impressed.

"Very. So close, I don't want to talk about it."

"Okay. I'll send up some prayers that it happens."

"That I appreciate. I believe in the power of prayer."

"Me, too."

Chapter Eight

Sondra attended church with Suzie. She was getting into some good habits of praise and worship, along with regular church attendance. That evening, as they relaxed around the house, Sondra began reading the novel Suzie's late hubby had penned.

The words sprung the story to life. *"Thunder rumbled, lightening cracked lighting up the sky as a sense of impending disaster filled his mind. Something sinister was going to happen tonight..."* It was 4:00 in the morning when she finally read the last page of the novel. "Riveting. Absolutely riveting." She spoke the words of praise aloud, despite the fact that Suzie had long since retired for the night.

The next morning at breakfast on the patio, the warm Florida sunshine caressing her, Sondra sipped gourmet coffee and picked at her omelette. "I can sure see why he's a New York Times best-selling author. I stayed up until 4:00 a.m. reading it. I couldn't put it down. How many books has he written?"

"One hundred and twenty-two."

"Unbelievable. Where did he get his inspiration from?"

"He claims his inspiration came mostly from God. But he also credits me for inspiring him. I made him laugh. He was incredibly witty. But he thought I was hilarious."

Danielle chucked. "What do you think it was about you that inspired him to write?"

"Aside from my wicked sense of humor? I really don't know. I always tried to find out... but I never really got a straight answer from him."

"I bet it was your passion for life...and your inquisitive nature... your love for nurturing flowers and plants...your beauty... your humor... and your generosity... and finally, your love for humanity."

"You sure you didn't leave anything out?" She chuckled. "Funny...I always felt inadequate around him. He was so superior to me intellectually, far more educated...and of course...thirty years my senior. Some of our friends thought I married him for his money. They don't know me very well. I married him because I loved him...deeply. ..passionately...and with every fibre of my being."

"What was it about him that captured your heart? I mean...aside from his...celebrity...and his great gift for writing?"

"I really don't know. Chemistry, I suppose. We just clicked the moment I met him...and I knew I wanted to be with him...wanted to get to know him better."

"And I think you told me that you met at a dinner party. Right?"

"Yes.... right here in Palm Beach. It was a memorable evening. Joan and Bob Saunders had a formal dinner for ten at their house...they just live a short stroll up the beach. Joan invited him as the spare man. I was one of three single women invited to the party. What I didn't find out until later was that Joan was playing cupid and trying to fix the famous author up with someone he could hook up with. He was rather shy, you see."

"What happened to his previous wife...or wives?"

"He was divorced twice. Not planning to remarry. That is...until Joan got her hands on him. Joan and her hubby met him at church. He had just become a Christian. All he had to do was mention to her that he was kind of lonely...and wham...Joan was on it. Three days later, she phoned him and invited him to a dinner party. She was determined to help him meet a special someone. Maybe head to the altar again."

"Enter. Suzie Allen."

"Exactly."

"She sounds like a real doll."

"You don't know the half of it. I have to say, one of the things I like most about her...is the fact that she has great empathy for single gals. She's been married since she was nineteen and, honestly...she's lived an idyllic existence, and woman living alone concern her."

"How extra-ordinary." Sondra smiled. "God promises to give us life abundantly. He promises prosperity, joy, peace...."

"Don't forget good health."

"Right. *"I wish above all things that thou mayest prosper and be in health, even as thy soul prospers. 111 John 11."* There you are.

"I really think that if we all meditated on the scriptures night and day, like God admonishes us to be, every dream of our heart would be realized. I just finished reading a book on the prayers of Jabez. It was riveting. The theme of the book is that we can come into great financial prosperity and blessing, if we press into the word and *ask. "We have not because we ask not."* That seems to be a recurring theme.

"Do you think that translates to asking favors from friends and acquaintances as well as asking God?"

"Sure. If someone you know is the recipient of great blessing, financial prosperity and all that, they should share it with others. If they don't, maybe the person in need should ask them to. There's a lot of power in asking for what you want. When I was young...last year...ha. ha...I found out years later that the man I wanted to marry was keen to marry me, also. He was just waiting for me to suggest it...to push him a bit. He kept hinting around, but he didn't come right out and pop the question. And I lacked the confidence to push it. So it never happened."

"Yes, there is great power in asking. In sales, they always tell you to *Ask for the order.* I think if we're asking our friends for whatever it is that we need, as well as asking God...I believe he will supply it." *"We have not because we ask not."* *"Anything you ask, believing, you shall receive.*"There's a couple scriptures... there are dozens more corroborating this."

Chapter Nine

Dana woke up feeling sick. She rolled out of bed and poured herself a glass of water in the bathroom. Momentarily, she threw it up. She was really sick today. So sick she didn't care what happened to her prize colt or the Derby, she wanted to crawl back to bed and stay there.

Jacob found it disorienting to exercise Flaming Sunset without the trainer. He counted on the input he got from Dana. Still, he put the colt through his paces and worked diligently. Maybe she would show up late. Maybe they would work twice as hard tomorrow.

He watched the other jockeys exercise their colts. He could feel the electricity in the air as the big day approached. He could hardly wait. He couldn't imagine doing anything else with his life. His dedication to the equines was absolute.

Dana pulled herself together, took a shower and drove out to the track. She would surprise Jacob. She was feeling a bit better and her stubborn spirit of determination fueled her to proceed. Soon, she was at the track coaching Jacob and everything was back to normal.

That night Graham told her he wanted to speak to her privately, without Violet or the boys. *What was he up to?*

In his comfortable den, Graham took a chair and invited her to do the same. "Dana. I don't know how to say this...but Jacob told me that he doesn't feel the colt is going to make it...he said...it's just a feeling he has about Flaming Bullet. He's a great racehorse, but not competitive enough...he said the only way you can know that it by training and following the typical training schedule geared for the big run."

"So...you're saying he's just concluded we've got a loser." Dana looked at him as though he'd just lost his mind. "*WHAT* are you talking about? What is all this negative stuff you're saying? Flaming Bullet is going to win. That's a fact. He will win. I won't hear of anything else."

He ran down the hallway after her. "Honey. I didn't mean to upset you..."

"Didn't mean to upset me?" She was fuming. "You just dumped a lot of negative stuff on me. But you didn't mean to upset me. Gee, I'd sure hate to be around when you deliberately want to upset me. If this is your idea of a joke... can it." Dana hurried away from the man she loved; the man that had suddenly become a virtual stranger to her.

That night Dana cried herself to sleep. *What was happening to her? To her marriage? To their mutual dream of winning the Derby? It seemed to be moving further and further away from her...from them. She wanted to physically run after that dream and say "No, no, no..."* She awakened suddenly, in the middle of the night. She was shaking. "I had a dream about the Derby. I dreamed that Jacob rode the colt to victory." She spoke with jubilation. "Honey...In the dream, we won."

Graham held her close. "Well, then, honey. That's what will happen. Our colt will win. Maybe God is showing you that so that you will have the steam...the passion to keep on keeping on...and not to give up. We're so close, I can feel it. If we seek God first and pray together and read the Word before the sessions, I think you'll find they will go much better."

"You know, honey. You're right. I've been so focused on getting to the track when the other trainers, jockeys and colts get there, that I've...well, I've left God behind. I haven't meditated on the word and prayed like I used to. *We* haven't. What's that scripture? "*I am the vine. You are the branches"*. We both know that we must press forward, but we also must remain connected to God, our source. Then, he will make our way prosperous."

"You know, I think if we do that, honey, we're going to see victory. It's tough and competitive, but if we seek Him with our whole hearts and listen for that still, small voice of the Holy Spirit to lead, guide and direct us...maybe we can snatch victory from the jaws of defeat."

That evening after dinner, Will and Jay engaged in an intense game of chess in the games room.

Graham and Dana snuggled on the sofa watching them.

"You know, honey, horse racing is like a chess game in a way. You have to look at everything, every angle, every nuance in order to get it right and inspire the colt to be so focused on winning... he just has to do it."

"I never thought I'd say this, Graham. But I just want it to be over. Win or lose. It's been such a long, hard road. What started out as a great adventure...has morphed into other things. Of course there's the underbelly of sleaziness in the business, which always makes for a sour taste in the mouth."

The day of the Kentucky Derby was warm for the first week of May. The air crackled with excitement. This was the first Saturday in May. The long anticipated day of the Kentucky Derby. The jockeys, trainers, owners and their colts had all worked hard. Someone would win the jackpot.

"All the contenders dream of taking the purse. But there's only one winner." Dana's good spirits had returned. Being pregnant wasn't bothering her as much as it had a couple months ago. She and Graham murmured to the colt, sending positive messages and prayers as they stood next to him and Jacob at the starting gate.

Jacob was in rare form. He teased the colt, whispering to him as though he were human. *"May you run for the glory of God. May the angels protect you and be with you.* He mounted the colt. They were poised and ready at the starting gate, waiting breathlessly for the starting signal.

"Boom." "Zero Hour. And they're off in the Kentucky Derby." The excited announcer's voice blared over the loud speaker, as the most exciting two minutes in sports began.

The gate flew open as the colts and their jockey's raced at fever pitch.

An excited crowd of magnificently clad spectators cheered wildly. Women in enormous hats, dressed flamboyantly and men elegantly attired watched, riveted to the action.

Jacob kept egging the colt on. A deep, inner confidence that could only come from God, welled up inside him. He was neck-in-neck with two other colts. Suddenly, as though Firelight Fancy had sprouted wings, he soared ahead of the other two colts, taking the lead by a nose. The bell rang. Jacob and Firelight Fancy had soared through to victory..

"And the winner of the Kentucky Derby is Firelight Fancy. His jockey is Jacob Jacks."

Jacob and Firelight Fancy blasted through to triumph. Jacob was floating a mile high in his mind. He was euphoric. Firelight Fancy pranced regally before the cheering crowd of spectators who were wildly applauding.

Thousands of excited spectators stood, cheering excitedly. There was a sea of enormous hats worn by the lady spectators, along with their elegantly clad gentlemen, as they continued to applaud the winning colt and jockey.

Jacob paraded the colt in the spotlight, while two young men heaped masses of vivid, red roses onto the winning colt. "We did it, Boy." Jacob grinned, elated as he patted the colt, whispering gratitude and blessings upon him. He grinned as the cameras moved in close, for all the world to see and share. Overjoyed, he felt like laughing and dancing and shouting victory, simultaneously.

In the owner's box, Graham and Dana were over the moon. The second their colt won, Graham grabbed Dana, kissing her fervently. "Honey, we did it."

"No, Graham, God did it. To God be the glory."

"Blessings and gratitude for Firelight Fancy and Jacob."

"You're absolutely right, honey." He swung her around, despite being in cramped quarters. Dozens of owners stopped by to congratulate them.

Dana knew in her heart that the well-wishers genuinely shared in their elation and joy of winning the purse.

Cameras moved around capturing the finest moments of colt, jockey and owners for the whole world to see. Firelight Fancy and Jacob had instantly become worldwide celebrities. It was heady stuff.

Graham and Dana were the toast of the town. They celebrated with fine champagne and caviar. Great food, music and a group of dedicated horse racing enthusiasts mingled in the owners' quarters popping corks of vintage champagne as everyone celebrated their win. "To Firelight Fancy. Jacob, Dana and Graham.".

Tippi Taylor, a local socialite and horse enthusiast, flamboyant and dramatic in her 1 outrageously enormous coral hat and matching suit and pumps, raised her glass in a celebration toast. "You're one up on me." She smiled. "But there's always next year."

Her escort, a debonair, older gentleman grinned. "We should retire to the South of France, darling. There are other things in life aside from the obsession of wining the roses."

"Ah, my dear." She flashed him a big smile. "You don't know me very well. *Until* I win the Derby, I won't be retiring. If I never win...I never retire." She smiled, lifting her glass in a toast, as her tiger eyes twinkled.

Dana could hardly miss the determined look in her eyes. *She'll win or die trying.*

"You'll change your mind, darling. Once you see my sumptuous villa on the French Riviera, you won't even want to come back here."

"Don't be so sure of yourself, Bill. Horses and winning are in my blood. Nothing and no one can change that."

Dana smiled at Tippi. "Did you grow up with the equines, like I did?"

"I sure did. Ever since I was knee high to a grasshopper, I've been riding them."

"Why is it so important to win?" Dana knew why *they* had to win. But Tippi hobnobbed in the rarified air populated sparsely by high society, hobnobbing with the elite in Palm Beach and watching polo. Dana knew she had a house in Lexington and one in Palm Beach.

"Because life, darling...is about winning. In life, there are winners and losers. I'm a winner. And yes, I'm stubborn. I will win the Kentucky Derby. No matter how long it takes, how many horses I have trained, how many years it takes...I shall win. My colt and I will take the roses. *Then,* I shall go on to other things. But not until then."

Her escort scowled, soon leading her away from the small circle of well-wishers who acknowledged them as they hurried out from the owner's box to join Jacob, Firelight Fancy, the heaps of roses and the cameras.

The world watched as Jacob and Firelight Fancy paraded before the cameras.

Dana and Graham as the owners were on camera as well. It suited them. They loved the cameras and thrived on the publicity.

Inside his cell, Tanner, a model prisoner, had been granted his request to view the Kentucky Derby on TV. due to his rapidly failing health, advanced age and the prognosis that he likely didn't have long to live. He watched "The fastest two minutes in sports" riveted to the screen. He was stunned as he watched Dana's colt, Firelight Fancy and his jockey, Jacob Parks, thrust into the spotlight as they embraced the enormous spray of magnificent red roses, smiling joyfully for the cameras. Tanner was fit to be tied. *If only he could slip out of this dungeon undetected. Danielle had done that twice. It was anybody's guess whether or not she would be apprehended a second time. He admired her guts.*

That night, Dana's emotions were super-charged. They watched a movie, propped up on their pillows in their king-sized, luxurious bed. A caller's name and phone number flashed on the screen. Dana deferred to Graham. "I don't know who this is. Do you?"

"No "

"Should we pick it up, Graham? It might be Mother"

"It's your call, honey."

Dana lifted up the receiver on the night table.

"Darling. Congratulations."

"Mother. Where are you?"

"Can you keep a secret?" Her voice took on a conspiratorial tone.

Dana was over the moon. They'd won the purse. She was pregnant. And now Mom was calling. Her prayers and the desires of her heart were being answered by God Almighty. Life was beyond amazing. "Sure, Mom."

"I'm in Palm Beach, darling. And I'm engaged to a wonderful man."

Dana couldn't believe her ears. She wouldn't mention the jail break or any negatives. She was flying high after the win. And she wasn't about to turn her Mom in. Oh, she and Graham had talked about it; but they'd both agreed to let sleeping dogs lie.

"I'm calling to congratulate you and Graham on winning the Kentucky Derby. You both must be over the moon. It's so exciting. What are you going to do with all that money?"

For just one moment Dana had allowed herself the luxury of dreaming that Danielle had changed. That she'd called to congratulate them with no hidden agenda. But, of course, it wasn't true. Danielle usually had ulterior motives with everything she did. This call was no exception.

"We're donating the money to Israel." Dana didn't try to

hide her disappointment.

Silence.

"Have you forgotten, Mother? The mandate we had. The money...all of it...will be given as a gift to help the aged Holocaust survivors in Israel."

"Well...you're a regular Mother Teresa, aren't you?" Danielle's voice took on an icy tone.

"It wasn't my brainchild. Graham has wanted to do this for ages. It's a dream he's cherished for decades. I think that's why God allowed us to win. I didn't actually think we would. I hoped we would. I prayed we would. But the colt...well, I just wasn't quite sure he'd make it. But he surprised us. At the last minute he soared ahead of the pack and ran like wildfire...won by a nose. Exciting stuff."

"Anyway, darling. I must run. I need my beauty rest. Big luncheon tomorrow. If you're ever in Palm Beach, look me up."

"Of course. Good-night and thanks for calling." Dana hung up the phone and turned to Graham. "It's incredible that she trusts us not to turn her in." Tears sprung to her eyes. "So much for a Mother who cares.".

"She called once before when you weren't here. She's met Donald Trump and been issued a pardon. I thought I mentioned it. Maybe not. I'm surprised she didn't tell you." Graham peered over at her. "I guess she thought I would have told you about it."

"That's incredible. How did she pull *that* off?"

"She's become a very successful fund-raiser for charities in Palm Beach. Almost overnight. She's known there...as a kind of phenomena. Seems she has a talent for extracting money from the rich and famous. Guess she called to see if we would give her the million we just won."

Dana chuckled through misty tears. "Well, I guess I can't blame her for trying. We *are* donating it to charity. Just not to one she's affiliated with."

"Oh...and the last time she called, she said she'd raised

several million for children's orphanages. She has a favorite one in Mexico."

"Well, she's certainly turned her life around. Does she know Jesus? Because if she doesn't, we better tell her about him. *"All your righteousness is as filthy rags."* springs to mind.

"She's like a different person lately. I swear she has multiple personalities. She's like...morphed into this high society dame...it's as though she's changed her personality...in one way, I'm fascinated by her, in another way, I want to shake her and ask if she's in there."

"She's a chameleon. No doubt about that. She sure landed on her feet." Graham shook his head in amazement.

"She used to yak about her girlfriend in Palm Beach. Frankly, I didn't believe she really existed. Turns out I was wrong. I guess they really *are* tight."

"Come on, it's late. Let's get some sleep. We'll talk more about this tomorrow. And, most importantly, we need to do a bank transfer to Israel for a million dollars."

"You know we're in for a big blessing for helping Israel, don't you?" Dana smiled and threw her arms around Graham, as she reached up to him and peered into his eyes. "My femme fatale Mom is off the scene. She's found her own man. Halleluiah. We won the Derby. And we're about to be blessed...big time. Hey, good things are happening."

But that night, sleep eluded her. She had a premonition that she hadn't heard the last of Danielle and a sense that she was going to make another play for the money. She chuckled softly. *Fat chance, Mom. The funds have been ear-marked for Israel.*

The next morning, bright and early, the buzzer sounded in the kitchen. It was hooked up to their newly installed security system, which included a manned gate guard. Dana set her coffee down, answering the intercom. *Who was stopping by at this early hour?*

"Ray here. You have an early morning visitor." He paused for effect. "Danielle and her driver."

Dana saw red. *How dare her Mom show up here uninvited? How dare she show up at all?* "Ray... Danielle is persona non grata. We've spelled that out to you and to her. I'm afraid you'll have to turn Mom away." *Unbidden, bitter tears trickled down her cheeks. Secretly, she dreamed of a Mother that adored her, that wanted to be her friend, someone she could rely on and trust. It wasn't meant to be. Danielle was none of those things.* "I better get over it." She whispered the words to herself. Shaking, she took another sip of coffee from her mug, as she sat at the kitchen table, fighting more tears.

Violet hovered nearby. "I'm sorry, honey." She came over to where Dana sat at the kitchen table and hugged her. "It's okay, Dana. You don't need her. You have me...and you have Graham and the boys. Some people are just plain no-good. Maybe she fits into that category. I'm sorry, honey. If it's any consolation, I will always be here for you. You and Graham are the children I never had." She smiled and patted Dana on one of her arms, affectionately.

"What a nice thing to say." Dana patted the chair next to hers. "Have a seat, Violet. Join me for coffee...and breakfast. Graham is in his office. He had an important early call to make to New York. He should be along shortly. *Lord, you are so good to me. When you close one door, you open another.*

Danielle never took no for an answer. She wasn't through fighting for the money Dana and Graham had won. She would intercept them and convince them that her charities were superior to any other causes, including their grand idea of gifting it to Holocaust survivors in Israel. If she could get her hands on their winnings and put it under the umbrella of her charities, it would thrust her name and image further into the spotlight. And she'd have more clout. Along with the funds she'd already raised for charity, this would be a nice feather in her cap. *But could she charm Graham and Dana out of a million dollars? Of course. She was invincible.* She smiled. She had fast become powerful in high society circles. She was so much shrewder than *Dana.* And men...well, she could wrap Graham around her little finger if she really wanted to.

Danielle instructed her driver to wait in front of the gate at Sugarbush. Sooner or later, the guard would take a break. Somebody from Sugarbush would drive out that gate. She would intercept them and talk them into inviting her onto the farm. She was Dana's Mother, after all, And with all their talk about the Bible and church...well, as Dana's mother, she should be honored, shouldn't she? Wasn't that the third commandment?

11:00 a.m. Three Hours Later.

Danielle's driver was getting itchy to move on. Horace had never been a patient man. He'd made an exception for Danielle, because, quite frankly, he fancied her. Sooner or later, she might need an escort to accompany her to one of the society parties or events. He would step up to the plate. He'd been blessed with his share of good looks; though sometimes he thought he'd trade them for a few more brains. He'd botched up a lot of stuff in his life. Becoming a chauffeur, though, was one of the smartest decisions he'd ever made.

He hadn't minded flying with Danielle from Palm Beach to Lexington, early that morning, renting a limo and driving Danielle to Sugarbush, but he was tiring of the waiting game. He wanted to get back to Florida.

Danielle turned to her driver. "That's them. Graham is driving the jeep; that's Dana next to him."

So what? They're going to keep driving, if you're persona non grata. But the chauffeur didn't say anything. He just nodded. He'd grown used to being subservient. Not that he liked it. But it was his survival.

Graham glared at the limo driver and Danielle, drove through as the gate clanked behind him. He sped down the road, ignoring Danielle's intrusive ploy.

"Follow them. We'll intercept them at the bank." Danielle didn't skip a beat as she instructed her driver to pursue Graham and Dana as they drove.

"I hope you know what you're doing, Danielle. So far, this seems like a big waste of money and time."

"I'm paying you to do what I ask. Not to think. Keep your opinions to yourself, if you don't mind."

Fine lady. Waste your money, if that's what you want to do. Ray didn't like being talked down to by this uppity broad. He'd get back at her. He just wasn't sure how. For now, though, he'd bide his time, despite the fact that he was seething inside. "Whatever you say, Danielle. You're the boss."

"Yes...I am, aren't I?"

Chapter Ten

Graham parked his white jeep in front of the
bank, in the only available space left, He opened the door for
Dana and they stepped into the ultra-modern Bank of
America.

Inside the bank, Graham, having phoned in advance, was
quickly escorted into the private office of Carl Trottier, the
bank manager. His assistant, Joy Annie expedited the
million-dollar gift, transferring the funds to the First
international Bank of Israel, where their designated
representative would arrange to receive and oversee the
distribution of funds.

Graham, with Dana seated next to him, grinned at Karl.
"That should make their day."

"Yes. I'm sure it will. I hope God blesses y'all real good
for this magnanimous gift. I wish there were more people
like the two of you...helping others. However,
philanthropists are a very small minority. I've been a banker
for over thirty years. In all those years, I've never seen a gift
to Israel or another country by an individual matching your
generosity."

"But surely there are wealthy Jews who are helping their
own. There must be many large financial gifts given to them
annually."

"Certainly there are monetary gifts given to them. But
it's from such a miniscule number of people; and without
giving away details, I will say these contributions are very

modest compared with your gift."

There was nothing she could do. Danielle had to face that. She'd been drinking too much fine wine and her brain was groggy. *What had she been thinking? Graham and Dana didn't trust her and barely talked to her. Why would they hand her the million dollars they had worked so diligently for so many years to earn? Money they'd earmarked for Israel ages ago.*

"We're going to an early lunch. I'm buying, of course. There's a fabulous restaurant called Villa de Vinci. It's private. The food is amazing. I'll give you the directions. It's a bit of a drive, but it's worth it. *I wouldn't be surprised if Dana and Graham showed up there today. I just have a hunch they will.*

Villa de Vinci was fabulous just like Danielle had promised. They dined on lobster with a Pouilly Fuse white wine. Just as the food arrived, in her peripheral vision, she saw them. Dana and Graham entering the private club they owned. She smiled across the table at her escort for effect. Graham and Dana might give her the recognition and respect she both craved and deserved. *How many other women could show up in that snobby town and rise to the top like crème...in a nanosecond? But she'd done it, and folks ought to take their hat off to her. Okay, she was a little egotistical. But show me someone famous who isn't?*

The lobster was superb, the white wine perfect. She glanced over at Ray and could see he was duly impressed. "Sondra" was distracted. She knew she looked amazing in the short designer dress. The vivid shade of pink was a flattering shade and enhanced her NEW Cleopatra look. That's why she'd chosen it. Botox and some excellent work done on her face caused her to look significantly younger that her chronological age.

She was bored with trying to attract Graham, though. The few available single men in Palm Beach, however, were significantly more interesting and wealthier than those in Lexington, except for the horsey set. In that small group, the majority moved back and forth enjoying dual homes. Most had a home in Palm Beach and one in Lexington, Kentucky; horse country. Some folks had large farms, others small properties. Once the Derby and celebration parties were over, the jet setters headed back to their Palm Beach residences.

She *was* engaged, after all. Still, her mischievous nature longed to kick up her heels and find a reason to celebrate. Flirting with Graham always got Dana irked. And since *she* was irked, and they hadn't respected the fact that she presided over world-class charities, she'd cause a little havoc. Graham and Dana had shown no interest in learning more about the charities she presided over. They'd declined her invitation to attend a charity ball in Palm Beach. Danielle and a few other local Palm Beach fundraisers organized and ran the event. Miraculously; it had to be her perfect timing...or maybe God's...the women organizing the charity events were burned out and encouraged Danielle to take over the reins It had been perfect timing. Timing that only God could have arranged. It was time to play a little game. Danielle thrived on games.

Dana and Graham noticed her simultaneously. Graham's first instinct was to take Dana and leave the premises. But after all, why should he? It was *his* restaurant. If anyone should leave, it should be Danielle.

"Sondra Silvers" smiled over at them, waving coyly.

Graham was losing his appetite. *He would ban her from the club. Let her enjoy her last meal here. "Mark."* He signaled the matre' d to come to his table. "See that woman over there?" He nodded in Danielle's direction. "She is Dana's step Mom. For reasons I won't get into, please do not allow her in the club. Or any of her escorts, for that matter."

"Yes, sir. Danielle Lockhart is persona non grata at Villa

Da Vinci. We'll make sure she never enters the premises. You can count on us." The handsome Latino, Juan Banderos grinned.

"Thank *you.*"

"Oh...and you might have to look closely. *Very closely.* She's been known to disguise herself."

"Really? Well...now this gets interesting."

"Yeah. Real interesting. She's like a chameleon...you never know who she is or what she's up to."

"I promise to do my very best to identify her and ask her to leave, I'll tell the staff, of course. But she won't get past me. That, I can guarantee."

Chapter Eleven

Dana threw up a lot of mornings and had a voracious appetite. Today she lunched with Graham. Violet served mushroom soup and a green salad.

Will and Jay bounded onto the veranda, apparently having already eaten lunch. Since today was Saturday, they were off to continue enjoying the day. "Hi Dad. Hi Mom." Will hugged Graham and then Dana. Jay did the same. They bounced in and out of the room, fueled by youthful energy.

She'd always marveled at how fast the boys had adapted to her and their father's new marriage. *Thank-you for that blessing, Lord.*

In the middle of the night, Dana began to have some fierce cravings. She wanted chocolate ice-cream and hot salsa and chips. She tried not to disturb Graham as she padded to the kitchen. Fortunately, she found those foods she craved. She sat down at the kitchen table and ate heartily.

Graham turned in their bed, placing his hand where Dana should be. When he realized she wasn't there, he was surprised. Groggily, he left the warm bed to go and check on her. *I bet she's raiding the fridge.* Sure enough, he found her at the table, gleefully gorging on chocolate ice-cream. He took a chair opposite hers. "Honey. ..eat up and let's go back to bed."

"Sure, honey…"She finished the ice cream, leaving the container empty. Then she started on the chips with salsa sauce."…soon as I finish."

Graham was already awake so he decided to keep her company. He waited until she had had her fill of the hot sauce and chips. "Ready for bed, darling?"

She nodded and together they headed to their bedroom.

The next morning, Dana felt better. She decided to answer some of the calls she had received requesting her services as a trainer. She was hot. That was great, except for the fact that she was pregnant. Staying healthy was a priority. She would carefully choose with whom she would work. She decided to kick back and relish their success. Next week, she would meet with horse owners who wanted her to train their colts for horse racing. Her reply was standard. "We'll meet. We'll talk about time frames, objectives, budget, etc., and once I've interviewed everyone interested in hiring my services, I'll make my selections. "

Graham was in the city doing business when she heard the blaring fire alarm. The sound was coming from the barn. "Violet. Come quickly. The fire alarm is blaring." She stared out from the veranda, shock overtaking her. Massive flames leaped from the barn. The neigh of terrified horses grazing on the nearby fields resounded throughout the farm. "All the horses should be outside, grazing. I sure hope none of them are in the barn. As far as she knew, none of the horses were in the barn. They were all grazing in the pastures.

Hurrying outside, she saw the leaping flames. And to her horror, she heard the terrified neighs of what was obviously a trapped horse. Why would a lone horse remain in the barn, when all the others were outside grazing? But as she glimpsed the magnitude of the flames leaping from the barn, with a sinking heart, she realized there would be little or no chance of rescuing the trapped equine. if one of them was inside the barn. "Lord. We need a miracle. I can hear the terrified whinnying of a horse."

Violet was with her. She phoned Graham, telling him to come home immediately. She was verging on hysteria. "I...I think one of the horses is trapped inside the barn, Lord. I don't know why he's there, but I can hear the terrified whinnying of a trapped horse. Lord, please help us get him out."

Violet had called the fire department when she'd first spotted the blaze. A massive red fire truck drove up, stopping near the barn. *Lord, please help us save the trapped animal.*

The blaze was escalating rapidly. Two firemen clad in fireproof bodysuits hurried into the barn. Dana knew she was witnessing a miracle when they emerged through leaping flames with the horse. Paramedics worked feverishly on him, treating severe burns. "We'll need you to load him up on a horse trailer and transport him to Park Equine Hospital at Woodford as soon as possible."

Another firetruck showed up. Both trucks continued pumping gallons of water on the barn. After some time, they managed to get the blaze under control. "Wonder how the fire started?" One of the firemen asked Dana. Any thoughts?"

Paramedics treated the horse as one of the men climbed into Dana's horse trailer to drive the equine to the hospital. She was torn between wanting to go with the horse and staying at Sugarbush. Graham was due any minute.

One of the firemen peered at Dana. "I've heard there is an arsonist in the area. No one has been able to catch him so far. I hope and pray we get him soon, before he causes any more damage. It is a miracle that we got your horse out before he died."

Dana peered at the fireman. "Yes, it is a miracle. The moment I heard the desperate whinnying of the trapped horse, I began praying the 91st Psalm over him. I know it by heart. Somewhere along the way I felt it was important to have that scripture emblazoned on my mind and heart. It has great, great power.

The fireman spoke up. "It does. There's an actress who had a home in Malibu, and when the fires started, she began reading Psalm 91 over and over again. Then, a miracle happened. "The blaze stopped in front of her house. Her house was not touched."

"Really. It's amazing these stories don't make the news. ..though maybe I missed it."

"It's all over the internet, you know." The fireman said.

"Really? Well, I'll be sure to check that out."

Wilbur and Ted, their ranch hands, gazed at the fire helplessly, as they stood next to Dana, a safe distance from the burning barn.

Dana could hear the terrified sound of the trapped horse whinnying. She turned to Wilbur. *He has worked on the farm since Graham bought it.* "Wilbur…why was the bay horse left in the barn, while all the others are outside grazing in the pasture? It doesn't make sense to me."

Then she saw it. The gleam in his eyes. She was horror struck. *Oh no. Don't tell me he's the arsonist they're looking for. Was she imagining that gleam in his eye? Maybe. But she sure didn't imagine the silence.* It spoke volumes. "Wilbur. Answer me." Dana's emotions rose, along with her voice. Tears sprung to her eyes. She loved every horse they had with a passion. *And Wilbur loves horses. He couldn't possibly be an arsonist, could he?* His continued silence gave her the answer she didn't want to believe.

"This morning's news said an arsonist was on the loose in this area. Several horses have been trapped and perished in fires in the area." The fireman kept talking as he hosed down the barn.

She stared at Wilbur, willing it not to be him. But she could not miss the fixated gaze in his eyes as though he were drunk.

Graham was on his way back from a meeting in Lexington. She'd called him immediately upon seeing the blaze. He hadn't arrived yet. She would get his take on it.

Graham's white Jeep roared onto the farm. He jumped out and hurried over to the scene. Wrapping powerful arms around Dana, he comforted her, wiping away her tears.

The remaining paramedic said he believed the horse had a good chance of surviving. "I think he's made it and will be just fine. God was watching over him."

Dana took Graham aside, as everyone remained fixated to the horror of the burning barn, which was getting under control. She whispered to him. "Graham... look at Wilbur. His eyes are strange, it's like he's under a spell. He's the arsonist they're looking for. He did this. I just feel it in my gut." She whispered her suspicion to Graham.

Wilbur was sobbing uncontrollably.

"Oh Dana...sometimes life is just so unbearably horrific. It makes me wonder how people get through it when they don't know the creator. We can call on Him in our hour of need; but those folks living in darkness, have to muddle through on their own. They cannot take refuge in that secret place like we can."

"I pray that the sheriff will catch the arsonist before more horses perish."

"They'll catch him...sooner than you think." Tears cascaded down Wilbur's cheeks.

"What makes you say that?" She stared at him, horror struck.

"I...just know. But you're going to be shocked when you discover who it is..."

"So...you know who it is?"

"Yes."

"But you're not going to tell me?"

"You...you'll find out soon." Wilbur turned his face from Dana.

"We'll let the sheriff do his work. We may learn something. Then, soon...enough...we'll know. Darling...there's no easy way to say this..." Graham herded Dana away from the others. His arm was around her, comforting her.

"Spit it out, Graham."

"It was Wilbur." Tears trickled down Graham's cheeks. "He gave himself up. Just called the sheriff on his cell. He's on the way here to pick him up."

Dana stared at Graham, horrified. When she found her voice, she spoke with acute sadness. "I always knew he was wacky." Dana shook her head.

"You *did?* Why didn't you say something?"

"I guess it's the old adage that a lot of people are crazy, but in different ways so it goes unnoticed." Dana sighed. "I didn't think he was dangerous. Never thought he'd hurt a fly."

"Wilbur was the first ranch hand I hired. He came highly recommended. Who knew?" Graham shook his head in dismay, as the sheriff and deputy sheriff dragged him away, sobbing hysterically.

They visited Wilbur at the city jail. He looked so forlorn, staring vacantly behind cold, steel bars. The sheriff told them that he'd been charged with arson once before. Dana and Graham exchanged glances, stunned.

Graham and Dana were shocked and devastated. "How could you do it, Wilbur? You loved the horses so, so much." Graham stared at Wilbur. He'd become like a stranger.

Wilbur stared back with hollow eyes. He was slumped on the cot in his cell, his hands covering his face as he sobbed hysterically. "I don't know. I don't know what made me do it..."

Graham had his arm around Dana, who sobbed. "Let's go, honey. The best thing we can do is pray for him." Graham guided her out of the city jail. "They'll do a psychiatric evaluation on him, no doubt."

Barn reconstruction was a major ordeal and took up a great deal of their time. Graham oversaw the project.

Dana got bigger every day; and her cravings and compulsive eating escalated.

Graham became concerned that she was gaining too much weight, too fast. They went for an ultrasound and soon learned she was carrying twin boys.

"From now on we are going to claim Ephesians 6:10 over the horses, the barn, our family and Sugarbush. Had we done that diligently, we might have averted the tragedy."

"It's a bitter lesson. It all comes back to putting God first and seeking his supernatural protection over ourselves, our loved ones and the horses at Sugarbush." Graham peered into her eyes as they kicked back in the family room, sipping iced tea from tall, frosted glasses.

The next morning, Dana was again besieged with morning sickness. However, despite her pregnancy, she had quickly arranged for all their horses to be transported to other farms during the reconstruction of their barn.

Trainers, colts and jockeys worked at fever pitch, adrenalin pumping through them as zero hour approached. Each competitor was determined to win the purse and bask in the glory of the roses. But as the date neared for the big race, Dana felt queasy. Not just her tummy from morning sickness, but a growing sense that they might not make it. Maybe Firelight Fancy would come in second. *Lord. I want to win the Kentucky Derby. With all my heart, I want that. We've been diligent. We've worked hard. This win is for You, Lord, for your honor and glory; and for Israel. But I give thanks in all things. You are in control. May your will be done.*

She was awake half the night. "I'm sorry I woke you, honey...but I just have to get some chocolate ice cream... and...I know this is weird, but I have this...craving for fried chicken."

"I asked Violet to buy a large variety of food. You might find fried chicken in the fridge." He yawned. "I'm going back to sleep." Graham reveled in her pregnancy, treating her like a delicate, precious orchid.

Dana loved it. She was crazy about him and the kids. She found chocolate ice-cream and remarkably a container of Kentucky fried chicken in the fridge. *Perfect.* She pulled up a chair in the kitchen and plunked down at the table, gorging on the food. Soon, she started to feel drowsy and headed for bed. Nuzzling up to Graham, she nibbled at his neck.

Dana arrived at the track at 4:45. It was brightly lit up. Trainers, jockeys and their colts were designated to do their training in the early morning hours.

Jacob was taking the colt through his daily warm-up when she arrived. Firelight Fancy was obviously in fine form and so was Jacob. They had as good a shot at winning the purse as anyone else. Better, she believed.

Soon, the exercises were over. Jacob dismounted and walked the colt to where Dana sat in the bleachers.

"In a way, Jacob...I'll be glad when the race is done. Then, we can get on with our lives."

"Dana. We're going to win. Please get that firmly implanted in your mind. Daily, I recite Mark 11:23 & 24. You know what it says. And it's always worth repeating. *"If you say unto this mountain, be thou removed and be thou cast into the sea, and shall not doubt, but shall believe that that which he saith shall come to pass, he shall have whatsoever he saith."* I claim Firelight Fancy is the winner of this year's Kentucky Derby."

"I know, Jacob. We were so sure we were going to win last year, but it didn't happen."

"We both know foul play was involved with the colt last year."

"At the risk of sounding like a pessimist, the same thing could happen this year."

Dana burst out crying. Her hormones were raging, her body was out of whack and her emotions were all over the map. She couldn't bear to hear anything negative about the upcoming race.

Jacob put his hands on her shoulders. "Dana. This is a clear attack of the adversary. Satan is out to get us. He wants to dampen our spirits, set up roadblocks and interfere with the focused, amazing progress we're making with Firelight Fancy. Because, Dana...we *will win.* We are going to take the purse."

"From your lips to God's ears."

He put his hands on Dana's shoulders. "Dana. You've been through an incredible amount of trauma in these last few years. Between Danielle's escapades, the kidnapping, the fire and now your pregnancy...it's understandable that you would tend to lose heart. But don't. Just remember, victory is just a breath away...well, a hoof beat away. It's so close you can touch it." He flashed her a confident grin.

A cheery smile lit her face, but a few stray tears trickled down her cheeks. "Thanks, Jacob. I needed that pep talk. I must say I am pleased that his conditioning has improved in leaps and bounds. He's a fast learner and becoming more focused daily. He's rounding those turns perfectly. There's a marked difference of improvement just in the last couple of runs. We're pretty much primed to compete fiercely and win.

"Yes. I've noticed his focus is becoming more intense as he gears up for the big race." Jacob smiled, confidently.

Chapter Twelve

Danielle had a ball in Palm Beach. Life had a new sizzle to it. She was hooked on the grand social scene she'd fallen into and hoped to remain in those circles indefinitely. She smiled *I am so blessed.* Or as Marilyn Monroe might have declared in her sexy, breathless voice, eyebrows arched, "It's just too perfect."

So perfect in fact that she wondered if it would last. As a fund raiser for charities in Palm Beach's high society, she regularly hobnobbed with the social matriarch's who had spent decades organizing the pricey dinners and events. She was well on her way to becoming a respected matriarch in those coveted circles. She was determined to push through the glass ceiling and transcend way beyond what had been achieved thus far by these reigning queens.

One afternoon, while working from her home office, which Suzy had graciously insisted she needed, she got a snarky e-mail from one of the premier, local matriarchs. "It has come to light that although I have given generously to your charity, I have recently learned that your character may not be what we thought it was. I have discovered you were previously incarcerated. This, of course, raised a red flag where I'm concerned. How do I know that you won't abscond with the generous gift I've made to your orphanage charity in Mexico? I hereby, therefore, revoke the contribution and expect to receive a full refund within 48 hours for the monies I have contributed. Had I known of your criminal record, I would not have entrusted these funds to you." It was signed Sincerely, Mavis Bloomgarten. P.S. I intend to inform my friends in Palm Beach of your background and I shall, of course, strongly advise them not to contribute or attend any events you organize."

Danielle roared with laughter upon reading the email. She was a force to be reckoned with and she was just beginning. She knew, of course, that Mavis was considered *the oldest and richest, as well as the most respected society dame in Palm Beach circles.* She stared at the e-mail for several minutes. Finally, she plucked up her courage, and strode down the hall to Suzie's office, to get her take on it.

She knocked on the door. She knew Suzie was in her office. She'd told her she would be working from her house this morning.

"Suzie. I just got a nasty e-mail from Mavis Bloomgarten, revoking the generous contribution she made to my new charity "Save the Orphanages.""

"Oh, don't worry about her. She does that sort of thing all the time. She gives — she takes back, she gives, she changes the amount, changes the check date...she's wacky. But she has a big heart. Just roll with the punches, and in the end it will all come out right." She smiled. "I think it's all about her retaining as much power as possible."

"I wish I had your confidence. But you know the dames here." She breathed a sigh of relief. Maybe it would all work out. "I'll take it all with a grain of salt, then."

"Sure. Just hold her hand. I think she likes the control; the status of giving away money. And she enjoys the attention and the power. I think she likes to give the fund raisers a rough time. She once knew a fund raiser that pocketed some of the cash for herself; and since that episode, she's been wary. There's a lot of greed in this town, even among the super- rich and most philanthropic." She put her hand up. "I know...it seems like a dichotomy...and really, it is. Everybody in this town needs the tax deductions. Their finances are usually complex. Most of these gals are under a lot of pressure with their financial advisors, husbands, family, accountants... attorneys...etc. Many of them have a huge outlay with their real estate investments, etc." She smiled. "If you roll with the punches, it will all turn out right."

"I guess if it was easy, everybody would be doing it." She smiled, her confidence returning. "This is your town, Suzie. You know the ropes. Thanks for your input."

She flashed Danielle a big smile. "So, are you going to make Palm Beach your home? Are you going to stick around and get married...and make a life here?"

Danielle moved closer to her friend. She hugged her, as much as that was possible, given that she sat at a desk, in her office working on the computer. "How can I ever thank you for introducing me to the power players in this town...for teaching me the ropes...for giving me...a very nice roof over my head?"

"Your success and happiness will be my thanks. I see no reason why you can't have what the majority of women in this town have; financial security and marital happiness."

"Well, you're optimistic. And thank you for that vote of confidence. Not to throw a damper on things...but it's no secret that there's a huge shortage of men...given the wars...the fact that men die off faster than women...yada, yada, yada."

"My dear. I rely on God. He promises to give us life and give it to us more abundantly. Those are sweet, treasured words to my soul. I rely on Psalms 37:4 *"Delight yourself in the Lord, and he will give you the desires of your heart."*

"Well, thanks, Suzie. I...didn't expect a spiritual retort from you. But having said that...I think I should get the fact that you have a big heart and...remarkably...you came along at one of the lowest points in my life and pointed me to a grandiose life style. I owe you a lot."

"Nonsense, Danielle. My reward will be just to see that

you make out good."

Danielle gave her friend a big hug. *Thank-you, Lord.*

Sunday morning splashed vivid rays of sunshine into her lovely room. Her second-floor window was slightly ajar. A balmy, tropical breeze wafted into the room. Danielle rose, stretched, smiled, and glanced heavenward. She spoke aloud. *"This is the day that the Lord has made, we will rejoice and be glad in it."* She peered out the window at the churning ocean, glimpsing soaring seagulls and a smattering of herons strutting along the beach. The turbulent ocean rose, crested and fell again. *How could anyone not get that the Almighty has blessed us with so much. She remembered the scriptures of how, some day, the trees and flowers would cry out and worship God. Yes. He was unsearchable, magnificent, omnipresent.* She fell to her knees in gratitude. God was faithful despite her being unfaithful.

Walter Nissan phoned Sunday morning just before Danielle was about to leave for church. She had the urge to whisper, "Not *that* Nissan." She didn't, of course. She'd quickly become accustomed to the caliber of folks residing in this prosperous town. He invited her for Sunday brunch at The Palms. "Sounds like fun. What time shall I meet you there?"

"Would 1:00 P.M. work for you?"

"Perfect. See you then."

Danielle worshipped at the Family Church in Palm Beach, and then drove to the Palm Beach Grill for her lunch date. The popular eatery bustled with energy and activity.

Walter Nissan was waiting in the foyer when she arrived. Soon, they were ushered to a nice table.

"Mind I order lunch for both of us? I think you'll like my selection."

"Please." A TV screen was perched in a corner of the eatery. Diners kept an eye on it as they dined.

"Did you consider leaving town; or you prefer riding out the storm?" Danielle glanced at her date.

"It's too late obviously to fly out now; and doubtful if we'd get out of town if we drove. Frankly, I left it too late. All we can do is ride out the storm here."

"Suzie says she always stays. So far it's worked out."

As if on cue, the sky darkened and tropical rains poured outside. The windows misted over. It was black and threatening outside. The umbrellas covered the tables of course; but the patrons quickly dispersed, demanding their checks pronto and hurrying to their cars. The car hops scurried around, quickly delivering vehicles to owners .A few chauffeur-driven limos and their clients were the first to drive off, since they didn't have to wait for the carhop to bring their vehicles around.

"May I see you home, Danielle?" They stood under the canopy at the entrance of the eatery.

"Thanks, I'll be fine. I'm sure we both want to get out of the storm and get into our houses and hunker down."

"True. I've got my storm windows up. I'm sure you and Suzie have yours in place, as well."

"Yes, and I don't know what I was thinking venturing out today, given all the storm warnings."

"Me neither. Though, I confess I wanted to see you." He grinned, flirtatiously.

She returned the smile. *Glad I haven't lost my charm.* "Thank-you for the lovely lunch. Fried oysters have always been my favorite."

Danielle drove home in the driving rain. *What had she been thinking making a lunch date, knowing a hurricane was looming?* As she drove up their street, she noticed a car parked directly across from the street entrance to Suzie's house. Someone was hunched inside it. It was dark, despite it being early afternoon. It's the stalker. Her heart stopped. Hands shaking, she pressed the garage door opener. Her heat beat like a tom-tom, she prayed as the door slowly moved upwards. In her peripheral vision, she saw him race toward the door. She watched it rise. It seemed to move in slow motion.

Suzie's Maserati wasn't in the garage. She wasn't home. The stalker reached the garage door with about two feet left to go. *Would he try to duck inside the garage?* Terror gripped her. *Lord, please cause the door to close before he gets in.*

She called 911 as she entered the house. She should have done it sooner. She'd panicked and hadn't been thinking clearly.

For a moment that stretched like an eternity, she held her breath. The garage door was only a couple feet off the ground. If he made a run for it now, he might be sandwiched in between it. Her heart beat so fast she thought it would pop out of her chest. "Lord, help me."

She breathed a sigh of relief as the garage door closed. He'd obviously missed the split second when he might have hurried into the garage before the door lowered. She called the police.

911 was inundated with calls because of the hurricane. She was put on hold. *Lord, I could be waiting for ages. What should I do?*

The storm was accelerating. Suddenly she heard it. "Crash." The heavy shutters on the windows acted as a buffer as the loud, churning sounds of the storm accelerated. They were in the eye of the hurricane. Anything could happen. Suddenly, everything went black. *Oh no. This is not good. But then she remembered that God was in control. He was always in control. She remembered a Word of knowledge spoken to her a long, long time ago.* "He knows our life from beginning to end." Peace swept over her in the midst of the hurricane. She would trust in the Lord with all her heart and lean not on her own understanding.

She could hear it raging, but suddenly, for her personally, it seemed to have lost its' power. She began praying unceasingly. *Why didn't I do that sooner?* But now, pushed to the brink of fear, stuck in the midst of the unrelenting storm, and wondering if the stalker would try to gain entry into the house...or worse, he could already be here. She knew she had to take refuge in the only place that guaranteed safety. *Jesus.*

Alone and fearful for her life, both from the cataclysmic hurricane, category five, and the loose cannon that had marked her for death, her only hope was to trust in the Lord. *Would she survive?*

The hurricane continued pounding relentlessly. She had no choice but to wait it out and pray the house didn't collapse or have significant damage done to it. Suzie had assured her that the house had been constructed to withstand hurricanes as much as possible. Suzy had assured her it was made of the highest quality materials available. She didn't know much about construction, but she could tell the home was solid. Though the fierce storm raged on, the house stood.

The violent, black storm continued to accelerate. Danielle picked up the Bible that remained open on the coffee table in the massive library. Her hands shook as she began reading and meditating on the scriptures. She knew that God was her only hope of surviving. She would hear the doorbell when the emergency workers showed up. She'd been told to expect a delay. *She knew the stalker couldn't drive off in the hurricane. He might be hunkering down somewhere near the house. Was he under te covered patio in the side of the mansion facing the ocean?* She couldn't peer outside, because all the storm window coverings were in place. She heard pounding on the patio doors. Instinct told her it was the stalker. The police would come to the front door.

She ignored it.

A couple hours later, she heard sounds at the front door. She peered through the peep hole.

"Police. Open up."

She opened the door, breathing a sigh of relief as she glimpsed the police officers. They looked exhausted. "We've done a search around the parameter of the house and adjacent properties. No sign of the stalker. We better check the house."

About twenty minutes later, the cops turned to her. "Nobody here. Try to relax. We'll keep an eye on the house as much as we can. We've have a lot of calls…"

The next morning, Danielle peered outside to a calm and peaceful morning. Bursts of sun peaked through the overcast sky, brightening the patio. She clicked on the TV. surprised it was working. She'd had the TV on all night, unable to sleep a wink. Reception had been poor almost non-existent due to the severity of the hurricane.

The local news confirmed what she already knew. The storm had receded and moved on from the Palm Beach vicinity. Empowered and encouraged by that good news, she ventured to open the sliding glass doors facing the beach. It was calm outside now. Of course, the rest of the house still had the shutters and emergency storm window coverings intact. She intended to leave them that way for now.

She stopped cold. To her utter horror, she saw him. *The stalker. The man that had threatened her life.* He lay on the ground. A fallen Palm tree lay on his head. *Was he dead? Playing dead?* He didn't stir so she hurried back inside, calling 911. *Let the sheriff deal with it.*

She watched for the sheriff's car, soon ushering him and the deputy sheriff into the house. And then outside. The sheriff confirmed that the stalker was dead.

Danielle breathed a sigh of relief. That evening, as Suzie barbecued steaks on the outdoor gas barbecue, while she chopped up salad ingredients and set the table, Danielle asked the question she'd been dying to ask. "Is Walter Nissan actually the heir to the Nissan car fortune?"

"Of course. You don't think I would waste my time with paupers, do you? And I wouldn't waste your time, either."

Danielle chuckled. "No. Of course not, Suzie. What was I thinking? I didn't know he was a friend of yours until today."

Suzie grinned and winked. "I don't tell you everything, Danielle. Only what...seems fitting at the moment."

Danielle had been on a steep learning curve since showing up in Palm Beach. "Thank you for sharing your glorious life style with me. I will forever hold you dear to my heart because of your grand hospitality."

"I know you will. We were bosom buddies in college...and then I moved here with my Mother and you were in Kentucky...with the horsey set." She smiled. "I'm so glad we've revived our friendship. I've been lonely since Mom went on to glory."

"Plus I'm your body guard, don't forget." She smirked.

"I'll tell you what, Danielle. If you observe my life style; which is pretty much the same as the other dames and gents in Palm Beach society, you'll blend right in. Don't despair if you have to dump a couple of guys along the way. Maybe things don't work out...maybe you're just not compatible. Remember… you have to kiss a lot of frogs to find a prince."

Danielle smiled. "I'll be sure to remember that."

A WEEK LATER

A cocktail party on a yacht, moored at the Palm Beach Yacht Club is in progress.

Danielle, clad in a stunning, short designer dress and open-toed pumps, is smitten by a short, rather good-looking gentleman. Deeply tanned, with a weathered face, he oozed practiced charm. He was dressed in white from head to toe. He grinned at her, showing off his pearly whites gleaming in the sunlight. He suited the white yachting cap he wore. He grinned at her, but circulated, grinning, it seemed, at practically every female on the yacht. Eventually, they were standing in the same small space. He grinned at her. "Britton Ziller."

Danielle was about ready to faint. Her heart accelerated for some strange reason. *My knight in shining armor?*

A small group of guests partied on the yacht, as it cruised lazily around the bay. She watched the long-necked, exotic, tropical birds strutting proudly around the pier. They scattered as the yacht purred out of the harbor.

"New in town, aren't you?" It wasn't a question. He grinned at her.

"I am. And you? Been here quite a while?"

"Grew up here. It's my home. I love it. I never plan to leave...other than little trips to Sicily and New York, mostly. Where do you like to travel to?"

Danielle's heart was beating a mile a minute. Had she lucked out? *He's just making small talk. It's not like he asked her for a date. She wouldn't be gauche enough to ask what business he was in. He would tell her if he wanted her to know.*

Guests hobnobbed with each other, sipping champagne and making small talk. It was perfect, tropical, balmy day. The yacht cruised lazily around the bay. Soon, he asked more personal questions, curious where she came from and how she'd become a fundraiser.

"You know...I really don't have an answer for you. It was kind of...I guess you might call it *supernatural.* Suzie Allen invited me to be her house guest. I met a lot of folks quickly and then...it just kind of evolved. I have a masters' in business... that helps a bit."

"Good for you. It's hardly a secret that...you...also have a...shady past." He flashed a wicked grin. He seemed to be sending her a silent message. *Nailed you, didn't I?* "I hear the President is about to grant you a pardon."

"That's right. I'm ...humbled by that gesture and very grateful."

"How did you wangle that?"

She smiled. *None of your business.* "News travels fast in Palm Beach. One of the President's assistants approached me after I broke all fund raising records in Palm Beach. He suggested it would be in order."

"When will you receive it?"

"I've been invited to Mara de Lago next weekend. I assume I will receive it then."

"Been there before?"

"No."

"You're in for a treat."

"So I hear."

THREE WEEKS LATER

A cocktail party is in progress at Mara de Lago. Danielle, hobnobbing with guests, sips champagne, chatting to guests as she flits from one cluster of folks to another. A discreet, courteous gentleman, elegantly attired, approaches her. "I have your presidential pardon ready, Ms. Lockhart. The president sends you his best wishes and his thanks for your stellar fundraising efforts."

Danielle could feel her face lighting up like the sun. "Wonderful. Thank-you so much. Is there a chance I could have a quick word with the president...and...uh...thank him personally for this?"

"Possibly. I'll let you know later this evening."

Danielle was over the moon. She could come out of the shadows and live a normal life. Finally. She didn't have to return to that rotten hole of a prison...ever. She determined once again to be the best fund raiser in Palm Beach. Even knowing it was a tall order and competition was fierce. She would eventually be known as *The Best Fundraiser in Palm Beach.* That was her goal and she would achieve it.

Later that evening, the president's representative found her hobnobbing with a coterie of folks. He whispered discreetly to her. "I'm sorry, the President won't be able to meet with you; but again, he sends his best wishes and thanks for the stellar work you're doing." He handed her an envelope.

She could barely contain her elation. "Thank-you. Thank you so, so much. Please thank Mr. Trump for his recognition of my work and of course, the pardon. I am inspired to achieve great things for charity." *Thank-you, Lord for your great mercy.*

The assistant grinned, shook her hand and soon disappeared into a sea of guests hobnobbing at the cocktail party.

Having received almost overnight celebrity status based on the enormous success of three high profile fund-raisers; $50,000 a plate dinners at Mara de Lago, she was on her way.

A newspaper reporter edged his way over to her. "Danielle Lockhart?"

She turned, startled to hear her real name uttered for the first time in Palm Beach circles. *She was legally free. No one could touch her. Why not tell the world?* They would know soon enough anyway; given her fund-raising celebrity status.

He flashed a *really, really big smile at the reporter. He sure is cute. Much too young for me, though.* Quickly, she dismissed that aspect of the meeting.

"Can you give me five minutes?" The good-looking guy with a mop of curly black hair grinned at her.

Her knees turned to mush. *I'd give you a lot more than five minutes if I have half a chance at it.* She smiled so big she felt like her face might crack. "I...I think I can do that. Let's find somewhere a little private..."

"I know just the place." His eyes twinkled with mischief and danger.

He moved away from the cocktail party crowd and outside onto a spacious patio. A short distance away, she could see an atrium, charming and quaint.

The handsome young reporter headed toward it, motioning her to join him. They sat on the bench inside the atrium. "Why do you think you deserve a presidential pardon, given your incarceration and subsequent jail break?"

"Thank-you for asking." She smiled. "I should not have gone to prison. The charges against me should have been dropped. They were trumped up…if you'll excuse the pun. My inept attorney, who has since been disbarred, did not present evidence which would have exonerated me. In plain English, I was imprisoned for something I did not do. My appeal was in the works, but you know how that goes; it may never have happened. I hadn't planned to escape, it was an impromptu thing, but once I was free, I knew God was calling me to contribute significantly to society and, in fact, devote myself to it. I've always had a flair for business. I hold a masters in business. At first, I thought I was supposed to help run an orphanage, but I believe God led me here. I mean, what are the chances of me knowing a fabulous woman like Suzie Allen? And yet, I do. And here I am."

"Fascinating."

She could feel his wheels turning, looking for the downside…digging for dirt. She was way too smart to be reeled in. She smiled.

He grinned back and she knew they had reached a silent understanding.

"I had a chance meeting with Gloria Turncott when I was shopping for steaks. Before you know it, she invited me to a fundraisers meeting. And the rest is history, as they say." She smiled. "I'm sure you know she's the reigning queen of fundraising, but she's ready to retire. She wants to pass the mantle on. Enter moi."

"Well, well, well. I don't believe in luck, but maybe you carry a horseshoe around." He peered at her, skeptically. "You're a real success story."

"Ah...but I'm just beginning. I have some remarkably...I think brilliant and unique concepts for fund-raising..."

"I'd love to hear more about that; but I'm on deadline." He handed her his card. "Would you call me next week? Perhaps we can do lunch."

"I'd like that very much."

"Oh...and I think I can get you a brief appearance on Fox News regarding your...stellar fund-raising events, and of course, your presidential pardon."

Dinner with Suzie on the patio was great fun tonight. Danielle was brimming with the amazing news of her presidential pardon and potential good press.

Suzie hugged her. "I knew it. You were never average, Danielle. You were always special. Of everyone I knew at school, you were the most brilliant, the most original...well, the gal I believed would make something great of herself."

Suzie cracked open a bottle of fine champagne, pouring the bubbly into crystal flutes. It was a night to celebrate. "My heart went out to you when you were on the run. I just knew in my heart that it was all going to turn around for you. I'm so glad I was here for you. It's been a great honor and privilege having you as a house guest. What a success story. Better than rags to riches. You showed up here with nothing, only a few, short months ago...and look at you now...the toast of Palm Beach. A local celebrity. Suzie proposed a toast. "To you, Danielle. To a stellar career in fundraising and...dare we hope? A new man and a new marriage."

"I'll drink to that." They clinked glasses. "Now, I'd like to propose a toast to you, Suzie."

"Bring it on."

"To God pouring out his favor and blessings upon you with such lavishness...that you will not be able to contain it."

"Why thank you for that." She flashed a big smile. "But as you can see, I already have the favor of God and great abundance. I work hard at staying in the center of His will. I put Him first in everything. *"In all your ways acknowledge him and he will direct your paths."* I live by that mandate.

"I must say I'm impressed by how much you read the Bible. It's a real inspiration for me. I'm particularly impressed that you read it first thing in the morning with your coffee."

"I wouldn't have it any other way. I put Him first and I

do not lean on my own understanding. Instead, I tap into His wisdom." She smiled, cheekily. "That's why people think I'm much smarter than I actually am."

"It really is an idyllic existence living here, isn't it?"

"Pretty much. No matter where I travel to, when I return, I look around and realize that it doesn't get any better than this."

"I guess that's why the President has a residence here."

"Exactly. And it's why some of the world's most incredible people call this place home."

"For sure. So, when do the polo matches begin?"

"Polo season is pretty much over. The next games will start in the fall."

"Do you usually attend?"

"If my social and travel schedule permit. Yes."

"I guess you met a lot of your friends through your fund-raising for the hospital."

"True. I'm glad I was able to launch you into that world. But no one could have predicted how fast your star would rise. You're like a racehorse let out of the starting gate. Determined to win. Imbued with a lazer-focus."

"I've always had the ability to totally focus on a goal until I achieve it."

"That worked well here."

"Suzie...you have a broad circle of friends from what I can see..."

"I do. And you can't have too many friends."

"True. But I'm surprised you haven't remarried."

Her chuckle was hearty. "Me, too. But I'm just about to take the plunge."

"What? You didn't tell me."

"Do I have to report to you?" She raised her eyebrows, smiling cheekily.

"No... of course not. I'm...I'm just so surprised."

"It's a secret engagement. Conner's Mom lives in Paris, and he promised her that there wouldn't be an official announcement of our engagement until she shows up in Florida."

"When will that be?"

"We don't know yet."

"Will you be selling this place once you tie the knot?"

"Possibly. We both have homes here. We'll sell one of them."

"Let me know if your house goes on the market."

"Why?"

"I might buy it."

"You don't have that kind of money."

"I'm just about to. If I marry the Nissan heir, it might be real soon."

"*Marry him?* But, honey, you just met him."

"So what?"

"So when did he propose?"

"He hasn't yet. But I've just made up my mind I'm going to marry him."

"Just like that." She snapped her fingers for emphasis.

"Yeah. Just like that."

"We'll see. I know a few things about that ladies' man that you don't."

"Such as?"

She moved back in her lounge chair. "Such as he's had several broken engagements in the last few years that I know about...maybe there are others, as well. He's a ladies' man. I'm sure you've figured that out." Suzie raised her eyebrows for emphasis.

"Well, I'll see how it plays out. Life is an adventure and I don't want to miss out on anything."

Danielle and Suzie dined on the outdoor patio, enjoying barbecued hamburgers and corn-on-the-cob.

"I'm starting to get a sense of who Walter Nissan is."

"Well, watch out. He might think you're rich. Maybe he's after your money." Suzie said.

"*My money.*" Danielle threw back her head, laughing

heartily. "I don't have any yet, as we both know."

"But *he* doesn't know that unless you've told him."

Danielle reflected for a couple of minutes. "I don't think it came up. And you know...you may be right. I haven't mentioned my financial position."

"You're here in Palm Beach as my house guest. You're staying in an oceanfront mansion at one of Palm Beach's best location. You're a fund raiser. Usually society gals, who are rich and bored, become fund raisers. Doubtless, he thinks you're one of them."

"I see." *Boy, did she ever see.* "So...he might think I'm as rich as he is... or maybe richer. And maybe...for whatever reason, he doesn't have much cash available...or something like that." Danielle bit into the corn. "And he's looking to marry into wealth."

"That' a distinct possibility. Let me explain how it works in this town. The super-rich here marry their own kind. They don't marry paupers." She smiled. "If he pops the question...why don't you ask for a statement of his net worth. Tell him you don't want to marry down; financially speaking." She smirked, raising her eyebrows for emphasis.

"Very clever." She chuckled.

"You learn the ropes when you live here as long as I have."

Chapter Thirteen

Dana and Graham were ecstatic about the coming birth of their twins. Dana continued to have morning sickness and was sometimes moody. Her body was doing strange things. Her appetite soared. She couldn't get enough ice cream and chocolate some days; other days she had to have pasta with red sauce. *It's a good thing we have a live-in cook. And Violet takes it all in stride.*

This morning she overslept. Graham was already gone. The barn was still under construction but usable. Soon, the horses would be moved back.

She slopped around, lazily, wearing her robe and slippers, drinking coffee and watching T.V. Glancing at the newspaper during commercials. After a while, she turned off the TV and began working on crossword puzzles. She peered outside. She could hear the comforting sound of rain. It was raining hard and steady. It was a perfect day to cozy up and watch soap operas.

The afternoon merged into evening. Dana stayed glued to the TV set. She was having a lazy day and relishing in it.

Graham didn't come home for lunch. She remembered he had a lunch date with his banker and some chores to do in town. She kicked back, still wearing her comfy, old robe. She made some popcorn, added lots of butter and settled onto the sofa to continue watching the soaps.

5:30 PM. Dana hasn't moved from the sofa. She's been eating practically non-stop. She polished off a box of popcorn, and then talked Violet into bringing her minestrone soup and salad into the family room where she continued to be glued to TV.

7:30 P.M. Graham appeared at the doorway to the family room. He stood there, staring at Dana. Stunned. Outraged. He was ashamed of her; embarrassed at this moment, that she was his wife. *What was happening to her? She looked downright slovenly. My beautiful, gorgeous wife, how could you let yourself go like this?* Oh, he got that her body was doing weird things, now that she was pregnant, of course. Her hormones were raging. But he didn't get how she'd suddenly become a slovenly creature overnight. Disappointed, and reeling from the shock of seeing her look so frumpy, he plopped down on the sofa, next to her. She didn't look up. She remained transfixed to the TV screen. She managed a little acknowledgment wave, reminiscent of the queen...and to him, just as condescending. Graham picked up the remote and clicked off the TV.

"Hey...whadda ya doin'?" She shot him a dirty look.

He had the remote in his hands. He waited a few minutes, pausing, for effect. "Dana, have you looked in the mirror lately?"

"I'm fat." She snarled. "Can we have the TV back on, please?" She scowled. "I'm watching something, if you don't mind."

"I mind. I will not have my wife turn into a slob right under my nose. You want to be treated with respect? Then, start by treating me with respect." He scowled. "You didn't even acknowledge me when I came into the room. Suddenly, the TV is your life? It's more important than me. Than us. I don't think so. You want to be treated like a lady? Then, act like one. This...slovenly behavior you're displaying right now... is just not acceptable in my house."

"Our house. This is *my* house, too." *He sure was snarky.*

"Maybe not for long...by the way you're acting now. Maybe we need to call the whole thing off. Get a divorce."

You could cut the air with a knife. Dana morphed into shock.

Finally, he had her attention. That was precisely the effect Graham intended to have on her. No way was he going to let her get away with being a slovenly couch potato, just because she was pregnant. His harsh words had the desired effect upon her. He watched as she slowly straightened up. Wordlessly, she rose from the couch, heading toward the master bedroom.

Once there, she threw herself on the bed and sobbed. Then, she looked in the mirror. "Ugh." After a while, she rose, took a shower and got into a gorgeous caftan in green and turquoise. A long dress Graham had recently bought for her, doubtless with the clerk's help.

In her private dressing room off the Master bedroom, she applied fresh make-up, applied a vivid pink lipstick, mascara and brushed on some awesome eyebrows. On a whim, she pulled her hair back into a chignon. She slipped on hoop earrings and finally, low-heeled gold slippers. Her walk-in closet with adjacent dressing room was both glamorous and practical.

She'd put on Maria Callas opera tapes and now listened raptly to the magnificent, inspired music. After some time, she checked her image in the mirror. Satisfied that she looked marvelous, she was poised to make a grand entrance into the dining room, when she remembered to spray on a whiff of Joy perfume. She took a last glance in the magnifying mirror in her bathroom, checked the back of her hair and strode regally into the dining room.

Graham was waiting for her. He had opened a very good bottle of red to go with roast beef. It was Friday night. The boys always had an early dinner with Violet in the family room, except on certain designated evenings. Tonight it was pizza with a movie. School was out for the weekend and the boys usually kicked back watching a movie or a sports event.

Graham stood when she entered the room. His face

beamed. "Honey, you look...ravishing." She took his breath away. "What a metamorphosis." He kissed her then. Gently on the lips. Respectfully. "Darling, my beautiful, glorious creature...how I love you. I...I'm sorry if I over reacted...but I was in shock...seeing you like that...slovenly...when you're always so beautifully put together...so elegant, so...conscientious about everything. I guess...in a way...I glimpsed the possibility that what we have could so easily go up in smoke if we don't take care of it..." Tears clouded his eyes. He kissed her then. "Can you ever forgive me, Dana? I was...in shock... and I over reacted. I see that now. Yet somehow God worked it for our good."

"It's okay, honey." She chuckled. "I probably needed a good spanking. I was acting like a spoiled, indulgent child. I think maybe because of all the discipline and focus with training the colt, then the headiness of the big win...all the parties and publicity...maybe it did kind of go to my head." She smiled. "But never again, darling. Never again. You...you and the boys...and Violet...you are all that matter to me. And before all of you, is...there is God Almighty. Without whom I am nothing and I have nothing. The win is for his glory."

It was a magical night. Reminiscent of their honeymoon. Tears glistened in her eyes. She heard the soft strains of Mozart in the background as they lay together, wrapped in each other's arms, ensconced in their luxurious, King-sized bed. *Thank-you, Lord. You've given us a taste of heaven on earth.*

She awakened with a song in her heart. It bubbled up inside her reaching the surface. Graham was already gone. Probably at the barn feeding the horses and doing other chores. The reconstruction was finally done.

She dressed carefully, praising the Lord, singing joyfully as she put herself together with great care. Suddenly, an idea sparked her mind. She spoke aloud, despite the fact that no one, except God, was present to hear her. "We need a vacation. This mini honeymoon we've embarked on doesn't have to end. Though, inevitably it will, because of pressures and responsibilities of daily living. The boys would be out of school in two weeks. Third week in June. Only two weeks away. It's a perfect time to take a vacation." She would broach the subject gingerly tonight. Maybe over dinner.

Violet served dinner in the dining room. It was liver and onions with mashed potatoes and gravy. She carefully broached the vacation idea after dinner as they sipped tea and enjoyed apple pie a la mode.

"Dana. We're not going on a vacation. We need to focus on getting the farm into a positive cash flow. We need to board some horses since we have the extra stalls. We have plenty of acreage for grazing. And we need to set up the equine consulting service we talked about. With your encyclopedic knowledge of training colts for the Kentucky Oaks and Kentucky Derby races...and now that we've won, there's no reason we couldn't co-author a book about it, too. I mean... given that we've won, the book might become a New York Times Best seller. That would put some money into the coffers. Maybe our phone would ring off the hook and you would need to hire an assistant. Wouldn't that be something?"

"And I'm supposed to do all this while being very pregnant and preparing to have my first child?" She peered at him. "Plural. I'm having twins, remember?"

He came around to her chair then and nibbled on her neck. "No, of course not, darling. You'll have the twins first. Knowing Violet she'll be a huge help to you. *She* might need to hire an assistant, though."

She wanted a vacation. She wanted to go to Palm Beach and surprise her Mom. Right after the babies were born. She would go now if Graham would let her. But he wouldn't, of course. She'd sent enough feelers out. They'd all fallen on stony ground. "Graham. I thought you were a gentleman farmer. I thought that with the ownership of Villa De Vinci and the fact that you bought this farm...and we mutually had the goal of winning the Derby...well, I thought finances weren't an issue. You've never shared your complete financial picture with me. And I don't care about that stuff. But what I do find surprising...is that you now tell me that it's mandatory that we rustle up some method of pumping up the cash flow on the farm. I assumed you were a gentleman farmer. That's what you led to me to believe before I married you. I wasn't aware that you had to earn money to stay afloat. And if that's the case, then why did we just give away the million dollars we won?" Dana was beginning to wonder what planet Graham was on.

"Honey..." He moved to her then. "My family have always been philanthropic. I grew up that way. I grew up with the philosophy that the greatest privilege and joy a person can have, is to give back to society...as much as possible...as often as possible." Graham peered over at her, gauging her reaction.

"Well, that's noble, Graham. But if *we* can't live graciously ourselves...and maybe take the odd vacation...a week or two off...then what's it all about?" She raised her eyebrows. "You know, enjoying the fruits of one's labor is biblical, darling."

"Okay, okay. Maybe you're right. I don't want to fight with you, Dana. I love you way too much for that. When we fight...I think it hurts me more than it hurts you."

"So we can go? We can go to Palm Beach for a mini vacation?" Her face lit with anticipation.

"Let's just say I'm not ruling it out. But no promises, okay? First on my agenda, is to get this farm into a positive cash flow. I'm thinking we should sell the inferior horses and upgrade to fine thoroughbreds. Maybe even get into breeding...though I swore I would never walk that road. I would like our farm to be one of the classiest farms in Kentucky."

"How can I get you to say a definite yes to taking this

trip?"

Graham paused before speaking. "Okay, Dana. I'll spell it out to you. I still don't trust Danielle. She may be a rising star in the world of charity; and I'm sure she is. Okay. Donald Trump has given her a presidential pardon. Great news. She's made huge progress. But honey, maybe we should just wait awhile and see how this whole thing plays out."

"What do you mean, Graham? She's got the president's stamp of approval. What more do you need?" She scowled. "Not to mention the clock is ticking with my pregnancy."

"It's just a gut feeling, honey. She might have a hidden agenda. You just never know what crosses her mind. She might be seriously dangerous, given her new social contacts. If she's the Danielle I know, success will have gone to her head. And she may be on some sort of power trip. Just what that entails, I really don't know." He put his arms around her. "Honey...why don't we go somewhere else for a vacation?"

"Like where?"

"Maybe a lake. Maybe take the boys fishing."

"Oh. Never thought of that. It would be great to take the boys with us since they're just about to be off for the summer." She thrust her arms around his neck. "You know, honey. I hate to admit it, but that's a much better plan. Maybe we should let sleeping dogs lie when it comes to Danielle.

"That's really what I'm thinking."

But that night, Dana had a dream that Danielle was in grave danger. She awakened in a sweat. "Graham...honey..."

"What, darling?" He moved his arm sleepily around her, pulling her close to him. He was only half awake.

"Honey, I know it's the middle of the night...but I had a nightmare. I dreamed that Danielle was fighting for her life. Somehow it seemed she owed a man some money and didn't pay him on time. He tracked her down, found her and demanded the cash. I had a sense that she'd been given an ultimatum. Something like: "Give me the cash within 24 hours or you're a dead woman."

Graham's lips came down on hers in a passionate kiss. He stopped for a minute. "I've warned you not to wake me in the middle of the night." He made love to her like she'd never been made love to before. Her eyes rolled back into her sockets after his passionate display of love. Soon, she sat bolt upright in bed. "Mother is in trouble. We have to help her. I don't know what she's gotten herself into, but she's in over her head..."

"What are you saying? That this whole charity success is a scam of some sort?"

"Maybe. I just know we've got to contact her. I think maybe we need to get her out of there."

"And then what? Invite her here?"

"Yes. She would be safe here. With the new security we have and the dogs and all that...she would be safe."

"You're kidding, Dana. Tell me you're kidding. After all the hell she's put us through, you're going to invite her here...so she can have a safe haven from...whomever?"

"Isn't that what Jesus would do?" Dana's eyes filled with tears of compassion for the mother she dearly loved. Despite all the heartaches, disappointments and betrayals, Dana loved her mother with a deep, abiding love. A love that neither time, circumstance, betrayal or dishonor could destroy. A love that was born of God and could only come from Him. A love that he designed and thus would last forever. Tears rolled down Dana's cheeks. "She's in trouble. Deep trouble. We must help her. She has no one else."

"What about the society gal she's staying with?"

"Maybe she's in on it with the gangster."

"In on what?"

"I don't know. I wish I did."

"We'd better pray on this. All I know for sure is that when big money and radical thugs are involved, anything can happen. She might be involved with some big pay offs...look, I'm in way over my head on this one. I think it's likely that Danielle is, also." Graham sighed.

Dana went back to sleep. The nightmares stopped.

But the next night, she had the recurring nightmare about her mom. She continued to have them. Her mom was in big trouble. That was the clear message.

Graham was just about to sit down at the long, round, country table to have devotions with Dana, over coffee. He wanted to offer comfort and solace to her, and a solution. That wouldn't be easy. "All right, Dana. I've made a decision. We *are* going to take a little vacation in Palm Beach. My curiosity is peaked. I might be able to figure this thing out, if we meet with Danielle and I find out who all the players are. After all, it's much like a chess game."

"So what about the boys?"

"They stay right here where they're safe and Violet can keep an eye on them."

"When do you want to go?"

"How about next Friday, Dana? You arrange the tickets for the morning flight and we'll go. Have you got her phone number?"

"I do."

"We'll be landing in sunny Palm Beach in exactly seventeen minutes. Fasten your seatbelts. It's been our pleasure having you fly with us today. Alaska Airlines is always here to serve you. We hope you have a wonderful stay in Palm Beach, whether you live here or are just visiting. Welcome to sunny Florida. Have a great stay."

A gunshot pierced the air as Graham and Dana alighted from the aircraft. Security men surrounded an apparent celebrity who had just disembarked from a nearby private jet. Bodyguards swung into action, dealing with the gunman swiftly. Four uniformed cops appeared seemingly out of nowhere. They caught the gunman and wrestled him to the ground.

As Dana and Graham hurried into the airport, wheeling their carry-on bags, they kept moving to the transportation area and then rented a car.

Graham drove them to the Palm Beach Colony Club. They checked in, saw to their luggage being sent to their room and headed downstairs for a snack. Dana spotted someone who looked vaguely familiar. He grinned at her and then looked away. They slept beautifully in their charming fifth floor suite overlooking the pool and a smattering of Palm trees undulating in the wind.

As Dana opened the drapes in the morning, expecting sun to stream through the windows, she was greeted by a dull, overcast day.

Graham had already turned FOX News on. "A category three hurricane is moving up from the Gulf of Mexico heading toward Florida…."

"Oh great…looks like we're right in the middle of a hurricane." He headed to the coffee maker, soon handing Dana a paper cup filled with coffee.

They both sat on the sofa, stunned, riveted to the freak storm accelerating in the area, eyes riveted to the screen, as they watched the eye of storm, waiting for updates.

"Relax honey. It's not even hurricane season. This is a freak storm. It could be gone by tomorrow." He clicked the TV off.

The next morning, the hurricane had intensified to a category four. The Palm Beach airport was closed. They were stuck here. Dana called Violet with the report.

"The two of you will be fine. If you have to go to a shelter, you'll do it. I'll lift you up in prayer. The boys are doing just great. Sybil dropped over and she's taking charge of them, driving them to school and generally spoiling them rotten. It's a blessing for me, because I have so much to do." Violet was an eternal optimist.

Right after breakfast, Dana called her Mom. "Mom. Graham and I are in town."

"Dana. This is not a good time. I wish you'd told me you were coming." Danielle was in fear for her life. She was still reeling from the surprise, brutal confrontation with the stalker. Now she realized there was a hit out of her. She had to get rid of Graham and Dana as fast as possible. Her own survival was at stake. Her days of shady living had returned to haunt her.

"Oh great. So we've come all this way to see you, but you don't have time for us?" Dana was feeling queasy and emotional. She wanted love and attention from her mom; not the cold shoulder. *What had happened to the Danielle she used to know?*

"I'm...dealing with a serious issue right now. And...with the hurricane and all...we need to hunker down. Maybe y'all should think about flying out while you still can. But if you don't leave right away, the airport could be closed down..." She paused. "Gotta go, Hon. Talk later." Click.

Dana cried in Graham's arms.

"Honey, I'm so sorry. We're going straight back to airport and get on standby. If we head out right away, we might be able to get on a flight going somewhere..." He started packing his carry on. "Come on, Dana. Move. If this hurricane becomes a category four, we could get stuck here for a while, with a lot of problems we don't need."

In minutes they were in their rental car driving to the airport.

At the airport, they peered at the overhead screen, praying for a flight out. But as they stood in the long line-up, a sense of foreboding overtook Graham. "I don't like the way this feels. Too many people...too few flights...too little time..." He glanced at Dana. "Maybe we shouldn't have turned in our car." He glanced at Dana. "Come on, let's roll our way back to the rental car agency and try our luck renting a car. We can drive out of the area. Though I know traffic is backed up from what we saw on TV."

The agent told them there were no available cars. Then they heard the announcement. "Palm Beach airport is officially closed. No more flights will be boarding or landing. Stranded travelers can hunker down here. Shuttled are on the way to drive folks to the nearest shelter. Hotels at or near the airport are fully booked. You'll be safer in a shelter, anyway."

"Oh great. So here we are, stuck in Palm Beach. I'm not going to say I told you so; but I had a bad gut feeling about taking this trip at this time to Florida." He put his arms around Dana. "Never mind, honey, God is in control and he said he would never leave us or forsake us. We need to know that and trust him with our whole hearts and not lean on our own understanding..."

"In all our ways acknowledge him, and he will direct our paths." Dana smiled and reached up hugging her husband. "How did I ever get so lucky to hook up with a man like you?"

"It had nothing to do with luck. God put us together. We've just begun a beautiful, spiritual journey together." He saw the emotion in Dana's eyes and knew how deeply the crass Danielle had hurt her. "She'll come around, honey. Our timing is just off." He grinned at her.

When the hurricane had moved on, Graham and Dana were transported back to the airport by shuttle. They couldn't wait to get home.

"I'm not saying one word, honey...okay just a short sentence. I had a bad gut feeling about travelling here when we did..."

"I know you, did. It was all my fault. I just *had* to get away." She smiled at him. "At least the hurricane moved swiftly from the area..."

Danielle sensed the sinister forces controlling the evil

monster that was following her out of the small parking lot. She'd intended to go into a specialty butcher shop, but he intercepted her as she stepped out of her car. She turned and looked him square in the eyes. "What do you want?" She put on a bravado she didn't feel.

"You." He smirked.

"And you think this is the best way to win my favor?" *Keep your voice steady. Never show fear.*

"Not really. But you gotta admit; I have your attention, don't I?"

"Yeah, you have my attention, but hardly my interest."

"Seems you owe fifty grand to a buddy of mine." He glanced around quickly. No one was in sight. In one swift motion, he grabbed her hair. "See... the way it is...if you don't pay up right away, I gotta put a bullet through your head." He actually lifted a Beretta and pointed it straight at her head. "Nothin' personal you understand. It's just business." His smirk was venomous. He hid the gun.

He spoke in a staccato speech pattern like he'd studied mafia speech patterns carefully. "You're telling me you're going to put a bullet through my head...but I shouldn't worry about it?" She stared at him. "What if I told you that I'm going to put a bullet through *your* head? How would *you* feel about that?"

He shrugged. "It don't matter what you say. Words are cheap." His grin was evil, Satanic. "You're the target, baby. Not me." His eyes were icy steel. "You're a rich broad now. But your past just caught up with you." He flashed that evil grin again. "You have twenty-four hours to come up with the fifty grand. Otherwise...you're dead." He flashed a sinister smirk.

Danielle had never been a wimp. Still, she began shaking. At first just a bit but then more intensely. She could feel the color drain from her face. She didn't recognize her own voice when she spoke. Her voice trembled. "I'll get the money. ..I'll have the money." She was sweating profusely.

"Where do you want me to deliver it to?"

He smirked. The evil scowl on his face darkened.

She stared, dumbfounded, into the face of Satan.

"48 hours. I'll notify you of the location where we'll meet. Make sure you're alone. If you try to avoid me, I'll go after you. I know where you live." His eyes narrowed to a slit of pure evil, his scowl emanating hatred. He was a viscous snake. He turned and walked briskly away, soon mingling with other pedestrians.

Danielle shivered despite the balmy weather. She gazed at the churning sky. It was dark and threatening like the monster that was slaking her. She slipped in behind the wheel of her jaguar. She'd purchased the racing green sports model at a recent auction.

She drove home in a daze, threatening black clouds looming overhead like a shroud covering her rapidly beating heart. "Lord, where am I going to get fifty grand?" She had no idea who the gangster was or how he'd found her. The claim was not legitimate. It was trumped up. But if women's intuition were to be trusted, the man meant business. If she didn't have the cash in 48 hours, she'd be dead,

Danielle drove down Ocean Boulevard to Suzie's opulent mansion, pressing the garage door opener as she entered the driveway. She performed a routine, cursory glance around her while in her car, peering in the rearview mirror to make sure she wasn't being followed. Satisfied that the coast was clear, she drove into the garage, her heart beating rapidly. Suzie's Mazarati wasn't here. Closing the garage door, she could feel sweat beads forming on her forehead. Shivering with fear, she stepped into the beach house. It felt massive and creepy tonight. *Suzy, please come home soon. I can see why you like company in this massive place.*

She was a moderate drinker and rarely imbibed alone. Today, however, she turned on some classical music and sauntered over to the ornate bar. She prayed Suzie would get home soon. The place seemed empty and enormous without her presence. Small wonder Suzie welcomed company. The place felt like a mausoleum. She poured a small amount of brandy into a snifter. Maybe it would take the chill off. The custom-made bar was ornate and opulent like everything else in the house. The large gold-gilded French mirror made a stunning backdrop for the bar. The brandy warmed her. Suzie had repeatedly told her that while she lived here, she should treat the house as her own and enjoy it to the max.

She waited for the sheriff to show up. She strode to the sliding glass doors, peering out at the dark skies and churning, black waters beyond. The sweeping patio was well lit. She gazed at the Palm Trees rocking back and forth in the high winds. She shivered. The turbulent ocean mirrored her turbulent spirit. *Lord, help me.* The sky overhead suddenly darkened. The waves cresting the dark waters became more turbulent, ascending and crashing with increasing intensity. She shivered. *Please God, let the sheriff show up soon.*

Danielle grabbed the remote, clicking on the TV. She had plopped down in the family room. *Where was the eye of the storm? And where was it projected to go? And where was Suzie?* She hadn't mentioned anything about evening plans. She'd assumed that Suzie would be home early so they could both hunker down and wait for the storm to pass. *She'll probably be home any minute.*

Still no sign of the sheriff. Susie had always said her house was like Fort Knox. No one could get in, unless they were invited. *Still...*

Two Hours Later. Suzie still wasn't home. She began tracking the storm on TV with mounting anxiety. They were close to the eye of the storm.

Danielle admired her surroundings, dreaming of the day when she would have a home here. Suzie's color scheme of lime greens and lemon yellows on a background of white and tan furniture was effective and inviting. The area rugs were exquisite. The entire house was outfitted with heavy, storm proof white shutters. They were decorative as well as functional. The shutters kept the sun out when it was scotching hot; and acted like a shield in hurricanes.

She remained riveted to the news. *Where was it going to make landfall?*

Tonight, she desperately needed to talk to Suzie. She tried her cell phone. It went directly to voice mail. Since Suzie was privy to all her secrets, she would start by running the deadly threat by her. She wouldn't wait another minute. She would call 911. She began to wonder if her lines were tapped. Could Suzie be in danger? A myriad of questions swirled around in her brain, unnerving her. She rarely bothered Suzie when she was out; because she was usually socializing, and she didn't want to interfere with her social life. This was urgent. It couldn't wait. "Suzie?" The call went directly to voice mail. *Oh great.*

Three hours later. 11:45 P.M. Suzie whisked into the house. Danielle ran to greet he. "Where have you been, Suzie? I've been worried about you."

"I was at my fiance's house. Sorry, I should have called to tell you I'd be late, so you wouldn't worry."

"No big deal. But this storm is. I guess it's too late to drive out of town. I guess we'll be hunkering down...until it passes."

"We missed the window of opportunity for escape. I'm sure you've seen the car lineups on TV. The airport is closed, of course."

She must be safe. The killer wouldn't stay in the area with a hurricane looming. He'd probably left town. If he had flown out of Palm Beach, he'd have had to do it immediately after issuing her the ultimatum. Her mind whirled. She hated to bring up the nasty encounter she'd had with the hit man, but given the fact that she was a house guest in Suzie's home, she needed to warn her. She might be in danger too. Quick witted and clever, she wanted her take on this.

Suzie listened attentively while Danielle recounted the

horrific encounter with the hit man. She was silent for some time after that. When she finally spoke, the words were not what she wanted to hear. "Danielle. I need you to pack your stuff and leave. Immediately. I was happy to befriend you... I've enjoyed having you as a house guest. But I didn't realize you still had criminal connections. I thought that phase of your life was behind you..."

"It is. Of course it is."

"Then who is this guy? And how dare he issue you an ultimatum, demanding fifty grand...or your life?" Suzie strode to the kitchen and picked up the phone on the counter. "Police?" She waited a while. When the police answered, she spelled out the threat. "My houseguest has received a death threat." She motioned for Danielle to pick up the other extension in the adjacent family room.

Danielle's hand shook so violently, she could barely lift the receiver. Tears stung her eyes. She had no idea who the man was, who put him up to it, and why she was being targeted. She started sobbing. "Officer...I don't know what this is about. It's a scam of some kind. He's trying to extort fifty thousand from me. He thinks I'm wealthy...or can get my hands on that kind of cash."

"We're on our way."

Suzie wrapped tender arms around her. "You'll be okay. Maybe the guy is high on coke...and...it will all go away."

"Why me? How does he know who I am? How did he find me?"

"You're joking right?" Suzie raised her eyebrows. "You're a high-profile Palm Beach fundraiser and you've just received a Presidential pardon. He knows your face. All he would have to do is make the rounds of the popular spots in town...and sooner or later he'd bump into you."

"But that's not what happened. I came out of the drugs store and walked toward my car and he was suddenly there...in my face."

"Why didn't you dial 911 then?"

"I did. I guess they're inundated with calls because of the storm."

"Of course,"

A short time later, the blare of police sirens filled the air. Suzie and Danielle simultaneously expelled their breath. Suzie wrapped comforting arms around her. "I won't abandon you, hon. The cops will nail this bad actor and put him behind bars where he belongs. Imagine. Showing up in Palm Beach and threatening my best friend. I don't think so."

Suzie had gone the gamut of emotions. She'd gone from shock to mistrust and then to outrage and protectiveness. "I've lived in this house for over twenty years and the Lord has watched over me all that time. We are blessed with a superior police force here in Palm Beach. No one is going to harm us." She smiled. "Every night I pray that angels will surround my house and protect us from harm or evil and keep us safe. And they do. Did you know that warrior angels are usually over ten feet tall?" She smirked at Danielle. "We won't worry. We'll just remember the stories in the Bible where warrior angels fiercely guarded the houses of believers against perpetrators."

The police asked Danielle a lot of questions. She told the truth. She was an American citizen with nothing to hide. Having received the presidential pardon, she was entitled to protection like everyone else.

They had moved to the kitchen and were drinking tea Suzie had brewed. They sat at the kitchen island bar. "I remember a story I read once...I think it took place in South Africa. Sierra Leone I believe. The rebels were burning down entire villages. A Christian family lived in one of huts in the village. They fasted and prayed fervently throughout the rampage, even while glimpsing outside at the horror and madness of a band of wicked men torching house after house. The couple sought the Lord fervently, asking him to surround their hut with tall, warrior angels." She smiled and paused before delivering the punch line.

"Their hut alone was left untouched, unharmed. All the other huts in the small village were burned to the ground. The carnage was unspeakably horrific. That Christian family alone survived."

"Incredible."

"Yes. It's a miracle from God, bestowed upon them in answer to their fervent prayers...their unshakeable belief." Suzie took a long sip of the tea. "An investigative reporter heard about the incident. He had a chance to talk to one of the wicked perpetrators who was currently serving a prison sentence." He asked "the Torcher" the question that was burning in his heart. "Why did you torch every hut except that one?"

"Give me a minute." Suzie flipped open her laptop which sat on the kitchen island. "I'm going to read this to you. Here goes..." She located the story on her laptop reading aloud.

The rebel scowled. "Hey, Man. We didn't dare go near that hut. There were tall, armed men surrounding it. They were... over ten feet tall. I don't know where they came from, but they held spears and wore helmets. They were like...from another era. They gave us the willies. We were terrified of them. The warriors surrounded the hut. We didn't dare go anywhere near them or the hut they guarded."

Scott Barlow was an American reporter and a good one. He didn't let the story end there. He returned to the humble family inside the lone, surviving hut, strangely intact, despite the rest of the entire village being torched.

Zarow Mitan and his family greeted the reporter with huge smiles, joy leaping from their faces. "It was the Lawd. The Lawd saved us. He caused the supernatural presence of warrior angels to manifest themselves during the unspeakably horrific torching of the whole village." Terena, the eldest daughter of Zarrow and Helena, was articulate despite having only a high school education, and thus was the spokesperson for the family.

The reporter was speechless and promptly returned to his hotel room where he did a study on angels. It would be many years later that Terena discovered the reporter had found Jesus and was following Him with a whole heart Suzie turned to Danielle. "Isn't that something?"

"It really is."

"We need to do spiritual warfare, also. It's easy to get involved with the fast pace of life and leave God behind. That's why I rise at 6:00 every morning and read my Bible. I bet that's why I've always lived in safety. It's the supernatural protection of God."

She was gone for a minute and then right back clutching her Bible. She flipped to Ephesians 6:10 and bound the evil forces and prayed for supernatural protection over the two of them.

"The cops are here." Suzie peered out the kitchen window and so did Danielle. She let them in.

The two burly cops greeted them and then hurried into the back yard. They checked the neighboring properties and came back to the house. "Gone, of course." George Scott, the more mature of the two gave Danielle and Suzie their cards. "We're going to drive the area real quick. He might be close by. Could be hiding on one of the properties, maybe behind shrubbery. We'll give it a shot, anyway." He handed them each a card. "If he returns or...if he calls...tries to contact you in any way, call us right away. After we've checked the area thoroughly, whether we find him or not, we'll be back. I need to get some information from you, Danielle. But right now, time is of the essence and we need to do our due diligence by conducting a thorough search for him in the area." He threw a couple of cards on the counter and they left.

The hit man had grown up in Palm Beach with wealthy parents. His dad had been a commodities broker and later played the stock market, making millions. But when Wall

Street stocks tumbled, and his folks lost everything, they went back to Oregon where their roots were. He stayed in Palm Beach.

His buddies called him "Jacko" a nick name for Jack. He'd just finished high school and had a few buddies in Palm Beach. Unable to fit into a regimented life style, he shunned regular day jobs and refused to do the bartender thing, as well. He lived in the shadows. Gambler by day, boozer and pool shark by night, he fell in with the wrong crowd. It wasn't much of a stretch. He hung out with shady characters and had no interest in moving in another direction. Once he got hooked on coke, it wasn't long before he lost all sense of right and wrong. His life was about getting that next fix.

He knew about Danielle through his contacts in the horsey set. Tanner had been a buddy until he made some stupid mistakes and got himself incarcerated again. He was determined to stay in Palm Beach and make a life for himself. But with no specialty and lacking a university education, he decided to marry into wealth, if he could He wasn't great looking, though he had a certain charm and a great sense of humor. Some women liked him, but not the ones he wanted.

Sally Mitford had been the first one. They'd had a fling. She'd gotten pregnant. He'd agreed to marry her and give the baby a name. When they split, he didn't get much because of the pre-nuptial she'd drawn, but it was a whole lot better than taking a day job. He had enough to live on for the better part of a year. After that, he survived by taking odd jobs. Working for moving companies didn't pay much, but it was better than nothing. He moved on, becoming a handy man and joining a painting crew. H did odd jobs, managing to survive. But when his old buddy Ben looked him up, together they started doing drugs again and that's when everything spiraled downhill. His life became about getting cash for the next hit. He didn't care how he got it.

His buddy, Rizzo Romano, a sometime chef, imbued with more than his share of wit and charm had shown up on his doorstep with some real good stuff. That was the beginning of the end. Rizzo was a buddy of Danielle's ex hubby. High on good stuff, they hit on a plan. They'd heard about Danielle's presidential pardon and could hardly miss the big splash she'd made as a fundraiser in Palm Beach. *She must have struck gold somewhere along the way.* Society papers hinted she lived in an oceanfront estate. It was time to cash in. They had some dirt on her that could ruin her despite the presidential pardon. If the circles she ran in got wind of her wicked background, they wouldn't want anything to do with her. Rizzo had been a co-conspirator with Danielle on Dana's kidnapping. The cunning Danielle had been the mastermind. If the press picked up *that story,* Danielle's stellar career would come to a crashing halt. She'd pay up all right. He was counting on it.

Fifty grand was peanuts in the upper echelon circles of Palm Beach society. They weren't greedy. A modest sum would be good, because all the bells and whistles wouldn't go off. It was small potatoes. They'd grab the cash and hit the road. They were tired of living on the fringes in this town anyway. "If we're too greedy, Danielle will create such a hullabaloo, we might be tracked down. Fifty grand won't alarm anyone. If she doesn't have it in her bank account, she can loan it from one of her rich friends."

Chapter Fourteen

Danielle awakened with a splitting headache. She'd been dreaming, but she'd had nightmares, the kind that was best to forget about. But she couldn't forget. Images and memories of the dream assailed her senses, crippling her, causing her to want to scream. She leaped out of bed and into the shower. Soon, dressed in a floral top and white pants with sandals, she padded down the stairs and into the kitchen.

Suzie was already there, humming a tune as she poured herself a mug of coffee. She greeted Danielle with a big smile and poured her a mug of it, also. "Well it still looks dark and threatening out there, but Praise God, the hurricane has moved on and we survived."

Danielle forced a smile, conjuring up bravado she didn't feel. "We really are blessed. It's gorgeous here, even when the weather is stormy. Unbidden tears sprung to her eyes.

Suzie noticed, of course. "Danielle. What's going on? What's wrong?"

"I..." She began shaking; at first just a little...and then increasingly more violent. "I...I had the most dreadful nightmare you could ever imagine." She hadn't intended to tell her. The words had just spilled out, unbidden. "I dreamed that monster hit man...got into the house...and found me. I dreamed he...was in a rage and tried to murder me with his bare hands. It seemed so real."

Suzie wrapped comforting arms around her. "Let's pray,

darling. It's an attack of the evil one. Have you been doing your daily spiritual warfare...and meditating on the Word day and night, like we are admonished to do?" She raised her eyebrows. "I never miss a morning of worship and Bible reading. And I always pray Ephesians 6:10, which of course is spiritual warfare."

Of course not. She'd been too busy planning her next charity event, and a myriad of other things.

"Maybe you don't realize that Satan can attack us even while we're sleeping. It's a hard concept to wrap our heads around. But there it is. We need to put on the full armor of God by claiming Ephesians 6:10 daily over our lives. God will fight for us. But we need to activate the spiritual forces available to us; and be constantly on the alert."

"I guess I should take one of the Bible studies being offered at the church. I'm loathe to admit it...but, I'm really not very knowledgeable on the Bible."

"I read it first thing every morning, as you know. That way, no matter what else doesn't get done...my prayer and Bible reading will prevail."

"Okay, okay, okay." Danielle didn't like being lectured to. Didn't enjoy being reminded of her weaknesses. But there it was. The truth. It was a slap in the face. A reality check. She turned to Suzie. "How did you sleep last night?"

"Strange you should ask. I usually sleep like a log. Don't wake up at all during the night." She paused, looking at Danielle, oddly. "But last night...I woke up a couple of times...now don't get alarmed...but I thought I heard something in the house. Then when I was awakened a second time. I was sure I heard something. We have the burglar alarm, of course. But it's not hooked up in the garage. It should be. That's my fault. I had a system that included the garage, of course...but it was malfunctioning...that was just shortly before you arrived. I knew it was a vulnerable spot in the house, but...it just kept slipping my mind. Whenever I thought about, I'd chuckle...call myself neurotic and forget about it." She stared at Danielle. "Danielle...I think someone *was* in the house last night."

Danielle's heart was in her throat. "Oh no." She began shaking, leaning toward Suzie and whispering. "Maybe...someone is in the house as we speak."

Suzie smiled. "Like they're going wait for daylight when if they'd gained entry, they could have...done the damage last night."

Danielle's mind was racing. "We were sleeping. An intruder would not have known which bedroom I was sleeping in. I don't think they would want to risk the noise of breaking into one bedroom, only to find it was not the intended target."

"Let's get out here. Now." She whispered the words to Danielle, ending with mouthing them. "We'll take my Mazerati and get out of here."

"What if the perpetrator is in the garage? If he's still in the house, he could be anywhere...couldn't he?" Danielle's voice was a shaky whisper.

"You know you're right. My purse and cell is here. Don't go upstairs to your room to retrieve yours." She leaned toward her, whispering. "I just have a hunch we need to hit the road. Fast."

"Call the police outside?" Danielle raised her eyebrows and started quickly walking toward the front door.

Suzie nodded.

They went outside, but not before Suzie swiftly activated the alarm system.

To the neighbors, they probably looked like they were out for a morning stroll. They acknowledge a sportily clad older woman touting a large, pristine, white poodle proudly strolling with his owner.

Suzie didn't wait. She phoned 911. "I have reason to believe someone may have broken into my house. They might still be there."

Danielle knew the questions they would be asking, so she wasn't surprised when Suzie predictably answered. "We're fine. My houseguest and I are outside the front door on the street side."

An unmarked car with two officers pulled up in front of the house. Suzie disabled the alarm system letting them in. One of the officers looked at Suzie and Danielle. "Hey Suzie. Would you gals mind waiting outside? Another officer is on his way. He'll keep an eye on you."

Twenty minutes later.

Suzie and Danielle, now being protected by a rookie cop, waited inside in his unmarked vehicle "

A flurry of gunshot sounds pierced the air.

Suzie and Danielle exchanged nervous glances.

In minutes, the pair of cops stepped onto the front porch, the perpetrator handcuffed, head cast downwards in shame, was with them.

Danielle recognized him immediately. She felt like screaming. *It wasn't a dream. He was really in my room. How did he get in? Why did he manage to break in…and yet allow her to live?* A barrage of thoughts raced through her brain. She knew the answer. God had surely sent his angels to watch over her and Suzie. *Did they look like ten feet tall warrior angels to the intruder? She remembered the story.* Chills of joy swept through her. That's it. Had to be.

"I know what you're thinking, Danielle. And I think I know the answer. I'll bet we both awakened at the same time. The moment I woke up, I felt burdened to pray for you. And I did." She smiled at Danielle. "We serve a great and mighty God."

"Is this the guy that's been giving you all that flack? Threatening you?" He had the perpetrator in cuffs, standing next to him.

Danielle peered into the coldest eyes she'd ever seen. Smokey grey ice. Devoid of all emotion. Chills raced through her. *Lord, thank you for removing him from our lives. Thank-you for letting us dwellin safety.* A barrage of words tumbled out before she could stop them. "You were in my room. What stopped you from...attacking me?" Icy chills swept through her. "Murdering me?" Tears of gratitude mingled with aftershock trickled down her cheeks. *God Almighty reigns supreme.*

"You're joking, right." He sneered. A glazed look swept over his eyes. "Ten-foot-tall guys guarded you as you slept. I don't know where you got them from. They looked powerful. I turned tail and ran out of your room. I was...traumatized and dog tired...I took a chance and slipped into the den and fell asleep on the leather couch. I intended to leave just before daylight, but I overslept. I awakened when I heard voices in the kitchen. I figured the two of you were up. I was going to head down the hallway and slip out the sliding glass doors to the beach. But as I glanced out, I spotted quite a few early morning dog walkers and joggers. I didn't want anyone to see me. I realized I was trapped. Plus I assumed the burglar alarm would be on."

Danielle and Suzie peered at each other. "So...how did you get past the burglar alarm in the first place?"

He smiled big. "That's easy. I slipped in yesterday...through the beach entrance. The sliding glass doors were ajar. I guess you were in and out of the house and left it that way."

"Okay. True confession time is over. Just remember what you said. You're going to be repeating it over and over." The older cop herded the perpetrator into the back of the paddy wagon. They locked the door, then turned to Danielle and Suzie. "We'll let you know the upshot...whether he's a lone wolf operator or works with a partner." He grinned. "Meanwhile, you'll be fine, now. He'll be behind bars until his court date comes up."

Six Months Later

Danielle and Suzie attended the perpetrator's trial. They still didn't know his real name or who sent him. He was charged with breaking and entering. In the absence of sufficient evidence pointing to intent to murder Danielle or anyone else in the house, the perpetrator was sentenced to two years in federal prison. A weapon had not been found. The judge contended that the perpetrator had broken into the house in order to steal cash, credit cards and jewelry. Something or someone had apparently intimidated him into abandoning his agenda. Fortunately, a neighbor spotted him fleeing the scene.

The judge raised his eyebrows in disbelief, rolling his eyes upon hearing the story about ten feet tall warrior angels guarding Danielle's door. "Utterly preposterous," he'd stated. But as he mulled over the sequence of events, he realized it could only have been something supernatural that had thwarted the plans of a perpetrator who had already gained entry into the house. Something or someone must have terrified him into abandoning his agenda.

Finally, Danielle could breathe easy again and get on with her life. With the failed hit man safely behind bars, she could move on with her life.

Suzie wasn't so sure. Rattled by the intrusion into her otherwise serene, nice life, she decided it was time for her house guest to depart. The next morning after breakfast she advised Danielle of her decision. "I'm sorry, Danielle, but this entire episode has me rattled. I've lived a nice, orderly life until the drama you brought with you wreaked havoc in our lives." She peered over at Danielle. "I think it would be best if you find another place to live."

Initially shocked, Danielle quickly adjusted. "Okay. No problem, Suzie. I know when God closes one door he opens two more. I would like you to pray with me, though. I need the favor of God."

"Of course. And just so you know...I've been praying. I didn't arrive at this decision easily." She smiled. "It will work out just fine. You'll see." She smiled confidently. "God is sovereign."

Three hours later

Danielle managed to lease a small luxury condo in downtown Palm Beach. She'd prayed fervently for something really nice. She'd been spoiled rotten since showing up in this town. Stepping down too far would not be comfortable. God heard that prayer.

Danielle moved into the furnished apartment. She felt good about making a fresh start. She intended to put her own touches on it and get settled in. She would make the apartment a cozy home.

She was barely settled in, when she heard a knock on the door. Looking through the peep hole, a man's face peered at her. A stranger. "I don't believe I know you." She spoke through the door.

"I'm your neighbor. Donald Jackson. Betty made me promise I would make you feel at home here." He grinned. "Betty and I bought in here when the project was brand new."

She opened the door and peered into a very pleasant face. Scratch that. A pleasant, *handsome* face. She smiled. Liked what she saw. She thrust her hand out. "Danielle Lockhart."

"Oh, honey. I know who are." He chuckled. "Quite a colorful character, aren't you?"

Danielle could feel a faint blush creeping up her throat. *She never blushed.* "What...do you mean by that?"

He chuckled. "Not much. Welcome to Seven Palms. You'll find folks here a friendly group." He thrust out a strong, tanned and somewhat wrinkled hand. "If you need anything, you know where I am." He grinned, showing even, white teeth. "Gotta run." He glanced at his watch.

"Thank-you so much. I appreciate that." *Thank-you, Lord. I feel less alone already.*

During the next few days she shopped for groceries, household items and various sundries. Her money was running low...real low. She'd been dropped from one of the premier fund-raising committees without a specific reason being cited. She was fast going from "The bright new star in town" to "Yesterday's tarnished goods." She'd always known the public...and people in general were fickle. With a teeny bit of bad press that had somehow filtered into the back pages of the local paper, her ratings had plummeted. She'd better get a job fast; or she'd be on the street pronto. With high rent to pay, the days of wine and roses were gone. She looked back fondly on the glorious time spent with Suzie in her opulent mansion. *Suzie will be the first order of the day. I'll have her over for steaks.*

Steaks and baked potatoes with a salad was the menu. She dressed in a casual hostess dress in tropical colors, served a fine cabernet and filled the house with opera music. Love for opera and the theatre were among the many things the two of them had in common.

As Lemon Meringue pie was being served, she heard the doorbell. She turned to Suzie. "Who would be ringing my bell? I haven't even given my address to anyone except you."

"Well, whoever they are...I guess they live in the building, since they didn't ring the intercom."

Danielle chuckled. "You know...you're right. I guess it's safe to answer. Or maybe I should just ignore them. It might be a well-wisher since I just moved in." She headed to the front door. "If you'll excuse me, Suzie, I'll look through the peek hole and see if I can get a clue."

Just as I thought. It's the neighbor. This town is filled with beautiful women, why is he pursuing me? There had to be a reason. She returned to the circular glass table with the dolphin beneath. "Suzie, it's the guy next door. I see no reason to interrupt our little dinner."

Suzie shrugged. "That's up to you. It's your house."

Yes, it is. And no one can tell me what to do. Still, his interest in her niggled at her. Something about his curiosity and the fact that he was pursuing her so quickly after she'd moved in bothered her. "So, have you set a wedding date?"

"No. Actually we've decided to wait. There are some issues we need to sort out..."

About an hour after Suzie had left, her doorbell rang again. She peered through the peep house. It was him. *Again, a strange hunch unsettled her. She wouldn't answer the doorbell.* She began to wonder if he would always know when she was home. He probably knew which parking stall was hers.

That night Danielle slept restlessly, awakening a couple of times during the night. At 9:30 a.m., she called the landlord. She would take the bull by the horns and ask her who the man was.

"Ann...I love it here and I want to thank you for everything."

"Well...how sweet of you to call. I appreciate that. Now, you let me know if there's anything you need..."

Danielle could tell she was about to hang up. She had to intercept her. "Wait...uh...there is something, actually..."

"And what is that?"

"The...gentleman next door, Donald Jackson...he...he's awfully friendly, considering this town is full of lovely ladies..."

The silence was palpable. When the woman spoke, her voice was noticeably cooler. "He...he's...just fine. I don't know him very well."

She smelled a rat. "No kidding. He seems extremely friendly...I'm surprised you didn't get to know him."

"Well, I didn't dear. I must fly. I have a doctor's appointment."

I bet you do. She couldn't begin to imagine what his

agenda was...only that she prayed it wasn't something sinister. Still, she had a weird feeling about him. *I'll ignore him, and tell him that my boyfriend likely wouldn't appreciate me being too friendly with the neighbors. My fiance. That sounds better. My fiancé is possessive. There. Simple. Succinct. Maybe I'll just ignore him.* Danielle had to find a job. Fast. She called Suzie. "Suzie, how tough would it be to become an interior decorator in this town?"

"You'd starve, honey. Decorators in this town are a dime a dozen. Clients are clever and fussy, fussy, fussy. Nobody can please them." She paused. "Oh...and uh most of them have some wholesale connections...they don't pay retail for anything."

"Okay. That's out. Any other suggestions?"

"What about managing a ladies' clothing store? You've done that before."

"Yeah, I guess I could do that."

"You don't seem very keen. Well, maybe the easiest thing would be to be a receptionist at a hair salon."

"Bingo. That might be a relatively easy job to nail."

"Maybe. Maybe not. A lot of gals like that job, because one of the perks is usually free hair styling, maybe color, etc."

"Well there are a lot of salons in town. I'll give it a shot."

Danielle made the rounds. After two days of hitting every hair salon she could find, she gave up. She called Suzie. "Another dead-end street. I'm running out of options."

"And you're tried ingratiating yourself with the society dames. it's like a romance that went sour. They're moving on." She sighed. "You were hot and now you're not. You soared to the top as a fund-raiser. What you probably didn't get, is that you invoked a jot of jealousy. Some of the older dames that have been the stalwart matriarchs in this town for decades resented a rising star like you."

"I didn't think of myself in those terms, Suzie."

"Well, think about it. You show up in town and within a short span of time, you're right up there with the seasoned matriarchs who have been running the charities in this town for decades." She paused. "Jealousy, darling. The green-eyed monster rears its ugly head once again."

"Of course. You know what? I didn't actually get that before. The dames I worked with seemed to like me because unlike most of them, I'm tech savvy and I move fast. They're from another era and they don't know how all the social media and PR stuff works; other than the same old...same old...so they embraced me, because I was able to fill a niche they needed. They must have found someone else; because...it seems, they just don't need me anymore..."

"Give them a chance to have a couple of flops and they'll be back looking for your promotional magic." Suzie said.

"They paid me as a consultant because of my tech savvy, but now that the new system is in place and they've picked my brain...they don't need me anymore."

"Well that's easy then. You have to create a need. Fill another niche they know nothing about."

"Right. Of course. Why didn't I think of that?"

"Let me lift up the situation in prayer. Remember; we have not because we ask not. I'm very big on that scripture; because I've found it to be profoundly true in my life."

Suzie lifted up the situation in prayer. "Now, I want you to sing praises to the Almighty and seek Him as never before. Forget yourself..."

"Hey, that reminds me of a Broadway tune. *Forget your worries, forget your cares...get ready for the judgement day...*" Danielle chuckled. "I need to go online and check the words. The tune in ringing in my mind...but I need a refresher on the lyrics."

"Right. Now I better get on the phone and hustle."

"Not so fast."

"What do you mean?"

"I want you to spend an hour praising and glorifying God. God lives in his praises. If you can tap into that spiritual level, you'll be well on your way to a miraculous answer to your prayer."

"How do you know all this stuff?"

"How does anybody know anything? They study. They read. They pursue knowledge. I've pursued biblical knowledge for decades. It was *after* I saturated myself in praise, by singing the Psalms aloud as a praise offering to the Almighty, that I began to tap into blessings. First, they came in the form of spiritual blessings...answers to prayers. Then, as I increased my giving to the Lord's work, as I felt led...and in the direction I felt led to donate to...that's when I met the society dames, who preside over the various charities...that's when I realized how selfish I'd been with the money I was so freely given, after the death of my husband; that's when I realized that I needed to do something significant for others. That God was calling me into a deeper walk with him and inspiring me to reach out to a lost world. I'd always known I had the gift for orchestrating major fund-raising events. I'd dabbled in it over the years; but now I threw myself into the work, developed a passion for various charities, and I must tell you, I'm a much richer person for the experience...and that's when I knew. Absolutely *knew* that God had bigger dreams for me than I had for myself. Suddenly, I wanted Darrell to be proud of me. I knew that he was looking down from above. I knew that he wanted me to live a big life...a grand life...I sensed that God had huge, majestic things in store for me, but I had been too focused on myself, too absorbed in day-to-day living, my social calendar...yada, yada, yada. You get all this, I'm sure.".

"Wow. So, actually...you're saying that huge blessings chased you down, once you forgot about yourself and your own problems and began focusing on others." Suzie said.

Danielle was really getting this stuff. It was a huge reality check for her. "You know what. I have been really, really selfish all my life...and somehow...I guess because I got away with it...I just blindly continued with my agenda." She was quiet for a bit, before continuing. "This is a reality check I have needed for a long, long time. Thank-you." She smiled. "Or, as Elvin Presley would have said "thank-you, thank-you. Thank you very much." Right then, in her new apartment, she peered into the gold-gilded, antique mirror in the living room and bowed, doing a stage curtsy, like the curtain calls at the end of a theatre production.

The lights had been turned on. She would spring into action. First, she dropped to her knees and repented, asking the Lord for direction. Immediately, she felt the tug to visit the Salvation Army center. They probably needed help. She was able bodied and available. She could start there.

She accessed the internet, determining their location, headed downstairs to the underground parking, and stepped into her Jaguar. God had prompted her to buy the older car no one would touch. She got it dirt cheap.

The car had been a dream. A joy. Truly, it was a miracle gift from the Lord. But she'd quickly forgotten this awesome blessing. She admitted to herself that success had swiftly gone to her head. She was the toast of the town, dubbed a fund-raising wizard. But as fast and furious as her star had surged; just that fast, it descended, crashing to the ground. She reflected on the day it occurred. "Your idea bombed, Danielle. Now, we're the laughing stock of Palm Beach; rather than the society ladies' revered do-gooders." Kate Scott spat the words out.

She'd been quickly snubbed. Well, she'd have the last laugh. She'd come back stronger than ever; launch a luncheon, maybe at Mar-a-Lago, invite a popular celebrity to be their guest. She'd find a theme that was powerful. One that resonated with the target market. She could do it, because God would lead the way. First, though, she would humble herself and spend some time at the Salvation Army, while she waited for inspiration from God Almighty.

She knew instantly she was on to something. She met the people that really counted. The folks that *weren't* written up in the society columns, but dedicated philanthropists and caregivers. Everyone she met had a huge, caring heart. They were compassionate folks. The real deal. The best of the pack.

By this time, she was well entrenched into society in Palm Beach. There were two familiar faces here mingling among the hurting souls from off the street. She couldn't believe it. The man from down the hall was one of them. Was he following her? And the other, was a much older woman she'd worked with or met at one of the charity events. *Eve Saunders.* Eve was a brilliant woman and had actually been a scientist before her retirement and subsequent involvement in the world of fund raising and other charitable activities. The two women gave each other a nod of recognition.

Just before her volunteer shift was over, and she was about to leave, Eve sought her out and greeted her. "Nice to see you here, Danielle. There are so many hurting folks here. We are so blessed to be able to provide some comfort for them."

"Yes."

"Incidentally, darling, I'm giving a small dinner party at my house next Saturday at 7:00. I'd like you to come." She handed her a small, square envelope. The address and details are inside. It's a semi-formal event." She smiled. "Last invitation...and I just happened to have it with me." She smiled warmly at Danielle.

Danielle returned the smile. *He is a rewarder of those who diligently seek Him.*

The party was a real eye opener. She'd thought she was in the right crowd when she'd been a fund raiser, despite the absence of certain snobby elite folks. They were all here. The quiet, revered inner circle of the crème de la crème of high society was present. They were more confident and relaxed, in contrast to the other charity events she'd attended. They were the real deal. She'd cracked the inner circle of high society simply because the society matrons liked her. However, she hadn't known how fickle they were and was stunned at how fast she'd lost their favor and been booted out, without any explanation. It had been a blessing in disguise, because the serious philanthropists had embraced her.

Harold Hopkins was a rotund, jolly man. Recently widowed, he seemed to take a fancy to her, occasionally winking at her across the long, elegant dinner table. Flirtatious by nature and habit, she returned the wink with a sexy smile.

That night, just before she was about to leave, Harold found her and handed her his card. "Would you call me?"

She nodded and smiled. As she drove to her new apartment, she knew the Good Lord was smiling down on her. She hoped she was about to step into a great and wonderful destiny. She had no idea how it would play out, but she felt that everything would work out brilliantly.

Chapter Fifteen

Dana gave birth to identical male twins. It was an ordeal she never wanted to go through again. If Graham hadn't been there every step of the way, she was sure she would have died giving birth.

Sybil moved into the house and helped with the twins. Violet, after talking it over with Graham and Dana, accepted a foreign exchange student from Israel. She was related to a couple that attended their church, but due to a family tragedy, did not wish to proceed.

Talia was an absolute delight. She brought laughter and gaiety into the tenseness of twin babies descending on an already busy household.

Graham and Dana named the twins Sal and Saul. No one could tell them apart. They both weighed 7 lbs 9 oz.

Dana was over the moon. Motherhood brought a new dimension into her life and somehow deepened her love for Graham, Will and Jay. *Four sons.* She felt blessed beyond anything she could have possibly imagined.

She spoke pretty good English. She fussed over the twins, changing their diapers and lavishing heaps of love and attention on them.

Dana adored her. They'd bonded instantly. She felt like Talia was her daughter, as bizarre as that was.

After several weeks, late one afternoon, after Talia had returned from school, she chatted with Dana at length. It was then Dana found out that Talia had been advised by her father and his assistant to move out of Israel. She told Dana that her dad was an ambassador to the United Nations for Israel and for political reasons she might not be safe in Tel Aviv. He'd arranged for her to become an exchange student, and she'd wound up in Lexington.

Because Dana had quickly bonded with Talia, Talia confided more details.

It turned out that her Dad, a widower travelled frequently and extensively and was currently based in New York, did not think it was safe for her to hang out with him. He wanted her safely tucked away.

It wasn't long before Dana knew she didn't want Talia to leave after the school term was over. Further, she learned that her Dad was seeking a semi-permanent refuge place for his daughter, where she would be safe from foul play.

Dana broached the subject gingerly with Graham and was struck down. He wouldn't hear of it. "Are you nuts? We've got our hands full with four boys; the last thing we need is another child."

That night Dana cried herself to sleep. She ached for Talia to become a permanent part of their family. Oddly, she felt as though she were her birth mother. The bond between them was so powerful, that Dana knew it could only come from God Almighty. He had thrust the sweet child into their path; and they needed to embrace her as a long-term guest or even adopt her.

Graham was adamant that none of this would happen. "I'm the head of this household and we are not taking on the responsibility of another child." It had been the last thing he said before falling asleep.

Dana cried bitter tears. She had never loved a total stranger like she loved this child. Her body still hadn't bounced back from the trauma of giving birth. She was willfully neglecting it in defiance of Graham's stance on turning his back on Talia. She determined to punish Graham by letting herself go, if she didn't get her way. She knew she was acting like a spoiled child. Regardless, she was determined to have her way.

Dana took to lounging around the house, deliberately sloppy, though not actually slovenly, when the babies were asleep. She was nursing them anyway and wore loose, comfortable clothing.

Talia, as always, provided great comfort and solace to Dana and the twins. There was nothing the child could not do. Nothing she would not do. She was incredibly resourceful.

Dana soon became obsessed with having her live permanently at Sugarbush. She was adamant about adopting her. She had to convince Graham that it was the right thing to do and would bring blessing and joy to Sugarbush.

Graham wasn't buying it. The next morning, over breakfast, they had it out again. He actually became snarky, to Dana's surprise. "Dana. Read my lips. We're not taking on any more responsibility. Talia can live here for now. Sybil, bless her heart, drives her to school and picks her up, along with Will and Jay, as you know." He placed brawny hands upon her shoulders, peering into her eyes. "But Sybil will be leaving soon, and I don't want the responsibility of raising another child, Dana. Surely you understand that four youngsters in the house is enough responsibility for us."

Tears stung Dana's eyes. *I want a daughter. I need a daughter, Lord. Why doesn't he get that?* Dana dug her heels in. They had a spat. Sybil had already driven the children to school. She hadn't returned yet.

A FEW HOURS LATER

"Ah, there you are, Dana. I've done the chores. Let's have some more coffee, honey." Graham smiled, moving into the kitchen.

Dana was downcast as she sipped coffee and sprung green grapes into her mouth, from the circular bowl of fruit sitting in the center of the table. "Graham...honey... I'm not taking no for an answer. I have bonded so totally with Talia, I just know God has sent her to us. Somewhere along the way, she will be an awesome blessing to us. I just know it. Trust me on this, Graham." Tears sprung to her eyes. "Please trust my judgement...my women's intuition on this one."

Graham was silent. It had all been said. He'd made up his mind that they couldn't handle any more responsibility. He wasn't about to change his mind.

"Well...aren't you going to say...anything?"

He peered at her, sternly. "It's all been said, Dana. We're at an impasse. And I'm not backing down."

"Fine. Have it your way. But just don't expect me to be the lovely, sweet...doting wife..." Tears sprung to her eyes. "You just don't seem to get how important this is to me, do you?"

"We're not adopting Talia. And that's the end of it." He rose, leaving his coffee unfinished. "I'll be in my study."

For the first time in four years of wedded bliss, they were not speaking to each other. Dana started it. Graham had no choice but to play her game. It made him furious. He dug his heels in even deeper. He showed a stubborn side to him she didn't know was there. Finally, after several weeks of barely exchanging a word, and their intimacy having ceased totally, Dana realized with a sinking heart, that due to her persistent demands, their marriage was in big trouble. *"Lord, what have I done? I've alienated Graham over this...dear, sweet, orphaned child..."* She couldn't help herself, she sobbed uncontrollably. She sat in the family room, feet propped up on the ottoman, feeling desolate. It was 8:00 in the evening She was alone. The boys were in their rooms doing their homework. Dana held Sal in her arms. He was so tiny and sweet. His trusting, little face peered up at her.

She was in awe of the two precious sons God had given them. Her heart swelled with motherly pride and love as she held Sal close to her, cuddling him.

Sybil sat next to her in the family room, rocking Saul. *Or was it Sal? She couldn't tell them apart.*

After some time, Dana's eyelids grew heavy. Sal wailed and wailed. Finally exhausted, he drifted off.

Graham strode into the family room. "I'll take him, Sybil." He lifted Saul from Sybil's arms. Immediately, the baby started wailing. "Well, at least he has good lungs. Thanks, Sybil. You look like you could use a good nights' sleep."

"I am rather tired." She smiled. "It brings back good memories from my days of working as a nurse. I love babies." She smiled, sleepily. "They make me forget I'm childless."

"I'm surprised you never adopted children, Sybil."

"Another time. Let's all get some sleep."

Graham led the way to the nursery. Each of them held a sleeping baby. Graham gently laid Saul down into his crib.

Dana laid Sal in the other crib. *At least I think he's Sal.* It was virtually impossible to tell them apart, since they were identical twins. *Thank God he still wants me, in spite of my temper tantrums.* But Dana was in for a big surprise. He turned away from her once they climbed into bed. Soon, she heard him gently snoring. He had not even given her a goodnight hug or kiss. Silent, mournful tears trickled down her cheeks.

Dana lay awake for hours. She stared at the ceiling, though she couldn't see much of it. A night light in the bathroom cast a flicker of light in the room. Just enough to cause her to dimly make out his sleeping form. Sleep eluded her. Silent, unbidden tears trickled down her cheeks. *Lord, I want Talia to be my daughter.* She loved that child. She had from the second they'd met. There was a powerful, invisible bond between them. *Couldn't Graham see that? Didn't he get that?*

Dana tossed and turned, unable to sleep despite being weary. The babies had disrupted their sleep nightly. Tonight

Dana prayed they would both be able to sleep without waking up and wailing. Maybe the lack of restful sleep had caused them to bicker about Talia. They'd had few disagreement during their married life; and never one that wasn't resolved before the sun went down. Dana had read that admonishment in the Bible and rigorously adhered to it. So did Graham. This refusal on his part to kiss and make up before the sun went down was enormously distressing to her.

Sybil wouldn't be around forever. She'd already mentioned she had a trip to Washington planned. She would soon be travelling, leaving her to cope with the boys. She had to talk to Graham about hiring a nurse or nanny; but would he? He'd suddenly gone penurious on them. Since she'd met him, money never seemed to be an issue; now suddenly, it was all he talked about. And for the first time in their marriage, they'd started bickering.

She glanced at the bedside clock. Exactly 3:00 a.m. *Lord, you said in your word that you give your beloved sleep. Please let me get some sleep.* She'd look like a rag tomorrow.

The next thing she knew it was morning. She glanced over and saw that Graham was already up. She'd been neglecting the TV exercises designed to get her body back in shape after giving birth. She had to get with it. *Lord, give me the strength to get through this day. "One day at a time sweet Jesus, that's all I'm asking from you."* The lyrics of that old hymn came back to her.

Though she'd overslept, she felt rested and better. She hurried into the nursery to see Sal and Saul. Sybil was rocking one of them and singing to him. She took the other and began nursing him. Maybe Graham will have a change of heart about Talia. *Hope springs eternal.* She doubted it, though. He'd been adamant about not adopting her. And to her dismay, because of that and other issues, there was a growing rift between them.

Dana entered the kitchen, soon spotting Graham at the

kitchen table, enjoying scrambled eggs and hash browns with crisp bacon. Lately, he'd begun eating breakfast before her, so he could do the chores. Dana often slept in, plagued with post-partum blues.

Violet was scooping fresh gourmet coffee into the coffee maker as Dana entered the kitchen. "Did you finally manage to get some sleep, Hon?" Violet smiled at her.

Dana peered over at Violet. *Thank God for her and her steady, calming influence on the family.*

"I did, thanks Violet. Good morning...and good morning, Graham." She felt like going over to him and giving him a peck on the cheek, but she thought better of it. He looked somber and unapproachable.

Violet moved out of the main kitchen area. Dana guessed she wanted to give them some privacy. She busied herself spraying water on a variety of the plants on the Baker's rack on the far side of the rambling, country kitchen. She moved on to the lower shelves, spraying them with water, also.

Talia entered the kitchen, her large brown eyes sparkling with vibrancy and mischief. But her eyes were filled with tears. "I...I guess I have to...to leave Sugarbush...because the...social worker..." She started crying. "Well, she...found someone willing to take me..."

Graham, she's only thirteen. Have mercy on her. Why can't we take her? We have the extra bedrooms? One more mouth to feed isn't going to break the bank, is it?

Graham was silent.

"At least he's thinking about it. I hope. He's fond of her, too. Oh Lord, open Graham's heart and eyes to see what a blessing it would be to have this precious child live with us. The words flew out of her mouth, unbidden. "She's welcome in our home, isn't she, honey?" *Dana had never been rude or presumptuous to Graham in the past; but her hand was being forced. She couldn't lose this precious child. She'd become deeply attached to her in the short time she'd been*

here. Oh please God. Please Graham..." It was a silent plea. Tears trickled down her cheeks.

Graham, finishing his breakfast, rose from the table, leaving a full mug of coffee. "I'll be in my office, Dana." He turned and walked out of the room, not willing to discuss the matter further. *Or was he inviting her to his office where they could discuss the matter privately? She wasn't sure. But one thing she was sure of, and that was that he was in a sour, disapproving mood. A stance he had never before taken with her. Alarm bells rang in her heart and mind. He was distancing himself from her. That was both frightening and hurtful.*

Tears sprung to her eyes. She rose from the table, throwing her arms around Talia. "Don't leave, Talia. Please don't leave. Give me a little more time. I...I'll talk some sense into Graham...I swear it." But even as the words tumbled from her lips, she knew she was not speaking the truth. For whatever reason, Graham had dug in his heels, and clearly had no intention of changing his mind. *Does money mean so much to you, Graham, that you would turn your back on this dear, sweet child? A precious, young women who needs a home, guidance...and a biblical upbringing? Parents she can count on.* "I don't want you to leave, honey. Give me...give me a couple more days...Graham will come around...I promise he will." *But even as the words tumbled from her lips, she knew they were untrue. He had dug in his heels and hadn't shown a crack in his steely armor of refusal. She was hitting a brick wall. She could hardly miss that.* She wrapped tender arms around Talia, lifting her sweet, innocent face toward her. Long, dark brown locks caressed her slender shoulders. That beauty contrasted starkly with her downcast mood. Tears rolled down her cheeks. Enormous amber-flecked chocolate eyes peered at her, tears glistening in them. It was a face filled with innocence and hope. Hope that she and Graham had unwittingly dashed to pieces.

Dana's heart broke. *I was adopted. I can't allow this precious child to leave here. She belongs with me...with us. Oh, Lord, I need a miracle.* "Even if I have to say goodbye to Graham, you're not going anywhere." The feisty, stubborn side of her had surfaced with a vengeance. It was that steely determination that had caused her to excel at jumping and go on to become an ace Thoroughbred trainer, with winning colts.

Violet was stone silent. She wanted to reach out to Dana, but she thwarted the impulsive. The issue was between Dana, Graham and God. *I will pray fervently. That is the one thing I can do.* "Excuse me, Dana. I'll be in my room for a while." Violet headed to the staircase leading to her room on the first floor. Soon, she was on her knees praying about Talia, Graham and Dana. She already knew their marriage was in trouble. Perhaps she'd sensed trouble brewing even before they did.

Dana took Talia by the hand, leading her into her private sanctuary. Sybil had the babies under control. She always took charge in the morning since she was an early riser like the wailing infants. And anyway, she had great joy in tending to the twins.

Once in her private sanctuary, words of truth sprung from her lips. "Have a seat, honey. Graham...is just scared. He feels overwhelmed right now. What with the farm, four sons, ranch hands, Violet and me to take care of; he's petrified to take on more responsibility."

Dana could see the poor child fighting back tears threatening to overwhelm her. "I'll work hard. I'll help do everything. I'll help with the babies, the horses...cooking, cleaning...anything you say." She started sobbing, big tears trickling down her cheeks. Soon, it bordered on hysteria. She threw her arms around Dana. "Please...please don't send me away...I had terrible things happen to me...at the last place I stayed...Oh don't send me away, I beg you... don't." She was sobbing hysterically and it broke Dana's heart.

Dana held her in her arms for a long, long time, soothing her, caressing her, murmuring encouraging words. "Oh sweetheart...even if I have to separate from Graham for a while...or divorce him...you're staying right here. I promise you that." *What have I just said, Lord? Disobeyed my husband?* Regardless of the consequences, the die had been cast; and Dana knew there was no turning back.

And so she prayed aloud, as she held the dear, sobbing child in her arms. "Lord, I am asking you to make a way where there is no way." Tears of love and compassion for the budding, young woman filled her mind and heart. Somehow it would all work out. *It had to.* Because one thing Dana knew for sure, she would not turn back. This child would remain at Sugarbush.

Graham was silent at dinner. The large group dined in the formal dining room tonight. Violet served a lamb stew. The silence was deafening. No one spoke. Not even Violet, though she puttered near them and the sideboard. Dana prayed silently, over and over. *We need a miracle, Lord. We need a miracle.*

But the next morning, Graham had his suitcase standing at the door by the time Dana entered the hallway on her way to the kitchen for breakfast. Her heart almost stopped when she saw it. He'd said nothing to her about travelling.

She walked into the kitchen with a heavy heart, soon pouring herself a mug of coffee. Graham sat at the table sipping coffee. One look at him told her he had not changed his mind about keeping Talia. His face was granite. "Have a seat, Dana. We're at an impasse. Either Talia goes; or I go."

Dana's mouth fell open in surprise and horror. "What? What did you just say?"

"Dana. My suitcase is in the hallway. I'm going to take a little trip. I'm flying out to Houston this morning to see my folks. I'll be back in a few days. If you haven't come to your senses by then and decided to obey me, I'll be filing for divorce."

Dana stared at him as though he'd just lost his mind. She opened her mouth to say something, but no words would come. She had been thinking about giving *him* an ultimatum, to smarten him up. it hadn't occurred to her that he might beat her to the punch. She had carefully planned her little speech. She would file for divorce, if he didn't agree to let Talia remain at Sugarbush and adopt her. He'd taken the play out of her hands. She couldn't change her mind about letting Talia remain at Sugarbush, though. She'd promised her that she could stay.

Violet was not her usual chipper self today. She sort of moped around. Presently, she was puttering around the country kitchen watering plants and humming strangely, like she was on another planet.

Dana watched in horror as Graham picked up his suitcase in the hallway and hurried down the front steps to his jeep. She stood at the door, watching him drive off. She was stunned. Speechless.

Violet plopped down on a chair next to Dana around the kitchen table. "He's serious Dana. It's over. The marriage is over."

Dana peered at her as though she had taken leave of her senses. "What are you talking about, Violet? What on earth are you talking about?'

"You heard me, Dana. The marriage is over."

"How can you say such a thing?"

"Because it's true. It just hasn't sunk in for you yet; that's all."

"But...what about our assets? The farm...community property...and all that stuff."

"I don't know. I guess that's what he's going to discuss with his Dad. He's a retired attorney, I guess you knew that."

"No. Actually I didn't know. Graham never mentioned it. How do *you* know about all this stuff?"

"I'm the little old lady everybody confides in. I'm surprised he never mentioned that to you, though."

Dana's body was out of shape from giving birth to twins and she hadn't been disciplined about getting herself back in shape. She'd been focusing on the twins...and Talia...leaving Graham in the dust. A mountain of tears gushed out.

Violet held her close. "Hush, darling. It will work out. God will work it out, somehow. I've been praying for a miracle. I saw the writing on the wall when this impasse appeared; I knew you'd come to loggerheads. The thing is, Dana, I don't see Graham changing his mind about adopting Talia; and I don't see you walking away from her."

Dana sobbed bitterly in Violet's arms. "What am I going to do Violet? There doesn't seem to be any solution to this problem."

"We're going to continue to seek God in prayer...and pray for a miracle." Violet smiled at her, hoping to cheer her up.

They prayed fervently and then cried together, holding each other. Soon, Dana focused on the exercise videos, determined to get back in shape after birthing twins. Not an easy task.

Graham was welcomed home at his folks' home in Houston. His Mom kept hugging and kissing him. His Dad grinned from ear to ear, as he kept repeating his welcome. "Welcome home, son. Welcome home."

Graham cleared his throat. "I'm warning you; I have a serious issue I want to talk to the two of you about." He glanced from his dad to his mom.

"That's French for "*I need cash and lots of it.*" His Mom continued to smile warmly.

"Actually, this is not about money, Mom."

"Really?" She raised her eyebrows, her beautifully coiffed silver hair barely moving. Inquisitive green eyes spoke volumes without a spoken word.

His Dad spoke up. "Let me guess, the headstrong Dana has pulled another caper...some sort of a power trip, no doubt."

Graham could hardly believe his ears. *His Dad was right on the money. How could he possibly have known?*

"I could use a drink." Graham glanced over at the bar, featuring fine wines.

"What would you like, darling?" His elegantly-attired Mom, clad in a turquoise silk sweater and matching pants, her size six figure still intact, stood waiting for her son's instructions.

"Mother...I'll have a glass of cabernet, please."

"Cabernet it is. Sure I can't get you something stronger?" She smiled conspiratorially at her beloved son. "Kalua on the rocks, maybe?

He was tempted for a split second. "A glass of Cabernet will be perfect."

"We'll join you, darling." She poured Graham a glass of cabernet, serving it in a Waterford crystal glass. Then she served one o her hubby and one for herself. "Now then, darling. Let's hear it."

Graham was on the hot seat. He'd put himself there. It was too late to turn back. He paused, organizing his thoughts. "I warned you before you married her, son. Told you she was headstrong. She's like an untamed horse...a wild horse...they're not easily cornered or broken in."

"I thought you were exaggerating at the time, Dad. But the truth is, that headstrong aspect of her personality is about to destroy our marriage..."

"Well, if it dissolves; it dissolves." His dad shrugged. "She's not the only woman on the planet."

"Harold. They *are* married. If they can salvage the marriage, it would be prudent financially. Besides, these kids are in love...so they've always claimed."

"So far, we've done nothing but support your gentleman farmer lifestyle; but we've warned you it's coming to an end. Either you get Sugarbush into a money-making proposition, or we...you might need to file for bankruptcy and move on to something else."

"Aren't you getting a little ahead of yourself, dear. You've just started laying the pressure on him lately. After we lost a bundle in our little investment, we started looking to you to make some serious money. The tax deduction for the Kentucky purse; which of course was gifted to Israel, was very useful; but now you need to make some serious money to continue supporting the lifestyle you've become accustomed to." His dad had always been a shrewd businessman, a talent that seemed to have evaded him.

"Give the dear boy a chance, darling. He's only had the farm for...a few years..."

"Fine. But more to the point, what are we going to do with Dana?" The wizened old coot peered into Graham's eyes.

"What do you mean by that statement, darling? Dana just gave birth to twins. She's going through a huge adjustment right now." His Mother took a sip of the Cabernet, then rose and headed to the bar fridge, soon returning with plates of cheese and crackers.

Next, his Mother strode across the room to the CD player, selecting Brahms Concerto No. Three, The music filled the room. "Darling." She peered at Graham, smiling as she raised her eyebrows, which she often did when she had something serious to say.

Here it comes. "What Mother?"

"I think divorce is the best option. That way, we'll pay her out; and you, Will and Jay can start a new life."

"Mom. I have *four sons* now, as you well know."

"Nice biblical names you chose for the twins. How are they doing, dear?"

"Fine, Mother. Just fine. We both know this conversation is not about them. I need to get a handle on the whole picture."

"So...what do you want to do, Graham? Patch things up with Dana and try to make it work or scrap the marriage?"

"Mother. You make it sound as simple and uncomplicated as… buying a new car or keeping the old one. She's not a disposable commodity. She's my wife and I love her."

"Then fight for her...and don't be such a wimp."

"How do I do that when she's determined to have Talia live under our roof; and I really don't want another mouth to feed."

"You can be so crass at times, darling. What difference does one more person living on the farm make, really?"

"We have four sons. We don't need a daughter, too."

"Maybe that's exactly what you *do* need." His Mother smiled, raising her eyebrows. "Tell you what, dear. Try to imagine life as a bachelor again. You weren't very good at it, darling. You're not suited to bachelor life."

"How do you know, Mom? I wasn't a bachelor for long.

"My point exactly." His Mother strode over to where Graham lounged on a bergere chair. She settled onto the luxurious sofa next to her son. "Darling, I'm your Mother. Mother's know everything, don't you know that?"

He chuckled then. "Okay, Mom. You win. What should I do?"

She laughed heartily. "Darling. I thought you'd never ask. Well, let me spell it out for you. So here it is. You go home. You tell Dana that Talia can stay. End of conflict. You live happily ever after. And we get five grandkids, including her."

"Give in. Just like that?"

"Harold. Tell him about all the times you gave in to me." She smiled. "And the fact that I was always right."

"That doesn't mean Dana is always right, you know." His dad scowled.

"Well I sympathize with Dana. I don't have a daughter. Of course...I was close to Myrna, but that's in the past. I welcome the young woman into the family." She looked over at Harold. "Remember...when we were young, and I wanted to adopt a little girl...and you wouldn't hear of it...?" Tears sprung to her eyes.

Harold glanced over at his wife, sadness etched in his eyes. "You...you've never forgotten...that little girl, have you, dear?"

His Mom had a faraway look in her eyes. When she spoke, the words came out softly. Her voice taking on a new warmth with a sentimental undercurrent. "No, honey; I've never forgotten her." She fought the onrush of tears. "I think...sometimes God gives us special people...people that we are assigned to help and bond with...on this earth. And it's up to us to...prayerfully figure it out...and not miss His leading and the blessing that comes with obedience."

"So you think I should eat humble pie, agree to let Talia stay, adopt her and focus on getting Sugarbush into a thriving operation." He peered over at his Mom. He thought he saw tiny droplets of tears trickle down her cheeks. *She has never gotten over the child she wanted to adopt.* Graham knew then. He knew what he had to do. Kiss and make up. Embrace Talia and bring her up as his own daughter.

When Graham reached home and walked through the front door, he saw Dana's luggage. Furious, he marched into the family room. Dana wasn't there. He went into the kitchen. Not here. He felt like screaming. He was ready to eat humble pie and Dana hadn't even waited for him to return. She was packed and ready to go. But go where with two babies in tow? Dana. Where are you, honey? Nothing.

He hurried into the nursery. The cribs were gone and so were the twins. That meant Dana had actually gone. Talia, also. What about Will and Jay? And where was Violet? "Violet." He called her repeatedly as panic welled up inside him.

Violet hurried down the staircase to Graham. He stood in the hallway, his face ashen. "Where is my wife? Where are my sons?" His voice kept rising. It was edged with hysteria."

And the babies. Where are they? And Talia?"

Violet was too quiet. Something had happened. Something terrible had happened. A premonition swept over him. "Violet. What is it? Where is Dana? What has happened?"

"She left you a note." Her countenance was sad. She spoke softly.

"A note. Isn't that her luggage?" He peered at it more closely. It was actually *his luggage. She was kicking him out. Was that it?*

He tore open the note. "*Graham. It's not going to work between us. I've had postpartum blues since birthing the twins. I'm also depressed about losing my figure. When I needed you most, you left town I've taken a walk. When you get this, Talia and I will be on a jet found for Tel Aviv. I've dropped Will and Jay and the twins off at Sybil's house. I'm sorry you just didn't get how much I loved and bonded with Talia; and how much I've always wanted a daughter. I shall try to help hr find her relatives. She said she doesn't want to be somewhere where she is not loved. Regardless, I'm applying to adopt her. You likely find it hard to understand that I would throw away our marriage over this issue; that should tell you how strongly I feel about it. You're not the compassionate man I thought you were. I thought you were a man of great understanding and compassion; but when you turned your back on Talia; you turned your back on me, just like Mom. I am saddened that I won't be there to see Will and Jay grow up. I know you'll be disappointed in me. But that's life, isn't it? Each of us must do what we have to do. God has called me to be Talia's mother. I don't really have a choice in the matter. That's why I can't abandon her, like governesses did. I'm truly sorry for this disruption in your life, Graham; but I'm sure God will give you someone more suited to you; a woman who will raise your handsome, precious sons. I'm truly sorry it couldn't be me. I wish you love and great, great happiness. Thank-you for the precious memories and the special time we had together. I shall treasure it always in my heart." Love, Dana.*

Graham flew around the house like a madman. "No. Violet. No. This can't be happening. I've got to get Dana back. She's lost all sense of reason…the silly fool. I came back with the idea that I wanted to embrace and adopt Talia. Must I now catch a flight to Tel Aviv and try to track her down? What am I going to do, Violet?" He covered his face with his hands and sobbed bitterly.

Violet held him close and let him cry his heart out. When he was spent, she smiled at him. "Feel better now, Graham? It's all going to work out; you'll see."

"All going to work out? She's …they've gone to a dangerous part of the world. I've got to get them back. When did they leave? When did their flight leave?"

Violet glanced at her watch. "A couple hours ago."

"Maybe…maybe the flight was cancelled…or delayed."

"If you're going to the airport, you better get going. I'll pray for a miracle."

Graham double parked his jeep and raced into the airport. If they towed him, he wouldn't care. All that mattered was reaching Dana in time. Heart racing, he rushed into the airport. Soon he was frantically peering up at the departure screen. He glanced at his watch. The flight had a stop in Chicago, maybe he could intercept her there. If not, he'd continue to Istanbul. He was determined to find her and bring her home. Glancing at his cell, he saw that the last flight headed to Tel Aviv with stops at Chicago and Istanbul . It was gone. His heart sank. *What was I thinking? I can't give Dana up regardless of her demands. I'm in love with her. I miss her like crazy. Lord, please let me find her, apologize, embrace Talia and welcome her into the family. And then start fresh.* He sank into the deep leather seats in the airport lounge area, covering his face with his hands and trying to avoid bawling. *"Lord, I need a miracle."* Soon, he took courage in hand, wiped away his tears, straightened up and got in line for a ticket agent. He would get the first flight he could. Then he would alert Violet and Sybil about his trip.

He heard the announcement. It was like manna from heaven. "All flights to Tel Aviv have been cancelled due to terrorist threats. Stand by for updates. *It was manna from heaven. They must be here. at the airport...or maybe booked into a hotel .No answer on hr cell.* He called the house. Violet had not heard anything. "Stand by, Violet. Maybe they'll come home. I'm going to hang out at the airport and try all the local hotels...see if I can find them."

"I'll be prayin' for a miracle, Graham."

Graham glanced at the time on his cell. 8:15. P.M. He'd called every hotel in the area and even drove to a couple of them. None of them had a guest registered under the names of Dana Van Rensellier or Talia Shaw. He began to panic. What if something happened to them? Foul play, maybe. Two, lovely young women travelling without a man...headed to Tel Aviv...anything could happen. His mind raced with possibilities. *Lord, I can't handle this. Only you can help me. I need a miracle. First, I need to find Dana; then I need to win her back. A recent sermon flashed back to him. The minister admonished the congregation to praise and worship God more. Rely on Him totally. Seek Him with a whole heart and do not lean on your understanding.* He'd told the congregation that was often a prelude to spectacular answers to prayer. *He'd do it, and count on God to help him.*

Thankful he hadn't been towed, he drove back to the airport praising God for a miracle he believed would happen. *I'm no Apostle Paul, Lord, but I shall praise and worship you and believe for a miracle.* If God could open prison doors super naturally, he could bring Dana and Talia back to him miraculously. He phoned Violet to tell her not to expect him. He'd checked into a hotel so he could be close to the airport. Then he called Sybil. "I should buy you a solid gold Bentley, considering all the favors I owe you."

She chuckled. "Just get your wife and your life back. It will happen, Graham...according to your faith, brother."

"Thanks for your encouragement and prayers, Sybil. I'm counting on a miracle."

THREE HOURS LATER

Graham fell asleep after many hours of praising and worshipping the Almighty. He'd read and sang various Psalms aloud. He kept remembering Paul when he'd been imprisoned. He'd praised God all night, despite the fact that he was prison. God had sent a mighty earthquake, miraculously freeing him as the prison doors flew open. For a fleeting second, he wondered what his miracle would look like. Then, he fell fast asleep.

He checked out at 4:00 a.m. the next morning, driving the short distance to Bluegrass International. Soon, he walked briskly into the airport, soon glancing at the screen and checking departures to Tel Aviv. As he peered at the screen, in his peripheral vision, he spotted his beautiful wife, Dana, peering at the arrivals and departures board, a frightened looking Talia, next to her. He was overcome with powerful emotions of love, as he glimpsed her. Talia looked so vulnerable, so lost...he just wanted to protect her. *How had he been so crass by rejecting her? He'd almost lost Dana over the rejection.* She hadn't seen him yet. Her eyes were glued to the departure board, like Dana's.

Graham hurried over to them. He thrust powerful arms around both of them, before they could object. "Come home, darling. I'm so sorry. Talia is welcome to stay as long as she wants. I welcome her into our family and Sugarbush. Please, forgive me...both of you." Tears of remorse trickled down his cheeks.

Dana had never seen him cry. She was deeply moved by the display of emotion. For a few beats, they stood staring at him. Speechless. Then Talia threw her arms around Graham's neck. Her eyes were filled with tears, but he knew they were tears of joy. "Oh Graham, thank-you. I've been praying for a new Mommy and surrogate Daddy, ever since Dad told me it would be best for my safety. God heard my prayer." Her smile seemed to light up the entire airport. He'd never seen anyone so overjoyed. *And to think he almost missed this amazing blessing.* He kissed Dana then, fueled by a new and glorious awakening; a fresh fire, a renewed love. He whispered softly in her ear. "I almost lost you, my darling. I will cherish you forever, Dana." He was overcome with emotion then. "I want to renew our vows."

Part of Dana was leery. Was he a Jekyll and Hyde? But as she gazed into his eyes, she saw only deep love and sincerity reflected in them. "What caused you to change your mind, honey?"

"Well, we both know that God moves in mysterious ways. I flew to Houston to see my folks hoping for sympathy and telling them we might both be...moving on. Well, they wouldn't hear of it. Mom, in particular, gave me a pep talk In a nutshell, she told me to grow up. She shared a great sadness in her life with me. There had been a child she'd wanted to adopt, just after she and Dad had married. Dad forbade it. Mom never got over it. She didn't want me to miss my chance at having a daughter. They said they would pray for a miraculous reunion and restoration of our cracked union. She reminded me that nothing was impossible with God." He grinned. "Well, after that long pep talk, I finished my glass of very fine Cabernet and knew I would move heaven and earth to get my family back; including; and especially my one and only beloved daughter, Talia."

Talia's smile lit her face. She beamed from ear to ear, her joy palpable.

Violet greeted them at the front door. She was not surprised. "I made lasagna, if anyone is interested."

"Oh goody. I love peanut butter cookies, aunt Violet." She'd quickly taken to calling Violet, aunt Violet. Violet rather liked the idea of being Talia's aunt.

Graham was determined to make up for past sins. He turned to Talia. "Want to learn how to ride horses?"

"Oh yes. I thought you'd never ask."

"We'll get you a Thoroughbred that's all your own." He winked at her. "But you have to learn to take care of him."

She jumped up and down with glee. "Oh yes, Daddy. I'll take such good care of him...you'll be amazed."

That night Dana didn't feel out of shape and frumpy, despite her extra fat. Instead, Graham made her feel like the most beautiful woman in the world. She loved how he made her feel. Cherished. Special. They'd retired early. Dana could have sworn she heard angels rejoicing in heaven, over a marriage restored, love rekindled and hearts that had expanded to make room for the sweet child that had been thrust into their lives.

At the grand, circular kitchen table in the colossal country kitchen, Graham examined his sizeable family. He needed a financial miracle to generate more income. Fast. He began to question his wisdom in giving the million-dollar purse as a gift to Israel, when they needed it to run the farm. He wouldn't think about that right now. He would enjoy breakfast with his loved ones.

"I'll be leaving tonight. I have some business at home to take care of." Sybil made the announcement over breakfast the next morning.

Dana threw grateful arms around her. "Thanks so much for helping out, Sybil. I don't know how we can ever repay you."

"Your sons give me great joy." She took her brother's hand, moving away from the group for privacy. I'll be back on Friday, for the weekend." She smiled. "Tell you the truth; it's a welcome change from spending so much time alone. And the girlfriends...well... I've already spent plenty of time with them. You might just have trouble getting rid of me."

Dana was overjoyed. She thought she heard the sound of

angels rejoicing again. *Was Sybil actually saying she would live in and help out with the twins? Seems like that's exactly what she was saying.*

That night Graham dismissed Will and Jay, sending them to their rooms and telling them he wanted to have a private chat with Talia. Graham and Dana sat in the family room with their new "daughter." Graham had a lot of questions. He hadn't asked them before, because he'd had it in his mind that she was a temporary house guest...someone who was just passing through. Now, he sought to know as much about her as he could. "Let's start at the beginning, Talia. So, Dana tells me you grew up in Tel Aviv with a governess after your mother died. And because your father, ambassador to Israel for the United Nations travelled extensively, and couldn't keep close tabs on you, he wanted you safely tucked away. He worried that you might be kidnapped or a victim of foul play."

Dana looked sheepish. She lowered her head. "Please don't be angry with me, honey, but I read about her plight in a magazine at my doctor's office and made some inquiries about her. The next thing you know, my doctor asked me if I would consider taking her into my home. I hadn't broached the subject with you at the time, and I hadn't given birth yet. The timing was all wrong. And I was preoccupied with the soon-coming birth of the twins. But when she told me Talia would have to return to Tel Aviv immediately, I felt...I don't know how to say it...I just felt this overwhelming sadness...like I just couldn't let that happen. So...I told my doctor...well, I said she could come to Sugarbush as a temporary house guest. Well, before you know it, Talia showed up and stole my heart. We bonded right from the start. I felt like...like she was somehow supposed to be my daughter." She smiled. "I know that sounds bizarre, but that's how I felt."

"God moves in mysterious ways."

"Well, with Dad's diplomatic missions, he wants me to be safely tucked away. As ambassador of Israel to the United States, he has a lot on his plate. Because of the unrest in Israel, he felt that leaving me there with a governess would cause me to be vulnerable. The previous ambassador was assassinated. And though dad never feared anyone, he wanted to make sure I was safe. He felt that I would be safer in America; but not with him. He wanted me safely tucked away. That's when we looked into living in Kentucky, since he has attended the derby on occasion and knew some people here. Mother died when I was five...cancer. So I grew up with a governess. She was okay. But in my heart, I didn't like her much. I was a very lonely child... so I started creating imaginary friends. One day when Dad came home from a trip, he saw me talking to an imaginary child. He became very worried about me, wondering if I'd lost my marbles. He wanted to find a proper home for me. He thought that would be best for my well being. Every night I cried myself to sleep, after praying for a new Mommy. I didn't need a new Daddy, because the one I had was wonderful, but I knew that they often came as a package deal. So I asked God and my dad if they minded if I had one Mommy and two Daddies. I got the feeling neither of them minded. Dad just wanted me safe and happy, whatever it took. Well, as soon as I set foot into this house, I knew in my heart that I belonged here. I can't explain it. It was just this...sense, that this is what God had for me."

"Your dad must have wrestled fiercely with giving you up."

"Yes. He didn't want to, but his hand was forced. There *was* an assassination attempt on Dad's life about a year ago. That's when he decided he had to get me out of the country. He wanted me to live in temporary foster homes until his stint as an ambassador was done. Then, he hoped to remarry and take me back."

"I see. Yes I understand he was...and is protecting you. And kidnapping does happen. We know that first hand...but I won't go there." Graham smiled at Talia.

Dana looked sheepish. "I hope you won't be miffed with me, honey."

"Life can be complicated at times." He grinned. "Well, I hope you'll be happy here for as long as you stay. We welcome you, Talia."

She leaped up from the sofa. "Oh yes. So very, very happy. I just love it here, with all the horses."

Graham and Dana spoke in the privacy of his office. "Talia is wise beyond her years." Graham grinned. "And obviously a very clever girl."

"Yes. She's actually part of Mensa. She's a major brain. And she loves children, especially babies. She wants to help me look after the twins. Can you believe it. We've just struck gold."

"My darling, I think you're absolutely right." His face lit up with a broad grin.

Talia peered at Dana and Graham. Her enormous, dark eyes held secrets and power.

Dana had known from their first meeting, that she was wise beyond her years. It would be a great privilege to share in her development.

Will and Jay bounced into the room, bubbling with mischief. Boyish laughter resounded around the room.

"You're timing is perfect, guys. So it's official. Talia will be staying at Sugarbush for an undetermined length of time."

"Cool." They chimed together.

Graham put a comforting arm around Will. "She's going to live with us until her dad finishes his time as ambassador of Israel to the United Nations. Her father is a diplomat and travels constantly. He wants her to be safe. He also wants her to be educated in America." Graham chuckled, thinking of her audacity." So, having grown up with the press and powerful connections, she called the newspaper and asked if she could write an article soliciting a surrogate family."

"What?" Jay could hardly believe his ears. "Come on, Dad. You're joking, right?"

"Do I look like I'm joking? She's a brilliant young lady and she knows what she wants. She asked God what steps to take to find the right surrogate family. She felt that He nudged her to write the article. I mean...she didn't write it personally, the journalist interviewed her and wrote it for the general public. That's how Dana discovered it...while waiting in the doctor's office."

"Wow. Cool. Very cool." He grinned. "So, now...like she's our older sister. Is that the deal?"

"You got it Kid. Smart boy." Graham flashed him a teasing grin.

"Wow. Hey Sis. Welcome to Sugarbush. If you twist Dana's arm, she might even teach you how to ride...if you want to learn."

"That would be amazing." Her smile was so sweet and refreshing, that Dana fell in love with her all over again. And she was thrilled that Graham was on the same page.

Graham reached over and hugged her. "Welcome to our family, Talia."

She thrust her arms around Graham, standing on her tiptoes to reach up. "I'm a lucky girl to have two Daddies and a new Mommy. God has been so good to me. And that's because I love him so much and talk to him all day." She smiled again, showing perfect, even, white teeth and dimples.

"What room are you staying in?" Graham hadn't even noticed.

"I'm in the turquoise room on the third floor, right across from the prayer room." A warm grin lit her face. "I've been spending a lot of time there. That's why God always hears my prayers...because...like... I'm so close to him. And

I read the Bible for hours...because I want to get to know him better." Her face was lit with joy and innocence.

Graham couldn't believe he had almost allowed this rare, treasure of a young woman to slip out of his home and their lives. Thank God he'd come to his senses before the opportunity had passed them by. "I need to contact your Dad, though and arrange for a meeting."

"Apparently he e-mails her his schedule on a secure server," Dana interjected. "Though sometimes his itinerary changes at the last minute. Then, he texts or calls her. He's in Switzerland at the moment; and then he heads to New York; so maybe after that."

Dana's heart soared. Graham and Dana kissed and made up and became blissfully close again. Tonight Dana nursed the twins, cuddled them, giving them lots of attention before setting them down into their cribs for the night.

Violet served Cobb salads with iced tea and fresh fruit for dessert.

That evening over dinner, Dana and Graham had a serious talk with Sybil. Graham's big-hearted sister had moved into the house and was helping as much as she could. Graham and Dana were starting to feel guilty about her doing so much work without being paid. Still, Graham had warned Dana that hiring a nanny just wasn't in the budget.

"I don't want to hear it Graham. First you basically tell me you're a gentleman farmer. Now, you tell me you're broke. Which is it?" She raised her eyebrows. "Not that it matters, darling... I love you either way."

Graham, Dana and Sybil dined together without the boys tonight. It had been Sybil's idea. Violet served roast beef with baked veggies and apple pie for dessert.

Graham finally got up his nerve to find out what Sybil's plans were. She was an enormous blessing to the household, but he was sure they were living on borrowed time. He didn't even want to think about the chaos that would ensue after her departure. He broached the subject, gingerly. "Sybil...you've been remarkably generous with your time and talents, I'm afraid to ask when you have to leave."

"Who said anything about leaving? I'll stay for as long as you need me...of course."

Graham chuckled, and it eased the tension. "Sybil...dear, dear sister...we will *always* need you. And I can't tell you how much having you here means to us. I dread the day you have to go."

"You're not listening, Graham. I don't have to go. Not now. Not ever." She smiled, her hazel eyes lighting up. The twins have given me...the French refer to it as a reason to exist. I won't attempt to say it in French. Dana needs my help. And it makes me feel wonderful to know that I can contribute something to your lives." She turned to Dana. "Having never given birth, I can't tell you what a joy and privilege it is to watch the twins begin their journey in life. You know how much I love children, Graham. It gives me great joy to be here. And I feel needed. That brings me happiness. So you see, Graham...and Dana, I've been secretly hoping you would invite me to...move onto Sugarbush." She flashed a knowing smile to Dana and Graham.

Dana jumped up from her chair. "Sybil, are you serious? You can stay and help us?"

"Only if you need me" She glanced from Dana to Graham.

Graham visibly relaxed. He let out a deep breath. "We're not going broke anytime soon. But in reviewing the budget the other day; I am reluctant to add a nanny to the payroll. Not to mention, I'm not fond of having strangers move into the house. Violet is family. And so is Talia." He smiled. He peered over at Sybil. "So what about your house? Will you rent it out?"

"I could do that. Or I could sell it and invest in Sugarbush." She winked, flashing him a cheeky smile.

A smile from here to eternity lit Graham's face. "I...think God just answered my prayers. I've been praying for a miracle...a financial miracle. Perhaps I shouldn't have given the million-dollar purse from the Kentucky Derby win to Israel. But that's what I felt led to do." He smiled radiantly. "Because I followed the prompting of that still, small voice of the Holy Spirit and gave away the money we needed, God has given it back to us.. *Nothing is impossible with Him.* He must have put that in your heart, Sybil. And I think it's a grand idea, don't you, Dana?"

"You don't have to ask, honey. It's a huge blessing."

"All right then. After I drop the boys and Talia at school tomorrow, I'll head home for a couple of days and do some business. Maybe put the house on the market. Pack some things...then I'll be back." She smiled and waved as she headed to the front door.

"You know what, Graham? I think God really likes us." Dana smiled and. sashaying over to him, she gave him a big hug. "This will give me a chance to get back into really great shape. Fast. And it will give us a chance to bond with Talia, without feeling overwhelmed by all the changes."

"That sister of mine is incredible, isn't she?" Graham grinned.

"She really is, honey."

That night Talia sang and danced around her room to music, before settling down to do her homework.

Later that night, Dana went upstairs to Talia's room, soon plopping down on her bed for a girl-to girl chat. She listened to Talia's plans and dreams, overjoyed with the good things God had bestowed upon them. "Sybil is moving into the house. She will be staying for an undetermined length of time."

"Doesn't she have a husband or any children? I didn't want to be rude, so I didn't ask her, Dana." The child smiled, peering at Dana with admiration.

"Oh, darling…you would never be rude. You're too well brought up for that. But no, she doesn't have any children; and it's a great sorrow for her. It turns out that being here with all of us has brought much happiness into her life. It's filled a gap she didn't know was there; except that she was always lonely. She said that good friends are valuable; but family is a rare and precious gift from The Almighty. And she wants to be part of ours. Is that okay with you, Talia?" She smiled, knowing the answer would be positive.

"Yes. Oh yes. I love Aunt Sybil." She smiled. "Is it okay if I call her Aunt:"

"Of course, honey. You're family now."

"Oh goody." She jumped up from the bed and threw her arms around Dana. "I love you, Mommy."

Dana fought the onrush of tears, overwhelmed by the love and joy the house overflowed with.

"I think I've decided on an occupation, Mommy."

Dana arched her eyebrows. *The kid moves fast.*" And what might that be? A diplomat? Like your father, perhaps?"

"No, a horse trainer. I just love horses. Sybil took me to the barn a couple of times and told me all about the horses. I want to learn to ride…really, really well. And then...maybe I'd like to become a jumper..."

What an odd thing to say. I've never told her that I was a jumper before I became a trainer. No wonder I've bonded with this young woman. Dana caught her breath. "What made you decide you wanted to be a jumper?"

"I don't know, Mommy. I don't know." Her eyes were lit with the joy of innocence and hope.

Dana held her in her arms. *Truly Lord, you have blessed me with five children. She remembered the scripture of how the Lord bestowed the blessing of children on couples as His precious gift.*

Chapter Sixteen

Danielle waited a couple days before calling Harold. She didn't want to appear too anxious. It was just after 10:00 a.m. Tues. She got a recording when she called his number.

Two days dragged by before he returned her call. It was Thursday evening. "Good evening Danielle. So nice to meet you at the dinner party."

"It was nice meeting you as well."

"Perhaps we should get together some time."

"Sounds good." *He wants to parry a bit before he makes his point. I can do that.*

"I was thinking...perhaps...you might enjoy having dinner with me...in my private dining room, at my estate. My chef will delight you, I promise you that."

Well, this gets more interesting. Danielle always lived boldly. Didn't follow the rules about dating or anything else in life. Rules were for other people. Dating sites always recommended meeting new men in a public place a couple times before considering going to their place or inviting them to yours. It was important to get to know the prospect first. She should know about that after the last fiasco. They warned folks that despite thinking you know someone; you might be in for a nasty surprise. She hated rules and never followed them. Maybe it would be her undoing. But that's the way it was. "That sounds...lovely. When were you thinking?"

"Whatever suits you, my dear. I have my day timer in front of me. If the date you suggest doesn't work for me; we'll pick another."

I rather like his speech rhythm. A bit odd, though. She was thinking Friday. But suddenly, she felt a hand in front of her, stopping her. It was like a powerful image. One that she could not deny. Oh my gosh. The spirit of the living God is warning me against this guy. He must be bad news. She suddenly starting shaking; not just a little...but actually, violently. Then she knew for certain. God was powerfully warning her against him. "You know what? In looking at my calendar, Friday doesn't work. Why don't I call you next week and we'll figure something out?" *I don't ever intend to call you, after the Holy Spirit has warned me with such power.*

"Whatever you like, my dear. But do keep in mind that I have a very busy social calendar." He chuckled. "Of course...we all do in this town."

"Of course."

"Until later, then, my dear." His voice had a smile in it. But she sensed something sinister beneath the charm, control and social graces. *Those who play with fire get burned.* "Okay, Lord. Thanks for protecting me. If he calls again, I won't return his call.

A week went by and he called again. "I've been invited to a small dinner party Saturday night. Leanna Trionis' home. Leanna hates it when I bring a date." He chuckled. "But she's used to it. Other bachelors do that sometimes, as well. She would like to exert more control over us bachelor...but she can't." He chuckled. "But that's not going to happen. I can pick you up; or if you prefer, I can meet you there. I'm really quite harmless, my dear." He chuckled. "You'll see."

You're lying. You're a snake. I feel God is showing me that. "Thank-you for thinking of me but I'm busy Saturday night." *I'd rather stay home alone and watch a movie.*

The silence was deadly. It was several minutes before he responded. She sensed his angry undertone. "Your loss, my dear. See you around town."

"Yes...perhaps you will. Bye now. Oh...and uh, thanks for thinking of me."

"I haven't been able to *stop* thinking about you since we met."

A chill zinged down her spine. She shivered. *He's a whacko. I just have a hunch he's a wacko. Maybe he's obsessed with me. That's all I need.* "Lord?" As she began to pray, she heard the voice of the Holy Spirit clearly speaking to her. "Run."

"Run? Where to? Why?" *I've been on the run quite a bit lately. I was hoping it would end.*

"Run." It hit her then, like a ton of bricks. *Of course. What had she been thinking? He's a plant. I thought I lucked in to the dinner invitation where I met Bob. It had all been carefully orchestrated.* Why hadn't she caught on sooner?

She glanced around the apartment. She wasn't settled in yet. Cozy but not complete. *I'll go on a little trip. Maybe not so little. Depending on what happens, I might just jump ship. If I leave everything as is and just disappear...well, the owner will be miffed. But she'll get over it and she'll rent it out. Thank God the place was furnished. She would get a couple of large, plastic garbage bags and throw everything into them, clean out the fridge, clean the apartment and take a walk. The owner would have no trouble renting the apartment. If she gave a month's notice, it would slow her down. The owner would be miffed but she'd get over it. I'll leave a note citing an unexpected emergency....*

The more she thought about the idea of disappearing, the better she liked it. Though she totally trusted and adored Suzie; she wouldn't tell her where she was going. She wouldn't tell *one person. That way it would be impossible to have a leak.*

Quickly, she packed a medium sized suitcase as well as

her carry-on. She got out her world map, spread it on the table and prayed. "Lord, I have a buddy who went to Indonesia and married a girl that runs a fruit stand. He was great guy. Good locking, smart. Educated. He just kind of opted out of society; never to be heard from again. *That's exactly what I'm going to do.*

FIJI would be exotic...or maybe the Grand Cayman Islands. I've always wanted to go there. Maybe that's where I'll go.

She headed to the nearest car lot and sold her jaguar to get some cash. She took a taxi to the airport, exhilarated. She would stay at a hotel near the airport tonight. Then, she'd fly out tomorrow on the first flight available. She retired early, rose early and got in the lineup for the American Airlines flight departing at 5:55 for the Grand Cayman Islands.

She was headed for a new adventure. Her past may have caught up with her in Palm Beach; but no way would they find her in the Grand Cayman Islands. She'd need to get a job right away, of course. And she would.

She flew into the airport, mesmerized by the tropical, exotic beauty of the island. Peering from her window seat on the jet, her senses were assailed by the majestic, sweeping vista of tropical vegetation. She'd never seen anything this exotic. Maybe amazing things awaited her.

As the jet came to a screeching halt on the runway, her heart soared with fresh hope and promise. *"Today is the day that the Lord has made, I will rejoice and be glad in it."* Joy was a choice. Stepping off the jet and onto a pull-down ramp, she was bathed in the warm, tropical weather. The air was scented with exotic vegetation. The tropical paradise was a balm for healing and renewal. *Good things were about to happen to her. She just knew it.*

She retrieved her leopard suitcase, which was a snap to locate on the luggage carousel. Swarms of people watched for their luggage as the belt rolled by. Soon she grabbed her suitcase and headed outside to hail a taxi.

The black driver was warm and friendly, like the welcoming arms of the exotic island. After setting her luggage into his vehicle, he turned to her. "Where to, lady?"

"You tell me." She raised her eyebrows and flashed him a big smile. She needed to mask the trepidation she felt in arriving at yet another new place. Alone.

"Ma'am?" He wasn't sure he'd heard her right. "Where do you want me to drive you? *Ah, it's my accent. She wasn't sure what I asked.*

"Any suggestions? I'm looking for a cheap hotel. But...I'd like it to be nice." She laughed at her own ludicrous request.

He nodded. "Ah. I have just the place for you."

"You do?"

"I do."

"Bring it on." Her humor and faith in God as well as mankind had just been restored. He would take her to an amazing place.

"It's a short drive from here... maybe seven or eight miles."

"What's it called?" *She tried to remember the hasty research she'd done. Maybe a name would click in.*

"Grass Shack"

"Grass Shack? No kidding?"

"You gonna like it. Trust me."

She raised her eyebrows. A total stranger just asked her to trust him. Her antenna went up.

About ten minutes later.

The cabbie pulled into a motel with an island motif. It *did* look rather charming and certainly quaint.

"Thanks." She shrugged. *I'm at their mercy, Lord. But I have prayed. I believe you are leading me.*

The driver came back out to his taxi where she waited. "We're in luck. You got the last room. Come on, let's go." He was holding the back door open for her.

193

Not so fast. "Give me a couple minutes, please. I want to...ah...take a look at the place."

"Suit yerself." He shot her a sour look. His mood had suddenly changed.

Danielle marched over to the front office and stepped inside to a small waiting area. "Good afternoon. May I see one of your rooms please? If I like it; I might be interested in a monthly rate, if you have that." She glanced around at the place. It was exotic. The office was a vivid shade of turquoise. A large red parrot squawked from his cage in the office.

The black guy at the front desk looked her over like she had a rare disease he might catch. "I show you a room. Come with me." She followed him to the upper level of the two-story wood structure. "Well?" He opened the door, and she glanced inside. She peered around. *This is the most disgusting, moth-eaten room I've ever seen.* "I won't be staying here. Thanks anyway." She turned on her heel, but as she glanced down where the taxi had been parked, she realized to her horror that he had sped off with her luggage. Against her better judgement, she'd given him cash upon his insistence, before climbing the wooden steps to view the room. She called 911. A husky female voice fired questions at her. "What is your emergency, Ma'am?"

Danielle took a deep breath and recounted the events.

"We have someone on the way, Ma'am. What was the name of the taxi company you dealt with?"

She couldn't remember. "I...I'm sorry, I don't remember." She sighed. "His car was yellow. Oh yes, *Fast Cab.* That's what it was called."

"A description of the driver, please."

Right. "He was medium height. Black. He had an island accent. I don't know if it's the local accent or not. I just arrived."

"Any distinguishing factors? A disability of any kind?"

She was glad she'd always been curious and observant.

It often came in handy. Like now. "Yes...his hand. His left hand was crippled...like maybe it had been burned or something..."

"Would you describe your luggage, please?"

"Medium sized suitcase... Leopard print... and a pink carry-on." She sighed. "My new, white laptop was in it and a camera...and a variety of clothing, including three designer dresses."

"I'm so sorry you had this happen to you, Ma'am. We're on it. Where are you visiting from?"

"Palm Beach."

"That's the problem. Unfortunately, you get drivers...some bad eggs...that are predators...they lay in wait for victims. They target visitors from high profile spots...like Palm Beach. Folks like yourself."

Well, at least I LOOK rich. I may not BE rich. But I LOOK rich. I guess that's a start. "We've had this happen before. They keep valuables and dispose of everything else."

"Oh great. So I'm stranded at a tawdry motel with nothing to wear except the clothes on my back." Her heart sank. She would have to replace cosmetics, lingerie and appropriate clothing for island life for starters.

"I'm sorry Ma'am. You're welcome to come down to headquarters and file a complaint. We recommend you do that. Giving us as many particulars as you can, will help us track down these nasty thieves and put them out of circulation. The company might just have one car. He could be a lone wolf operator. We get that here sometimes."

Her heart sank. "Do folks usually get their luggage back...or some of it?"

"I'm afraid not, Ma'am. It's just one of those things. We *can* recommend a safe, clean motel for you, though."

"That would be great. Thanks."

"Island Hideaway is a decent place. Not cheap, though."

"Where is it? And what cab company would you recommend I use?"

"Pink Flamingo Cab. Only female drivers. They're well established on the island."

"Now we're talkin' " *Finally a glimmer of light.* "Do you have a phone number for them?"

"I do." She rattled off the number.

A chunky, gregarious gal, probably in her fifties, stepped out of the pink taxi after pulling up to the motel office. She flashed a bright smile. "Welcome to the Cayman Islands. Where is your luggage?

"Stolen by the last driver."

"Oh, I'm so sorry."

Danielle was grateful for the sympathy. She managed a smile. "It was a terrible shock. Take me to Island Hide Away Motel, please."

"Just a short drive. You'll be there in no time." The driver smiled, raising her eyebrows. "I'm warnin' you though...the place is a little pricey."

She just had to say that, didn't she? Danielle hopped in the back of the cab, while the lady driver pulled out. "Where are you from?"

She hesitated for a couple of beats. *Maybe this woman intended to rip off her cash and credit cards. I'd better not say I'm from Palm Beach.* "A few places, Ma'am. I...uh...travel around quite a lot."

"The name is Pixie. It must be devastating to lose your luggage."

"Yeah, it is. I'm Danielle." She smiled, feeling somewhat better.

"Tell you what... you're in a pickle. I don't want you to have a sour taste in your mouth about the Cayman Islands. We cater to tourists. That's how we make our living. I own a small mobile court. I have a furnished vacant unit that I rent out from time to time. I'll give you a good monthly rate, if you're planning to stay for a while."

Lord, this is an answer to prayer. "Well...Pixie I...uh...I think that's a real nice offer. I'll just take you up on that." She breathed a sigh of relief. She had a place to stay. Now all she had to do was find a job right away and she could enjoy living here.

"My daughter is a budding singer, though; I must give you fair warning. She works on an aria every day after school...sometimes for long hours at a stretch." She smiled. "Your unit is right next to ours, so you'll hear her doing her scales and rehearsing arias at all hours. Pippa's real sweet, though. You'll like her. Pretty too. ..and ambitious. She's destined for big things. I think you'll like her...and she has a great sense of humor. Don't know where she got it from. Not me. Not her old man." She shrugged. I guess sometimes God just...likes to surprise us with...attributes that are real nice."

"Yeah. I guess so." Danielle peered out the window which was partly open. The aroma of tropical vegetation wafted over her. The scent was intoxicating. Palm trees lined the street they turned onto. "I know what that hotel charges... $150.00 a night plus tax. I'll just charge you $300 a week. If you stay longer than a month, I'll reduce that quite a bit. I own the Pink Flamingo Cab Company, by the way. "

Danielle smiled. "It's nice to make some new friends. I don't know a soul in this town."

"Well, Pippa and I will keep you from being lonely. How long do you plan to stay in town?

"If I find a job, I'll stay for a while. Do you enjoy living here?"

"Crazy question. It's paradise, hon. Look around you. It don't get no better than this."

Danielle nodded. "You're right about that." She smiled. "Absolutely right." She liked this lady. She called a spade a spade. She needed a friend in this town. It would get lonely real fast if she didn't have friends. "Do you go to church on Sunday?"

"Church. What a crazy question. 'Course not. Does anybody still go to church?"

Maybe I better think hard about what I'm getting in to. She's a nice woman. I think; although I don't know here from Adam. Now I know where she stands in her beliefs. Maybe I better run the other way.

"Maybe we don't have much in common, Ma'am. You see, I'm a believer. One of those Born-again Christians. Jesus is Lord of my life. And I like to hang out with like-minded people."

"Oh. So you think you're better than us. Is that it?" She took her eyes off the road for a couple of scary beats, glancing back a brief moment at Danielle in the back seat of her cab.

"I didn't say that." *She'd better shuffle out of this relationship in a quick hurry.* "...I just don't think we'd have much in common."

The woman was quiet for a bit. "Well, we need the money. We're trying to raise money for Pippa to go to New York to study opera. She's got that kind of talent, ya know."

"Oh, well in that case." *And because I don't have any other options, I'd better give it a shot.* "Maybe we'll give it a shot." She liked the woman and had a good gut feeling about her. It might turn out to be a great blessing. And she adored young people. Besides, she had no other option. She'd better lose her uppity stance in a hurry. "How old is Pippa?"

"She's only thirteen, but she knows what she wants. She's very focused...very serious about her goal."

"She sounds really special. Were you a singer at some point in your life?"

She chuckled. "Funny you should ask. I love singin'. Not sure I'm much good at it thought. Certainly not like my daughter. I have a pretty good range though..." She stopped talking as she turned the wheel into the trailer court. A sign read Pink Flamingo Mobiles and Taxi's. "Here we are. Home, sweet home." She drove down to the end of a road and parked the pink cab. Her trailer was larger than the others and had extra land around it. Two Pink Flamingo taxis were parked there. The other three were obviously on the road. She was in one of them.

Pippa greeted them at the door. Glorious opera music played in the background. She'd heard Pixie telling her daughter that she was bringing a new renter over for coffee. The child was exquisitely beautiful. She had startling blue eyes and a smile so radiant, it was downright alarming. *The child is special. No question about that.*

"Danielle is going to rent a mobile on a monthly basis." Pixie announced as she motioned for Danielle to come inside her mobile.

"Hi. Welcome to the Cayman Islands, Danielle. You'll love it here." She smiled. Her piercing blue eyes assessed Danielle. "Do you like opera music, Danielle?"

"Very much. I haven't spent much time listening to opera, but I find them thrilling." She smiled at the child. "I hear you're going to be an opera singer."

"I hope so. I've got a real good memory. My teacher says she's never had a student with a memory as good as mine." She got real serious, suddenly. "That's real important if you're studying to be an opera singer... because you have to learn those long arias in other languages."

"And I bet you have a large vocal range, as well." Danielle had seen enough operas to know the basics.

"Oh yes, Danielle. Do you want to hear me sing?"

Danielle had no luggage to unload, but she was grateful that she had her Tote bag with her. In it she had her Bible, make-up and sundry items, including her wallet. She was glad she'd worn white laced sporty shoes. She usually wore that type of footwear when she travelled. The white cotton slacks and T-shirt she wore were comfortable. *My favorite clothes are gone. She'd have to go shopping right away...at a thrift store.*

The mobile was basic but clean and sparsely decorated. But it was a place to live; and for that she was grateful. It smelled fresh. There were a couple of exotic, flourishing plants near the front windows. That lent an air of charm to the place.

"My cab business is doing pretty well. When Pippa becomes rich and famous, we'll lead a better life. Right now, everything I make goes for expenses."

"I'm on the day shift. I start at 8:00 a.m." Suddenly, she glanced over at Danielle. "Hey, until you decide what kind of business you want to get into here, why don't work for Pink Flamingo? I'm always hiring good drivers. " She smiled. "I'll help you get your license. It should only take a couple of days."

"Sounds real good. I'll need to think about that, though. I have some other things in mind."

"I'm sure you do. I'm just sayin' that it might be an option for you."

"I appreciate that."

Danielle slept well, despite the trauma of losing her pricey clothes. *I'm alive. Unharmed. God has opened an unusual door for me. Pixie is an interesting character. I knew that the second I laid eyes on her. You don't raise a daughter that is focused on becoming an opera diva unless you've got something going yourself.*

Danielle awakened to the vibrant sound of multiple, exotic birds, chirping. The cacophony of sounds on the island were incredible. She peered out the window. Exotic, colorful birds flitted from Palm tree to Palm tree. She moved to the window, still clad in the long, cotton nightshirt Pixie had loaned her. Peering out the kitchen window, she spotted a bevy of birds flitting from Palm tree to Palm tree. The birds chirped together, as though in a chorus. She smiled.

Pippa was warbling her scales before going to school. She'd been warned. God had miraculously provided for a place to live and job. She was supposed to be here.

The next morning, Pixie invited Danielle over for coffee. She knocked on her door. "Hey, Danielle. How did you sleep?"

"Great."

"Come on over for coffee. I need to tell you what you'll have to do to become a taxi driver here."

Over coffee, Pixie told her she would have to marry a resident or become a permanent resident.

Pixie went with her to fill out the application for permanent residency. Given her presidential pardon, she was able to quickly obtain it. She passed the special driver's test required to become a taxi driver in the Cayman Islands and was awarded residency immediately.

THREE MONTHS LATER

Danielle thrived as a taxi driver for Pink Flamingo. She decided to stay on at the trailer court, since Pixie gave her a deal that was hard to beat. Plus she enjoyed hanging out with her new friends.

She intended to reinvent herself. She was a master at doing that. What did she want her new life to look like? She had absolutely no idea. So she prayed and sought God's counsel. *"Lord what would you have me do with my life? This was not a town for raising big money from charity events like Palm Beach was. The Grand Cayman Islands was a tropical paradise; a favorite vacation spot. Tourists showed up to vacation; others fell in the love with the island and made it their home. She was in the latter group. After all she'd been through, she wanted to settle down and relax.*

What do I really want out of life? What are my goals? Those were questions she needed to answer before she could proceed to invent her new persona. Soon, she figured it out. I want to buy a gorgeous house here and make it a home. I want to entertain. Invite interesting guests to my dinner parties and...accomplish what? That was the question niggling at her mind. *Lord, what would you have me do?*

Pippa tugged at her heart. Maybe there is a reason I've met her. Maybe I'll fast and pray for a couple days and see if I can hear that still, small voice. Maybe then I'll be able to figure out what it is I'm supposed to do with my life. She'd thought it was to work at orphanages; then she'd felt called to be a fundraiser. She adored being a socialite. She'd skipped out of that prosperous town, opting for the simple life here. She shivered as she thought about how close she'd come to becoming a victim. First, there was the would-be assassin, and then the odd man down the hall at her Palm Beach apartment. She knew it was a warning from God to move on, despite the fact that she had just moved in. Palm Beach was certainly Suzie's home; but it wasn't hers. She was tired of being a gypsy. Maybe she would find a hubby and settle down in the Cayman Islands.

Chapter Seventeen

Graham, seated at his Louis Fifteenth desk in his
office, was on a conference call with his folks. "I'll be flying
out to Lexington to see you as soon as I can get a flight." His
dad had insisted on a conference call with Graham, himself
and the banker. The meeting was designed to help set up and
the farm in general; and then analyze the current operation.
Graham had dreaded this day of reckoning for a long time.
Though he hoped he had enough knowledge to pull off
running a horse farm; there were many times when he wasn't
so sure. But where could he go for help? His dad had told
him quite some time ago, that attempting to run a horse farm
in Kentucky was a fool's errand; and not one he should be
privy to.

Lawrence Van Rensellier was a man to be reckoned
with; Tough. Smart. Educated. Nobody's fool. In fact, his
friends had often commented that rivals had to get rise early.
No one could outfox the fox so far. A retired criminal
attorney, he'd seen it all and claimed he could write a book
about his experiences. It would probably be a New York
Times Best-seller.

Lawrence got settled into a guest room upstairs. It was,
in fact, the last room available in the house. He'd arrived late
on Monday evening, and Violet had shown him to his guest
quarters. "If there's anything you need, Mr. Van Rensellier,
please let me know." She smiled, admiring the tall, courtly
gentleman.

"Please call me Lawrence." He smiled at Violet. "I know you're like family."

His presence and persona were charismatic. Accustomed to being a fly on the wall, she was delighted he'd be staying here. *What amazing secrets would she be privy to from a man like this?*

Lawrence Van Rensellier brought vibrant energy and adrenalin into the house. "Breakfast is very nice. Thank-you. Love the hash browns." He grinned at Violet.

"Glad you enjoyed breakfast. More coffee?" Violet held the pot in mid-air near his place setting,

"Thank-you." He grinned. "Uh, it's real good too. They sure were lucky to find you. Ever get tired of them...you give me a call." He winked at her.

Violet was delighted. She wasn't sure quite how to take the back handed compliment. Still, it was all good...the man apparently appreciated and liked her...and if she ever wanted to live in Houston...well, there was an open door.

Graham and Dana, mesmerized with each other, sort of waltzed into the kitchen. They stared at each other, reluctant to pull apart and join the family at the table.

Ah love. Sweet, blissful love, Violet mused.

"Good morning, Dana and Graham. Did you sleep well?" Lawrence grinned over at them.

Graham winked at his Dad. "Good morning, Dad. Glad you're here. Violet makes a mean breakfast. Guess you've already found that out."

He grinned. "Yes. Actually, I told her that if she ever gets tired of hangin' around Sugarbush with y'all; she's welcome to come on down to Houston. We got a real nice room for her. She wouldn't have anywhere near the amount of work she's got here..." He grinned. "Ah shucks...I'm just kiddin' you know. I know she's entrenched here; but as the sayin' goes...you just never know in life."

"Well...that *is* quite the sayin'; it really is." Violet peered at him, flattered by his interest. She filed the invitation into the back of her brain. He was absolutely right...you just never knew what life might throw at you.

TWO WEEKS LATER

Graham's dad had scrutinized every detail about the operation of the ranch. He was horrified. They were running a negative cash flow every month and headed for a big fall. Bankruptcy was just around the corner. He quickly realized that everyone at Sugarbush was oblivious to the fact that the farm was quickly heading into the direction of receivership; failing a miracle. No one had bothered to state the obvious.

It was Thursday morning. Graham and his dad were sequestered behind closed doors for several hours. Violet knocked on their door at noon handing them sandwiches and fruit at their request.

Friday morning, just as they were leaving, they glanced over at Dana in the nursery. "Honey, we'll be at Bank of America. We have a meeting with the loans officer and mortgage department."

FRIDAY DINNER

Lawrence Van Rensellier stunned everyone present with an announcement at dinner. "We are putting Sugarbush on the market immediately."

The kids were having dinner in the family dining room. In the formal dining room, Graham, Lawrence and Dana convened, somber- faced. "So...as I said earlier this morning, we have to make the farm into a stud farm immediately or sell. It's your choice, Graham...and Dana."

Dana peered at Graham in a state of shock. *This is the equivalent of the world caving in. Her world.* She'd been living in La-la land oblivious to the need to have Sugarbush turn a profit. It was time to pay the piper.

That night, as Dana and Graham sipped iced tea on their private deck overlooking a gargantuan Hanging Moss tree,

Graham bared his soul. "Dana. Ever since I can remember, I've wanted a horse farm and all that it entails...I knew about stud farms, of course, but I've always found the concept repulsive, as I'm sure I've told you. Now, we're faced with a brutal dilemma: Put Sugarbush on-the-market or turn it into a stud farm." His lips quivered.

Dana knew he was horrified at the thought of it. She came over to him the and cradled his head in her arms. "Darling, oh darling...neither of us want that. We love the equines too much to turn them into money making machines. What are we going to do, honey?"

"We're going to pray for a miracle and never stop believing for one." He turned his face from her and she knew he was fighting bitter tears. He had failed.

He knew it and he knew that she knew it. His big dream had gone up in smoke. Though to his credit, he'd lived up to the family tradition of being philanthropic. He'd cheerfully given a million dollars to Israel, designated for the poor of that country. He'd done it, despite knowing he couldn't afford it. Dana had questioned him at the time. "Graham, this is crazy. We need that money for the farm. We need it for operation costs. I know we'd *like* to give it away; but I don't think we can afford to."

Graham had silenced her. "I choose to live in the supernatural, honey. We must trust God for everything. I have discovered that the more we trust him, the more he boggles our minds with incredible, even grandiose answers to our problems and dilemmas. He will never leave us or forsake us. Jesus never fails. No one can know the mind of God. His ways are not our ways; they are so much higher."

"We've become a large family, Graham. I sure hope your Dad comes up with a solution for how we can continue living at Sugarbush. I'm attached to this place, and I know you are, too. I don't want to lose the farm. I don't want to step down. What can I do to help? Ask your dad? Maybe I can whip myself in shape and hire myself out as a professional trainer again; and aggressively seek a lot of clients. But we're in such trouble, it would hardly make a dint in our finances. We need a miracle."

"Let's not panic, honey. Dad is here to help us get the farm into a positive cash flow. If we can accomplish that; we're good to go."

"Yeah. Nice dream, Graham. I think we're too far behind the eight ball to recover."

"You're correct in theory, honey. But remember, God always has the last word. Nothing comes as a surprise to him. And nothing is impossible with Him. He knows our life from beginning to end, as incredible as that is." He turned to her and kissed her. But he needed to be alone. "Darling, I'm going into prayer; even while Dad is here. Don't expect me at breakfast. Tell Dad I'm in my prayer closet. Ask him if we can meet at 8:00 in my office. Tell him...tell him that I'm expecting a miracle."

A miracle? No question; that's what it would take. She'd known for a while that they were living on borrowed time. She'd often questioned Graham's sanity, given that he joyfully gave away the million-dollar purse they'd won to Israel's poor. That infusion of cash would have helped Sugarbush get out of the red and thrive. Then, by turning it into a Dude ranch or boarding horses and running constant riding classes, training and jumping lessons, they could survive. They had the extra stalls. Now the debt was so enormous, bankruptcy seemed like the only option. It was either that or a miracle.

She'd never had a mind for numbers, though she did have common sense and a good head on her shoulders. She'd always thought so, anyway. The first thing she needed to know was how much it took to run Sugarbush a month. There were salaries, horses' feed, taxes, security, etc. While Graham and his dad conducted a meeting in his office; Dana conducted her own meeting with Violet.

The boys were in school. Sybil had gone. Dana and

Violet coped with the twins. Graham and his dad remained sequestered behind closed doors in meetings. Early afternoon they emerged. "We're heading downtown. We have a meeting with our banker."

Dana and Violet prayed earnestly for a miracle. And to Dana's delight and surprise, so did Talia. Talia was a tower of strength. It was as though she was born for major challenges. She seemed to emerge, like a diver bubbling to the surface having rescued a drowning man. She had strength when Dana felt weak. She had courage, while Dana wavered. She had hope, while Dana was fast losing hers.

Talia asked Dana if they could go to the prayer room and pray together. She also asked for permission to stay home from school for a couple days to focus on seeking a miracle from God.

"I can't say no, Talia. You're a straight A student. It won't hurt you. And if this is what you want to do, okay." She paused, studying the child. "You have understanding and compassion way beyond your years. It's as though... you've been born for a crisis.

She turned to Dana. "I can help. God has prepared me for such a time as this."

In the privacy of her room, Talia fell to her knees and wept before the Lord. "Father, you are a great and mighty God. There is none like you. You have given us this wonderful farm and great old house to enjoy. It's a blessing to all of us. I believe you want to save the farm. I bet you have a great and mighty plan for it. Father, please reveal this plan to us swiftly."

Talia returned to the nursery where Dana and Violet kept an eye on the twins while they prayed. "It's going to be okay. I just know it is. God Almighty is going to step in and save the day. You'll see. It will happen just as I say."

Dana could only hope Talia was onto something. She

could only dream that something amazing would save the farm from bankruptcy.

The next morning, bright and early, Talia was on her cell to her Dad in Israel. As ambassador of the United Nations to Israel, a visible diplomat, he'd wanted Talia to be safe in America and assume a different last name than his. He knew that if evil adversaries wanted to get at him, kidnapping his only daughter would be a possibility they'd consider. He had to make sure she was safely tucked away. He would even consider giving her up for adoption, if it meant safety for her. He would always love her and look after her financially. He would always keep a close eye on her. But he had seen too much and knew too much in the rarified atmosphere he moved in, causing him to watch his back. Nothing must ever happen to his only, beloved daughter, Talia. He could not allow a crack of vulnerability anywhere to undermine him. His love for his daughter was deep and powerful, his mandate to protect her, unrelenting.

Talia prayed in the privacy of her room for hours. Finally, she closed her bedroom door and headed downstairs to the kitchen. The coffee pot was on. She poured herself a cup of the brew and plopped down on a chair around the massive, circular oak table.

Dana had been in the nursery for hours. Violet showed up to give her a break. "Thanks, Violet. I need a cup of coffee."

Talia sat at the table, sipping coffee. A big smile lit her face as Dana entered the room. "It's going to be okay, Dana. A miracle just happened." Talia smiled.

"What are you talking about, Talia?' Dana poured herself a mug of the steaming brew and plopped down on a chair next to Talia.

"I phoned Dad on my cell. He's transferring two million dollars to your bank immediately. He just needs you to give him the name of the bank and bank manager. For security reasons, he doesn't want to know your bank account number.

He'll contact the manager by phone. He said it was no big deal. I know it's true. Dad is...like...super rich...oil money...he wants to help. He is so relieved that I'm happy and safe here at Sugarbush." She smiled. "He said it was his privilege to help. No big deal. He wants to know that Sugarbush will continue to thrive and that I will be here where I'm safe and he can count on finding me."

Ambassador Louis Stein was Graham and Dana's houseguest. He'd come to meet Graham and Dana and the family. He graciously declined being added to the title of Sugarbush, despite his magnanimous contribution to it. He insisted it was his pleasure...a great privilege to invest in the farm where his daughter was growing up.

Lights twinkled in the Milky Way as Talia peered outside into the night from her bedroom window. God was in his heavens and he would make everything turn out right. He was a God of miracles and she saw them day after day, rejoicing in Him. She hugged herself and smiled. Big. She felt safe and happy. She had prayed unceasingly for a miracle so she could remain at Sugarbush. It had not even occurred to her that her Dad would invest in the farm. She'd just kept on praying and believing for a miracle. God saw to it that her prayers were answered. And now she would get to see her Dad as well. She could hardly wait. She jumped up and down with youthful glee.

Louis Stein, their honored guest sat at Dana's right. He was the first dignitary she had ever had the honor of being hostess to. She was glad his assistant had e-mailed them information he felt they might want to know, prior to his arrival. He was ambassador of Israel to the United Nations. He'd been a general in the army and was from an oil rich family, Educated at Ben-Gurian University of the Negev and other prestigious universities, he hobnobbed in a rarified atmosphere. Dana was thrilled to pieces.

Graham and Dana had far more in common with Louis than they might have guessed. It turned out he was an avid horse-racing and polo enthusiast. An ace polo player in his youth, he adored the sport. "Polo is a tough game, but once you get the hang of it, and get comfortable with it, it gives you an incredible high. There's something truly magnificent about the sport. No wonder they call it the sport of Kings. I try to catch the polo matches in Palm Beach whenever my schedule permits."

"I would love to try my hand at polo, when I get back in shape," Dana smiled at their honored guest.

"Me, too." Graham grinned, glancing over at Dana. It was one of those secret desires he'd never shared with her.

"Honey ...I didn't know you had a yen to play polo."

He winked, mischievously at her. "Gotta have a few secrets."

"Maybe I'll play polo, too." Talia piped up, grinning.

Will and Jay did not jump on the bandwagon. They'd been brought up with manners and grace. The last thing they would do is to try to upstage Talia, their parents and their honored guest.

Graham and Dana exchanged a knowing look. A silent understanding flashed between them.

Talia sat next to her dad, stealing side glances at him, and alternatively gazing at him with admiration. "How long can you stay, Dad?"

"Honey, I'm afraid I have to leave tomorrow. I have a meeting in New York and one in Washington and then I'll be flying back to Israel."

Tears sprung to Talia's eyes, but she quickly recovered. "That's okay, Daddy. A lot of people need you. I'm just glad you came here to visit." She flashed him a big smile. "You can always find me here." Gentle tears trickled down her cheeks. "I love you Daddy. Thank you for implementing the miracle I prayed for."

"Oh, honey. I didn't have to think twice about it. God

spoke to me very clearly. *"Your little girl needs a miracle. And you can be part of it."* He grinned, as his eyes misted over. "And that's when I heard the still, small voice prompting me to write a check for Sugarbush."

"Well you certainly saved the day." Graham was determined not to mention their lavish gift to Israel of a million dollars; the purse they'd won at the Derby. He'd felt led to be philanthropic and God had caused his gift to be doubled and given back to him. They served a great and mighty God. Truly he reigned in the supernatural. He was a God of constant miracles.

"My pleasure. And now that I've met all of you and had the tour of Sugarbush this afternoon; and now that I see how very happy Talia is, I know I've done the right thing."

Talia's smile lit her face with joy. As soon as her father stood from the table, she threw her arms around his neck. "Oh Daddy, I'm so happy. So... so happy. It's like I totally belong here. I feel more at home here than I even did in Israel."

"I know you do, honey. And out here in the country...with these fine folks, and the horses...you'll have a wonderful, rich life. And when you get a little older, I'll maybe take you on a trip with me. Provided, of course, that I am confident that excellent security is in place," He grinned. "We'll take one day at a time."

Lawrence Van Rensellier had flown back early this morning, satisfied that everything was under control.

Dana, Graham and Louis socialized in the pristine, elegant living room. Dana felt proud that she'd had a hand in the décor. Though Graham had bought the house turnkey, she'd made certain suggestions that Graham had taken, after checking with an interior decorator. At that point, Graham had agreed to give Dana carte blanche for the living room.

They both loved the Queen Anne dining room set in the formal dining room, and they'd both loved the comfy pieces in the sprawling family room. Further, they'd agreed that the vast living room had to be refurbished. It was tired and had a dated, tawdry look when they'd moved in. It was glorious now.

Dana noticed Louis didn't mention anything about the women in his life; though she assumed, of course, they existed. Perhaps that was because it had only been three years since his wife's fatal car crash. Almost as though their honored house guest could read her mind, Louis suddenly began talking about his past. Talia and the boys had long since vanished to the games room, presumably to play chess. Violet was out of earshot.

Dana, Graham and Louis socialized for some time. Everyone was compatible. They felt honored that he invited them to call him *Lou* instead of the more formal *Louis.* After all, they were family now.

"When Melissa was suddenly...taken from us, I mourned bitterly for a long time. But there is a special someone in my life, now." He smiled, as a look of tenderness crossed his features. "To be frank, I'm very much in love." He grinned. "I never thought it would happen again. I felt blessed to have had such a glorious, glamorous, charming...and yes...even brilliant wife..." He grinned. "And I'm humbled that I've found love again."

Dana thought she saw a misting of tears cause his eyes to appear glossy. She smiled over at him. "I'm happy for you. A wonderful man like you deserves to have a special lady in his life."

Graham grinned. "Do I hear wedding bells?"

"That's what *she* wants. And I think that's what I want, also. I haven't told Talia yet. But once I make the decision to propose, I'll break the news to her."

Dana peered over at him. "At the risk of stepping on toes...do you think...maybe you should drop a hint to her, so that she isn't totally shocked when you pop the question?"

"I would. But I'm really not sure I'm going to propose. I

haven't heard from God yet; though I have been praying."
He grinned. A tinge of nervousness played across his
features. "There are a few questions...and issues that must
first be resolved." He ended the sentence with a sense of
finality.

Dana knew the subject was closed.

Chapter Eighteen

Danielle was happily ensconced in her new digs. She looked forward to a blissful future despite not knowing what lay ahead. She slept poorly, waking early to the sounds of chattering, squealing noises from fleeting tropical birds. Unfamiliar sounds. She slipped on the new robe she'd bought, admiring the vivid, tropical flowers on the white background. The ocean wasn't far away. Maybe she'd ask to borrow one of the Pink Flamingo cabs and park by the ocean and enjoy the view. She longed to meet a new man. Waves of loneliness washed over her as she thought about how lonely her life was. How could she meet a good man? Did they even exist?

Prayer. Of course. Only God could help her, given the discouraging odds and her high standards. She closed the sliding glass doors, flicked the blinds closed and fell to her knees. She began praising God. Praising Him for the great and mighty God he was. King of the Universe. Name above all names. He had miraculously arranged for her to get her freedom back. She had escaped some dangerous situations. Even now, she'd landed on her feet, despite showing up here without knowing a soul.

Then it came to her. It was like a flash of blinding light. She would open a dating service. Of course. Why hadn't she thought of it sooner? Then, when the guys started appearing, she would, hopefully, have first choice. She patted herself on the back for the innovative idea.

Three Weeks Later

Moonlighting driving cab and running the dating agency during the day, she could earn a pretty decent living. She would keep her fees high to sort out the riff raff. She was going for that top five percent of the market. She'd take a series of photos of the client and make up a dossier of each prospect. In no time, she'd have a thriving operation. She gave herself a mental pat on the back.

Three Months Later

The operation is buzzing. She has twenty-two women and seven men on her roster. It was a start. One of the men was older and more distinguished looking than anyone she'd met in some time. Rolf Harrison, retired ex pro golfer. An interesting man. He claimed to be a widower. She would accept that information until and if proven otherwise. She fixed him up with two gals, neither of whom he liked. Danielle asked him to come back to the office. She needed to flesh out his profile. If she had it wrong, she would fix it. That's when it happened. He looked at her, straight in the eyes, grinned and, putting his arm around her, started kissing her...passionately.

"Wait a minute. This is not how it works. I run this agency, remember? If you can't conduct yourself like a gentleman in my office, I will be happy to give you your money back and you can look elsewhere."

He shot her a sour look. "What...are you gay, or something?"

Danielle laughed. "No. I am not gay. And I am not interested in you, personally. I'm running a match-making business here in case you hadn't noticed."

His eyes narrowed. A scowl flashed over his features. They had suddenly hardened, his eyes darkening. "Oh, I'm not good enough for you, is that it?"

She'd better get him calmed down. He could be

dangerous. The sudden shifting of his mood unnerved her, sending up red flags. "Actually, it's the other way around. I'm not good enough for you. You're urbane, handsome and charming...you can do much better than me."

He seemed to settle down a little. "Well, I guess I misread your signals."

She smiled. "Maybe you did. No big deal. No harm done. I'll find Miss Wonderful. Just leave it with me. I have several new gals joining in the next week. Plus there are new prospects signing up all the time. I'll find you your perfect match. Leave it with me."

Danielle drove home from the office she shared with another small company, her mind racing. It was time consuming matching up the right people. She was already getting bored with it. Still, the front money clients paid would pay the rent, though there wasn't much left after expenses. Pixie had graciously given her the use of a Pink Flamingo taxi for temporary transportation. She needed to buy a car soon.

Driving cab, she met all sorts of people, occasionally giving out her dating service card. It would take time to build a roster of eligible bachelors and bachelorettes worth working with. Her thoughts often flashed to Graham and Dana. Would she be persona non grata forever?

She stayed in touch with Suzie who formally announced her engagement. Danielle was thrilled to hear the good news. The nuptials were set for September 9th. They were thinking of coming to the Grand Cayman Islands for their honeymoon. She welcomed them, but later had second thoughts about it. She trusted Suzie but she didn't know her intended; and the fact remained that the perpetrator was still at large. What should she do? Suzie had been the most gracious hostess imaginable when she'd arrived at her grand estate while on the run; the least she could do was accommodate her here and show them some sights. After all, she could pop in to the fine hotels; see which one was best, visit the board of Tourism, and research the most romantic places to visit. She would be "hostess" when they came to town. Of course she knew they would likely be incognito most of the time, as newlyweds.

Suzie and Trevor arrived, all smiles, doting on each other, unable to keep their hands off each other. They'd had the church wedding in Palm Beach. Danielle had never felt twinges of envy when in the presence of an ecstatically happy couple. Until now. There they were: Handsome, tanned, deeply in love and poised to enjoy an idyllic future together. Here she was, barely scraping by. Still, she wouldn't let them know that. She'd put on a brave front; making sure they wouldn't see her humble home at the mobile park.

They checked into the Hilton and invited Danielle to join them for champagne at 5:00. The rest of the evening, it would be just the two of them. A twinge of envy raced through her. Seeing her closest friend deliriously happy with her new hubby made her realize how alone she was.

Suzie shot her a certain look at the champagne event. Danielle knew she understood how lonely she suddenly felt. She really cared, and it was a great comfort to her. When Danielle drove home to her mobile unit, she knew she had to find a good man to enjoy life with. But this time, she wanted God's best. Her Bible promised her that anything she asked for in His name, she would receive. It was time to implement the Bible promises she believed, but had not focused on. She made a pot of herb tea, kicked off her shoes, changed into an orange silk robe she'd bought at the thrift shop and plopped onto the large, white wicker chair with her Bible. She read Psalm after Psalm and meditated on the Word until her eyelids grew heavy and she knew it was time to turn in.

The next morning, Danielle awakened, brimming with fresh enthusiasm and high energy. She would make her dating service sparkle. Unlike all the other dating sites, hers would be an exclusive, unique operation. She had a clear concept of what she wanted to do. Run some TV ads soliciting male clients only to begin with. Rent a small, posh office to interview the prospects. Charge them a healthy fee; though she hadn't come up with a number yet. She would befriend them, getting to know as much about them as she could. Once she had ten good men on board; she knew she could quickly line up a roster of available females. Sure enough, with a couple of ads, her phone started ringing. Incessantly. *Romance was in the air.* Her unique spin was that her company was *not* online. Called *Exclusively Yours, Danielle* only dealt with clients she had personally met, interviewed, checked references, etc.

Soon, her operation began to thrive. Then it took off like a speeding bullet. Everyone in the Cayman Islands was talking about the new dating service.

Three Months Later

Danielle continued to moonlight as a taxi driver. She managed to interview clients and match make around her night shifts driving cab. She was very fussy with whom she would work. She was determined to make the agency as exclusive, sought-after, and elite as possible. Though she gave almost everyone who called an interview, she only accepted about half of those applying. She was determined to make her agency as elite as possible. It would take time to build a stellar reputation, and she was determined to begin that process. As the weeks ticked by, she began to develop a deep understanding of what both sexes were looking for. She believed she had a flair for this new business. And like every business she'd ever had, she had dreams that it would excel.

·

She would have great satisfaction when she found an ideal match for one of her clients. Maybe even be invited to celebrate their nuptials if it came to that. Danielle was certain it would be easier for her to find her own dream man, given the new business.

She had dossiers on twenty-five women and eighteen men. It was a great start. She intended to launch her business formally through TV coverage, if she could swing it. She hoped the agency would take off and in the process she would find a great guy for herself. A girl can dream.

Robert Manning was her last appointment for the evening. It was 9:00 P.M. on a Tuesday. Ten minutes to 9:00 he showed up.

She hired a couple of students to man the receptionist desk

Sylvia, today's temp receptionist, had masses of unruly, dark hair, black eyes as big as saucers and a quick mind. She was eighteen but seemed much older. She greeted the prospect. "Good evening. And you are?"

"Robert Manning, Ma'am. I have a 10:00 appointment with Danielle Lockhart."

"You're right on time, Mr. Manning. She's expecting you, of course." She stood, quickly flashing a shot of his face with her high-tech camera, despite knowing there were cameras which were obscured. I'll let her know you're here." She made the announcement and shortly ushered the tall, urbane gentleman into Danielle's office. She looked him over, carefully scrutinizing him.

He looked somewhat uncomfortable. He chuckled. There was an edge of nervousness about the laugh. "I feel like I'm being...scrutinized."

"And I'm just the gate-keeper. Wait 'til you meet my boss." She smirked. She was glad she could do her homework at the desk, as she sat through the appointment. It was security for Danielle to have someone else on the premises, given that she was meeting with a lot of total strangers.

The man flashed a grin at Danielle. He extended his hand. "Hi. Robert Manning."

"I'm Danielle Lockhart of Lock Hearts Agency. I must warn you that there are security cameras in this room as well as the reception area. Our conversation will be recorded, primarily so that I can replay it later to make sure I didn't miss any pertinent information. Your references have been checked, and you appear to be an excellent prospect for the right, lucky lady." She smiled. "Please, have a seat and make yourself comfortable. Given that the 21st Century has ushered in dangerous times, I trust you will not take offense at some of the security measures I have implemented."

"Can we just get on with it? I don't have all day." The macho man snarled.

A virile, robust man with a cocky attitude gazed at her with contempt. He had a thick mop of unruly dark hair. She was taken aback at his rude remarks. She waited to see if he would apologize, change his mood...whatever. Nothing. He squirmed slightly in his chair. "Look...Danielle, I'm under a lot of financial pressure. My time is extremely valuable. Can we just cut to the chase? I'd like to view the videos of the female prospects you've selected for me."

Danielle smiled. She liked the gorgeous hunk despite his outburst. There was something vulnerable, charming...even amazing about him. "I'll run the tape." She pressed a button on the video machine and momentarily, a curvaceous, honey blonde, as sweet and charming as the late Marilyn Monroe, appeared. She ran the short clip and then handed him her dossier. "She has a Master's degree in political science." Danielle smiled. She sensed he was excited by her.

"I think I've met her before. Does she hang around bars?"

"Good heavens, no. None of my clients do. I put everyone through a rigorous interrogation process. I'm shooting for the top 5% of both sexes. My female clients are much too busy and discreet to be common. Most are well educated from good families..."

He smirked. "Like yourself, Danielle? I know a little

something about you." He pointed a Beretta at her head. "It's game over, Danielle. Cough up the fifty grand or bye-bye."

Danielle could feel the color drain from her face. She pressed the emergency button on her desk, praying it would work...praying the sheriff would find her in time. "You're on video. This is not a wise move on your part." She didn't know where the cool control came from. Only God himself could have orchestrated it. She screamed to her assistant, despite knowing there was a wall between them. "Sally...call 911."

She heard a muffled sound. He held her hands behind her back with the steely power of a large, muscular hand. He peered at her, sinisterly. "Quite a little scam you have going here." He sneered at her. "Thought you could run from us, didn't you?"

"What are you talking about? You've got the wrong person."

"We know who you are. Does kidnapping Dana Van Rensellier ring a bell?"

His evil gaze sent shivers down her spine. "This is all a terrible mistake. Let me go. The police are on the way. I pressed the emergency button."

"You idiot; I dismantled all that stuff before I came here. Do you think I'm a fool, Miss High Society dame...from Palm Beach?" he laughed, sinisterly. "You can't run from us. Surprised you didn't know that. You owe somebody like us money..." He sneered at her. "We're going to collect it... one way or the other..." His eyes were evil, grey slits.

Suddenly, the door burst open and two uniformed cops burst inside. "Police."

Shock and horror were etched on the man's evil face.

Two cops, one younger, one more mature, strong armed him and then spun him around, clamping handcuffs on him. "Let's go, Buddy."

Danielle wiped the sweat off her brow.

"I'll follow you out of the building. We need to make

sure the receptionist is okay."

But when they reached her desk, it was vacant. "Guess she raced out of here when the confrontation occurred," The younger cop said.

The older cop spoke. "Yeah. And she called us, even before you pressed the panic button…said she had a hunch the guy was bad news. She'd read some bad press about him somewhere."

Danielle smiled. *I knew I liked that young women. So much for building a career in matchmaking. So much for my brilliant concept.* The incident had given her the willies. Was it a precursor for more weirdos showing up? She wouldn't stick around to find out.

The next morning when she arose, knowing the bad dude was behind bars, she picked herself up, dusted herself off and started all over again. *No two-bit gangster was going to keep her away from a burgeoning industry like match-making. She'd try again.*

This time Danielle took her pepper spray with her. If her life was in jeopardy, she'd use it. Also, she would have her assistant present during the interview. Further, she would inform the cops of the time her male clients would be arriving, particularly the evening appointments. She invited them to stop by unannounced or use surveillance. If she was attracting the wrong kind of guys, maybe she could smoke them out early on, get rid of them and move forward with bona fide clients. The local Ladies' man was off the scene, they told her there were a couple more shady types they guessed might contact her. They agreed to keep an eye on her new operation.

Danielle had a 10:00 a.m. appt. with a stunning brunette gal in her forties. That would give her a breather.

Tips were good with the Pink Flamingo Cab Co. She was making better tips now that she'd learned the area. *Maybe I should stick with driving cab and forget the match making job.* But there was a part of her that wouldn't quit. She was a survivor and a winner. She'd decided on those labels a long time ago. Plus, she could use her cab to recruit occasional clients for her matchmaking company.

Chapter Twenty

Dana was in seventh heaven. What could go wrong? They'd been given a windfall, which not only restored their faith in humanity; but also in the principles and edicts of the Bible. They'd been given double what they'd given away. You couldn't out give God.

Talia had a boyfriend. A young man she'd met at school. She wanted to bring him home. She wanted him to be able to hang out at Sugarbush with her.

Warning bells rang in Dana's mind. She told Graham they needed to have a meeting with Talia to lay down the parameters she would need to adhere to, while living at Sugarbush. Further, they wanted to talk about her goals.

"Talia, we need you to get settled in. We need to solidify our relationship with you. You're a brilliant student, and we need to discuss your future... and what path you intend to take. Getting sidetracked with a cute guy from school will not only complicate *your life* but *ours, as well.*" Graham and Dana wanted to err on the side of caution, at least until they got to know her better.

"Are you saying that I can't have any friends? That I can't bring my friends home?"

Alarm bells rang in Graham's head. The sweet, charming Talia had suddenly become demanding. He knew she'd been spoiled and had led a privileged life. But he hadn't expected her to be a rebellious teenager. "We need to talk about boundaries...and that sort of thing."

"Boundaries? What don't you want me to do?" Talia's large brown eyes seemed to grow larger.

Dana rolled her eyes. "Now is not a good time, honey. We'll talk tomorrow." *She needed to have a serious talk with Graham to figure out just what parameters they would expect Talia to adhere to. She was rich, brilliant and...she'd just discovered... spoiled rotten. That fact was quickly coming to light. As long as she'd been striving for something; in this instance;* taking up residence *at Sugarbush; she was affable; but as soon as that goal had been achieved, she'd staked out her territory, with little or no regard for her guardians. This is not going to work.*

"So, when *is* a good time? I hope I don't have to be a prisoner in my room?" Talia's voice had an edge of irritation to it.

Dana rolled her eyes. She told herself to calm down. Teenagers were famous for being difficult. She forced a smile and made an attempt at sounding affable. "Talia...communication is a major key to remaining a happy family. I understand that it's not easy for you to adapt to having many other people to consider; but I'm afraid you will need to do that here, for this arrangement to work out." Dana tried hard to remain loving, but firm. "We deeply care about you. You quickly got under our skin. And we are humbled by your father's magnanimous gift. But since we are now responsible for you...and we take that responsibility very seriously.... we need to sort these issues out as soon as possible."

'So...like when?"

Dana felt like smacking her. The impertinence of the child was incredible. She knew she had to remain cool. She and Graham had prayerfully agreed to be her guardians until such a time as her father thought it best to revise those arrangements. Meanwhile, the plan was to infiltrate Talia into the American way of life, get her education here, and use "Van Rensellier as her last name. In the unique contract, which had been Drawn up by Louis's attorney, and accepted by both parties to the contract, the Ambassador stipulated that when his Ambassadorship stint was completed, he would have the option of taking Talia back into his life; depending on circumstances. Meanwhile, he requested a written monthly report from Dana and Graham regarding her behavior and studies, etc.

Dana recalled the private dinner meeting she and Graham had with the distinguished ambassador. Oddly, the conversation came back to her almost verbatim. "It would not be fair for me to attempt to look after her and guide her through the teenage years and on into university, because due to the nature of of my work, I am constantly socializing at cocktail parties, dinner parties and meetings, as well as having a very busy travel agenda. She doesn't take well to having Nannies. And I believe Sugarbush is an ideal setting for her to grow up in. I believe she'll thrive here. Of course I recognize the responsibilities that would fall on the two of you, but you have my assurance both verbally, as well as in writing, that the compensation I am offering should make the venture appealing. If at any time, something about her or the arrangement in general...is seen to be a problem, you have only to contact me, and we will arrange to discuss the matter in further detail...and hopefully resolve it in an amicable way."

Dana carefully reread the contract they'd signed with her father. *He is such a remarkable man. And he's been magnanimous to us.* "Lord, please give us wisdom to deal with this... spoiled child." Her new mindset came as a total surprise. She'd been so affable up until now. "Lord, please help us to cope with her...along with everything else...I know there's no turning back. The die is cast. We'll just have to take the good with the bad...and trust in you, because I know Talia is destined to live with us."

Thank God the twins are down for a nap. I need this time of refreshment with you, Lord. Father, please pour your wisdom... and joy and favor into my mind and heart. What seems impossible or daunting for us mere mortals, is absolutely nothing for you. You created us all...fearfully and wonderfully. You created this entire universe. It is mind boggling to think that you can hear billions of prayers simultaneously; and yet at the same time, answer those prayers...maybe not answer some of them...and oversee everyone's situation and deal with each person according to their relationship with you and the extent of their faith...and commitment to you. And so, Father in heaven, right now...I ask you to help us deal with Talia's new mindset. Thank-you, Jesus."

When Dana emerged from the prayer room, she felt better. It was as though a weight had been lifted from her shoulders. "Lord, I can cope with this." She spoke with resolution and certainty. Yes, He would make a way where there was no way. She knew that she could count on him.

Quickly, she freshened up and headed to the nursery. Violet was making funny faces at the twins and causing them to gurgle happily. *God bless that woman.* "Hey, Violet. I can take over from here." She smiled, picking up one of the twins.

Violet picked up the other, since he instantly began wailing, raising his cries louder than his twin's. "Mommy loves you, honey. And so does Grandma Violet." She hugged the baby, singing sweet melodies to him.

At dinner that night, Talia was unusually quiet. *Sulking maybe? Because she didn't get her own way. Maybe can't call the shots.*

Somewhere Dana had read that when bad behavior occurred, ignore it. She'd give it a shot. She didn't bring up the conflict. Instead, she acted as though nothing had happened. "Did Violet make the steak the way you like it, Talia?"

"Yes. Thank-you."

So her manners are back. That's a good sign. "How was school today?"

"Okay." She fiddled with her dinner. "I don't think Mrs. Carruthers likes me, though."

"What an odd thing to day, Talia. Why would you think that?"

"Because we had to turn in an essay. So...like... I based it on some of my experiences."

"And?"

"And she said I made up the experiences. Then she smiled at me, and said it was very interesting, though. And that maybe I should become a writer. She gave me...like...kind of a weird look."

"Well, perhaps she finds it difficult to relate to your... somewhat grand beginnings. Maybe she thought you were exaggerating."

"Maybe." Talia dug into the steak. "The steak is perfect. You sure know how to cook, Violet."

"Want me to teach *you* how to cook?"

"Cool. How did you know I love to cook?"

Violet shrugged. "Just had a hunch."

Dana and Graham exchanged glances, a silent understanding flashing between them. Will, Jay and Talia excused themselves, moving in the direction of the family room.

"Well, Talia seems to have settled down considerably since her little temper tantrum."

"Yes. But I don't trust it. She is a girl of many...faces, like a chameleon. I don't think we have any idea what she's really like."

"Well, whatever she is or is not; we're stuck with it and we'll have to deal with it. We'll just take one day at a time. That's all we can do, really." Graham shrugged. "I do, think, though, that possibly...once she feels secure and gets really settled in...she'll settle down and be just fine." He peered over at Dana. "It must be emotionally wrenching for her to have lost her Mother at such a young age. And now...in a way...she's lost her father, too. Maybe we just need to cut her some slack and love her a lot more than we have been." Graham sipped his tea and finished his generous slice of Boston cream pie.

"You're probably right, honey." Dana sighed.

Graham could hear a quarrel in progress in the games room as he sauntered by, intending to glance in and see who was winning at chess. Talia's voice sounded shrill. "You think you know everything about chess. Well, you don't. My Dad is the best chess player ever..."

Graham stood at the door to the games room. "It's not a competition, in terms of who is better, Talia. I'm sure your Dad is a fine chess player. Just enjoy the game." He winked at her. "And don't underestimate my sons when it comes to playing chess."

Will and Jay did the thumbs up gesture, grinning.

Talia peered at Graham, stony faced.

What happened to the sweet gal Dana fell in love with? Graham sighed, grinned and glanced at his watch. "A half hour...then everybody heads to their rooms to do their homework."

"I've already done mine." Talia flashed Graham a saucy smile.

"Have you? When did you do it?"

She scrunched up her features and shot Graham a look. *None of your business.*

Okay, have it your way. "May I see it?"

"Sure. It's in my room. I'll go get it." She hopped to it.

Graham was getting mixed signals about this girl. He wasn't sure how to read her.

She bounced out of the games room and down the hall and then upstairs to her room, returning with her homework. She smiled, as she handed it to him.

Graham peered at the typed sheets. The Math was done. The assignment was printed from the computer with today's date. He glanced over her answers. "Okay. Fair enough. You're welcome to go back to playing chess...provided Will and Jay have done their homework, as well."

The boys looked sheepish.

"You're not going to let a girl upstage you are you, are you?" He already knew they hadn't done their homework. *Maybe Talia would turn out to be a blessing, after all. If nothing else, she would bring out the competitive spirit in the boys, who would then want to beat her at doing their homework, hopefully.*

That night as Graham and Dana lay in bed, Graham aired his thoughts about Talia. "You know, maybe we're making a big deal out of nothing. It's got to be a tough adjustment losing her Mom and then having her Dad...basically farm her out."

"You're right, honey. We'll give her time. Anyway, we really have no other choice."

"Good-night, darling." He kissed her and kissed her and kissed her...

Chapter Twenty-One

Danielle had trouble sleeping most nights. Though she hated to admit it, the ugly incident in her office had rattled her. Maybe she was walking directly into more traps. By the time the end of the week arrived leaving her haggard from lack of sleep, she decided to close down the match-making service.

Driving a cab with Pink Flamingo was fun at times. She'd make the best of it and trust God to bring the right man into her life.

Six Months Later

Danielle still hadn't met a man she really liked. She hadn't had a date since arriving in the Cayman Islands, but she remained hopeful that would soon change. She hadn't heard from Dana and Graham and she missed them. Carving out a new life in the Grand Cayman Islands sounded exciting, and in a way it was; but it was also challenging. Still, she'd always thrived on challenges.

She needed an infusion of new adrenalin. But what would it be? That's when she heard the voice of God. *"Have you forgotten me, my daughter? I love you with an everlasting love. You have not sought me, though it is I and I alone that hold the answers for your abundant life. You have sought me in your darkest hours; and vanished when I poured out my favor and blessings upon you. Return to me and I will return to you saith the Lord Almighty."*

Wow. God was pouring out his Spirit upon her. She remembered that brief time not long ago when she sought him with her whole heart, because her life had flipped into an unmitigated fiasco during her brief, disastrous marriage. But after that nightmare, the prison stint and then the glorious utopia at Suzie's mansion in Palm Beach, she had forgotten God Almighty. Oh, she'd attended church a few times while there, but that was the extent of it. A sermon she'd heard at a church in Palm Beach flashed into her mind. It was about being on fire for God, and how He despised lukewarm believers, even to the point of spitting them out of his mouth. A shiver ran through her. *Was that her? Had she slipped into a kind of spiritual apathy? Oh Lord, forgive me. What had she been thinking?*

"Return to me, and I will return to you." As the scripture flashed into her mind, she knew what she had to do. Repent and seek God with a whole heart. *Then,* he would hear her prayers. She picked up her Bible and brushed off dust she couldn't see but suspected was there. She would start at the beginning of the New Testament and read it right through. She would read several chapters a day. Then maybe God would give her the desires of her heart. *"If you delight yourself in me, I will give you the desires of your heart." Ps. 37:4.*

Christmas was just around the corner. Other than Pixie, the owner of Pink Flamingo Cabs, she hadn't made any friends. She knew whose fault that was. She had popped into church occasionally, but hadn't committed herself to a Bible study group or attending church regularly. *Did God notice everything? She knew the answer to that. The Almighty was omnipresent.*

She decided to do something creative to bless the folks at church since a Bazaar was coming up. She made some puppets. That led to the idea of doing a Puppet Show for children. A huge smile flashed across her face. "Lord, I think I can bless the children and amuse them." She did and once again she sensed the voice of the Holy Spirit leading her into a ministry with children. First, there had been the orphanages, and then the fund raisers. Now she sensed that God was prompting her to once again use her theatrical skills to entertain and amuse children.

Thanksgiving was a special time of the year. She offered her help in the kitchen at church, preparing the dinner. That's when she met Carrie. Carrie was a gourmet cook, happily married to a property developer. She liked Danielle instantly and invited her and a couple other gals from the church to her house for a private Thanksgiving dinner party.

Danielle drove up to the glorious estate owned by Carrie and Bob Sherman. A massive, contemporary house, it was perched on a hillside surrounded by what appeared to be a few acres. She parked her pink cab and rang the front doorbell.

Two darling little girls, obviously Carries' daughters greeted her. They were dressed in festive outfits and welcomed her.

Soon, she was laughing gaily and meeting new people. *Lord, I didn't expect your blessings to chase me down so fast after returning to you. I'm impressed. Thank-you, Lord.* There were ten people at the table. It soon became apparent to her that she was the only stranger. The newcomer. She was amazed at how many jokes were exchanged and how quickly folks burst into joyful laughter. *They have the joy of the Lord and their lives are overflowing with happiness.*

"Esther is six," she smiled in her direction. "This is Lana, she's five… and the baby, Veronica, just turned three."

"I'm not a baby." Veronica wailed.

Mommy hugged her. "Of course you're not, honey. Sometimes we just call the youngest child in the family *baby.* We don't mean it literally, honey. You're a big girl. And you're all grown up." She smiled, leaned forward and scooping the child into her arms nuzzled her. "I love you, honey. And you look so beautiful." Carrie put the child down and she soon settled down.

"They are dressed...just beautifully." Danielle gushed. "And the children have lovely manners. You and hubby have done a stellar job of raising them."

"Why thank you, Danielle. What a nice thing to say."

Dressed gloriously and imbued with the finest of manners, the children passed around hors d'oeuvres, doing a curtsy after serving them to the guests.

After dinner, Danielle surprised and delighted everyone by giving a mini puppet show. With few friends and having dropped her dating enterprise, she'd rehearsed for hours in front of a mirror.

Danielle waited on God, seeking him diligently, reading his word daily and worshipping him on Sunday. She kept praying and believing that he would send her a glorious hubby. But time was marching on and she was becoming impatient. Finally, one night, after she'd prayed for many months and still hadn't even had a date, she felt the Holy Spirit nudging her. She was led to read Malachi 9. In it, she read about tithing. *"Lord, you know I can't afford to tithe. I'm just getting by as it is."* But then she heard the spirit of God speaking to her very clearly. *Trust Me. Trust Me with all your heart and lean not on your own understanding."*

She was speechless. Coming from a believing friend or even reading God's word, she might have been able to justify not hearing correctly. But maybe that was why He spoke to her so clearly that she could not miss the message.

That night, she made a decision. She would trust God with all her heart, mind and soul like the Bible admonished her to do. And she would not rely on her own understanding. Somewhere in the Bible she had read that if one followed God's edicts to the letter, he would open the windows of heaven and pour out a blessing that she would not be able to contain it. She really liked that idea.

When she got her paycheck from Pink Flamingo Cabs,

she found an early Christmas bonus in a nice card from Pixie. The check was made out to her but signed by a name she was unfamiliar with. She was stunned. Maybe there had been a mistake. She'd better check with her friend before she deposited it into the bank.

"Oh no, honey. There's no mistake. An anonymous donor showed up at my office. He had your cab number, your name and your description. Of course we both know you go by Dottie as a driver. And that's what he called you. He said he wanted you to have this bonus. He went on to say that he was terminally ill and would soon be hospitalized. He asked if you might consider visiting him there. It seems he took a shine to you; though I suspect, more in a fatherly fashion. He appeared to be…maybe over ninety."

Danielle was overcome with emotion. "Oh Pixie. It's really true that God works in mysterious ways. Thank-you for this envelope." She felt it for a second. "It's thin. Must be a check." She opened it, there, in Pixie's small office in her mobile unit, she stared, stunned at the check. Speechless. When she finally found her voice, she smiled at Pixie. "Oh my gosh. What a generous gift. It's…like a miracle."

"Well, bless your heart, honey. I know you need it. Maybe you're closer to getting that new car now."

Danielle started dancing around the office. "God is real. His promises are real. He said he would never leave us or forsake us. He meant it. Look at this. A financial miracle, that's what it is." She laughed. "This is the start of my new, glorious… prosperous life. I just feel it in my bones."

"Well, I wouldn't doubt it one bit. I told you…you start doin' the Bible and church thing…sure as can be, you're gonna have real good things happen for ya. That's what my Mom used to say. Now, I'm beginning to believe it myself."

Danielle hugged Pixie. "I'm taking you for dinner tonight. That is, provided you're free."

"I'm not; but I'll avail myself." She chuckled. "I want to celebrate what God is doing in your life. I'll tell my daughter

I'll be home later. She won't mind makin' her own dinner tonight." She flashed Dana a happy smile.

"You might be right. I think God really likes me, after all." Danielle smiled.

"Ya, he does." Pixie smiled. "Where you takin' me?"

"I dunno. Where do you suggest?"

"I was thinking steaks. That new steak house is real good...so I'm told. Sam's Superior Steaks." She smiled. "Catchy name, isn't it?"

They ordered porterhouse steaks, baked potatoes with sour crème and chives. Just as they were being served, Danielle couldn't help noticing two burley guys sauntering by their table and glancing at them.

Danielle had a sour look on her face. "Too young," she whispered, to Pixie." They don't have dates but they're too young for us."

"How do you know that? They're not that much younger. And...actually...I noticed the taller of the two checkin' you out when they walked by..." She flashed Danielle a cheeky grin, eyebrows raised for emphasis.

"Oh come on...you're just sayin' that."

"No, I'm not. You know by now that I'm a straight shooter."

"Ya, you are."

As soon as the server brought the steaks, she heard one of the guys from the next booth over, call the waiter. Moments later, he returned to their table. "A gentleman at the next booth over asked if he could send over a glass of wine for you two ladies."

Danielle's eyes sparkled. A radiant smile lit her face. She glanced at the waiter. "Sure. Ah...Cabernet for me. Pixie?"

"Make that two."

The waiter served two glasses of Cabernet to them. They glanced over at the booth where the guys sat. "Thanks guys...To...life and good health." Danielle lifted her glass in a toast.

The taller of the two men peered directly into Danielle's eyes. "To you lovely ladies."

Later that night, the two macho guys strode by their table. The taller man leaned over, handing Danielle his card. "Text me, would you?" He grinned at her. The guys turned and left.

"Well...there you are. Just like that. You've met a guy. How easy was that?"

"That's God raining down his blessings on me. Has to be." She peered at the card. *Brandon Scott, computer geek.* There was a phone number and an e-mail.

"Well...I think you're absolutely right, Danielle."

Chapter Twenty-Two

Dana and Graham settled into the routine with the twins. Dana was a natural mother and loved her role. She adored the twins. When she wasn't tending to them or helping the boys with their homework, she continued bonding with Talia. Life was good and getting sweeter all the time.

She worked hard to get back in shape. The discipline and focus she'd learned as a professional jumper and trainer stood her in good stead. There was big money in training horses for competitions. The sooner she got back to it, the better. She'd already begun private riding lessons and group lessons. And having placed an ad in a horse magazine, they began boarding horses. Still, she knew that without the massive infusion of funds they miraculously received, they would have been in big trouble. It was an ongoing challenge to keep the operation running smoothly. But with everyone doing their share, it hummed along.

Talia, Will and Jay, sparred constantly. "How do you know how to speak French? You're from Israel. It's not predominantly French speaking." Jay questioned her, one morning at breakfast.

"Of course it isn't. But Dad is a diplomat as you know, and that's the preferred language they speak. Also, I grew up with a French governess."

"Cool." Jay was satisfied with her answer.

Dana returned to the house after a full day of teaching

group riding lesson, followed by private lessons.

"Zoltan Boraz is hanging out in the games room with Talia." Violet had a skeptical look on her face as she relayed the news.

"Thanks Violet." Dana took a deep breath and headed down the hall to the games room. She found them there, doing crossword puzzles. *Lord, give me wisdom...and calmness to deal with Talia's new male friend.*

But as Zoltan extended his hand in greeting and grinned at her, flashing dark, amber-flecked eyes which radiated warmth and intelligence, her resolve to banish him from Sugarbush instantly evaporated. Instead, she began blubbering. "How old are you?" "Where are you from?" "How did the two of you meet?" Interrogation flew from her lips, while she tried emotionally to assimilate the scene playing out before her. She soon realized she was acting like a blubbering idiot.

Zoltan was short to medium height. Maybe 5' 7".Talia and he were about the same height. He had swarthy skin and a smile that lit up the room. *What was she to do? What questions should she ask? If she and Graham forbade Talia to see him, would she find a way to meet him secretly?* She decided to say very little, until she had consulted with Graham and prayed with him about the matter.

That night when Graham heard the news that Talia had a boyfriend, he fell silent. It was well over an hour before he spoke. "Dana, I had a hunch something like this might happen. Actually, that's one of the many reasons I was reluctant to welcome her into our home. But the die is cast for better or worse. We have to find a way to reach her, communicate with her, get and keep her respect and guide her in her life. Lou expects nothing less. And frankly, darling; we are well paid to do it."

His calmness and analytical mind caused her to relax. "Well, maybe it will all work out." "We'll pray that it does."

They sipped their tea in the family room, both of them pensive.

The boys were nowhere around. "I guess I should check on the twins. Violet tells me that she checks on them every time she thinks of it; or if she hears them crying." Dana smiled. "Violet is a wonder woman. As you know...she does the work of three people."

"She really does. We need to pray that God will keep her in good health. I don't know what we would do without her."

"Well, she seems to be healthy as a horse. I hope it stays that way." Dana smiled and edged her way over to Graham. She was falling more deeply in love with him with each passing day. "Oh, honey. I'm so happy. God has truly blessed us." She jumped up from the sofa and kissed him on the cheek.

"Yes. But we must never take his blessings for granted. Remember the scripture *"The Lord giveth and the Lord taketh away?"* He peered into her eyes. *"We must always be thankful for what we have. And remember...that without Him we are nothing and have nothing."*

"I know, honey." She sighed. "Do you think we have even a chance of getting Talia away from Zoltan?"

"Not even a sliver of a chance. We'll pray about it tonight... and again in the morning. Meanwhile, I think the best we can do it commit them to the Lord and ask for his protection over them...and, of course, wisdom and favor to deal wisely with them."

"From the conversations I've had with him, I've learned that he's an exchange student from Israel. Maybe they knew each other there. So far, she hasn't been forthcoming about any further information about him."

"She's very secretive at times. Perhaps part of that comes from having a diplomat for a father. She's grown up being aware of that mindset." Graham rose from the sofa. "Maybe I'll make a pot of tea. And I'd like something sweet. I'll see what's in the pantry." He headed for the kitchen.

"I'll check on the twins. Then I'll join you for tea."

"Sounds good, honey."

Graham and Dana sat in the enormous kitchen sipping tea.

Talia and Zoltan strolled into the kitchen, holding hands.

Graham saw red despite his resolve.

Dana put a hand on Graham's lap under the table and then shot him a warning glance, which said. "Don't go there." Was Talia trying to irk them? Was she trying to provoke a fight? Why? What would be her motivation? She'd begged to stay here. Would she put the goodwill she'd built with them; and the trust in jeopardy? Dana smiled. "Join us for tea?" She gestured to both of them.

"We're going to a movie. We have to leave right away." She seemed to edge closer to Zoltan.

Graham took a deep breath. "Really? Where? And...who is driving you?"

"Zoltan's hostess. He's studying to be a filmmaker, so it's mandatory that he sees as many films as possible."

Graham worked at staying cool. "Sounds like fun." He glanced over at Zoltan before addressing Talia. "But Talia, you need to *ask permission* to go out. You're only thirteen. And though that may seem ancient to you...and you may feel as though you know everything...trust me; you don't. The least we require as your guardians is courtesy and respect. I'm sure you were brought up to adhere to that."

"Spare me the lecture." Talia spat out.

Graham's voice was steel. He was stunned, but not so stunned that he didn't think fast for her punishment for disrespecting him. "You won't be going tonight, Talia. You're grounded."

Talia's eyes filled with contempt. Still, the swift punishment seemed to bring her to her senses. "That's not fair. I didn't do anything wrong."

"Disrespecting your guardians is wrong and very rude. It is not acceptable behavior in our home."

"Are you threatening to kick me out?" She raised her voice. Irate.

Graham lost it then. "Maybe that's exactly what I'll do. I'll return the money and you along with it."

Finally, she had his attention. She looked befuddled. "But...but you signed something...a contract with my dad. You said I could stay here...that Sugarbush was my home..." She burst into tears. "I'm going to my room."

The macho Zoltan had been silent during the heated exchange. He spoke up now. "It's *my* fault. Not *hers*. I...I told her I wanted her to join me to see the movie...and she said she didn't usually go out during the week; only on weekends...but...but...I insisted and finally she caved."

Dana came to his aid. "Look, you're clearly a fine young man. I think maybe we need to have a meeting with the couple you're staying with and...set up some parameters...make it clear what our house rules are for Talia."

"Ya. Like...sure." He shrugged. "Whatever you think. Uh...maybe I won't go to the movie tonight, after all. Maybe...maybe I'll wait until I get your blessing to take Talia with me."

Graham was quite stunned by Zoltan's gentle spirit. *He's a fine, young man. And Talia is a spoiled brat.*

His cell rang. "That's probably Lila now. My...uh...hostess." He spoke into his cell. "Hey, Lila. Are you outside? The gate man will need to open the gate."

Graham flashed a signal on the ground line. "Bob...please let Lilia in."

"Ask Lila to come in for a few minutes. We'd like to meet her." He turned to Dana. "Wouldn't we, honey?"

Dana smiled. She was on the same page. "Very much."

Lila was loquacious and curvy, though chunky. A large woman. An older gal with masses of red, wavy hair, she sparkled with life and big personality. "Well, hi there. I've heard so much about y'all." She smiled. "Guess you didn't know I bought that dilapidated house over by False Creek." She smiled, like she had a joke or some mischief up her sleeve and raised her eyebrows. "Got me four exchange students. They love the place. I make stew or a huge pot of soup every night...then some nights, though..." She flashed a big smile. "Well...sometimes I make roast beef, turkey...you name it. See I jest love to cook. Hubby number four owned a couple of restaurants...I did all the cookin' but one day...well...he jest up and left." She chuckled and shrugged. "What ya gonna do? Life goes on, don't it?"

Graham grinned. *She is some piece of work. Where is this going? And how do I get rid of her?"*

"So where's the girl? Talia, I believe her name is." Lila peered around, obviously expecting her to surface.

"She won't be going to the movie tonight." Graham's voice was stern.

Lila raised her eyebrows. "And why is that?"

"It's a homework night." Graham said, flatly.

"I bet that girl has next week's homework done already, from what I've heard." Lila arched her eyebrows.

Graham grinned. "She's pretty smart. I'll grant you that. But we have house rules around here...that need to be adhered to."

"Adhered to?" Lila smiled. "What kind of word is that? Adhered to? Why don't you say...ah followed? You know... rules that have to be followed."

Graham had a hard time to keep from breaking out with laughter.

"Well, I guess I better *adhere to* the fact that it's time for us to go." She smiled like her life depended on the size of that smile. "Thanks for havin' me in now. We'll see y'all again...real soon. "Let's go honey." Lila smiled at Zoltan. "We'll go home for dinner and then I'll go with you to the movie."

"Good night." Zoltan said, as he left.

Violet served spaghetti and meat balls with a salad. "I couldn't help but hear that conversation. She's quite a character, isn't she?" Violet sat at the table with everyone. She always did, at Graham and Dana's insistence.

"Well, from what I can see, Zoltan and Lila are as different as chalk and cheese. But he seems real happy there."

Talia piped up. "He says she's a great character to study...because she's bigger than life. He wants to be a filmmaker and he says the film medium loves extreme characters."

"Yes, I suppose that's true." Violet mused.

"Anyway...I've already done my homework. I don't really care about the film. I just wanted to go to hang out with Zoltan."

Dana opened her mouth and started speaking without having thought it through. "Well, maybe he could come over here for dinner tomorrow night and the two of you could watch a movie together on T.V."

"Yeah. That would be awesome." She gave the thumbs up gesture to Dana. Her face was lit with youthful joy.

Zoltan came over for dinner the next night and the next and the next. Finally, Graham put his foot down. After the third dinner, Graham took Dana aside. "Honey, I thought maybe they would get tired of each other; but it seems spending a lot of time together has only drawn them closer. He's what? Fifteen? And she's thirteen." He peered over at Dana.

"That's exactly why...I know what you're thinking...that's exactly why I want him under our roof. That zany Lila character...Lord only knows what her story is...the kid...Zoltan is better off here...than with her."

"Honey, I agree with you; but we can't adopt the whole world. Talia is a handful as it is."

At that moment Will and Jay burst into the room. "Why

doesn't Zoltan go home? Its...like he...well, he practically lives here..." Jay sulked.

"That's about to end. Trust me." Graham shot him a serious look.

"Good. I get my chess board back. That'll be nice."

"But you've had some good games with him, haven't you?"

"I guess. It's just...well...he acts like he lives here..." Jay sulked.

"Yeah. And then we have to wait to use our own chess board." He grinned, peering at Graham." If we weren't so well mannered, we would have told him to leave ourselves."

"And to your credit, son...you *are* a gentleman. God is watching. Maybe he doesn't have parents that are living. Did you ever think of that?

"No." He looked at his brother. "But Jay said he had a hunch that...well, maybe he has foster parents."

"Well, for whatever reason, God has brought him into our lives and we need to be alert to see why that is. We just never know where the paths may wind. I mean...did we think that having Talia live with us...would bring about the miracle that it did?" He grinned. "We both know the answer to that. God moves in mysterious ways. And his ways are not our ways. His ways are so much higher. So...rather than try to figure out what God is doing...we need to go with the flow. Right now, I see a young man with fine manners, obviously brought up well...but I have a hunch there's a lot more to his story..."

Graham and Dana went out to check on one of the thoroughbreds that had shown signs of ailing. They rarely went to the barn at night, except to make sure the barn doors were locked. Dana heard a noise in the background. It was coming from the haystack. "Hold on, Graham. I'm going to investigate that sound...it seems to be coming from the haystack. Suddenly, as she peered upwards, she saw the top of two heads, the rest of their bodies were hidden by the haystacks. They were necking. She moved closer to them, straining to get a better look. There they were...Talia and Zoltan entwined together in the haystack.

Graham whispered to Dana. "It's incredible that we happened to come out here after dinner. We rarely do, as you know. If that colt hadn't shown signs of being sick, we wouldn't have come out here tonight."

"True. And yes, I think we should call the vet to have a look at him." She peered over at Graham. "Are you thinking what I'm thinking?" Dana rolled her eyes and whispered to him. "I've done the girl talk thing with Talia. I've told her how God feels about sex outside of marriage. I've spent hours instructing her and corroborating it with scriptures. She has no excuse."

"Well maybe they're just...necking." Graham said.

"And why wouldn't they do that in the house?"

"More privacy? Excitement? I don't know, honey." Graham leaned toward her. "We're going to pretend we didn't see them...and go back to the house..."

"Honey? Are you sure that's what we should do?"

"I'm sure. Come on...let's go."

Graham and Dana talked about their strategy for bringing up the sensitive subject. They decided not to say anything tonight.

Lila picked up Zoltan later that evening.

The next morning Graham set down his newspaper at the table, when Talia showed up for breakfast. "You're grounded, Talia. I'm sorry it has to be this way. We saw the two of you in the haystack yesterday. No hanky-panky is allowed at Sugarbush; other than us...old married folks."

"Hanky-panky?" Talia seemed confused.

"Okay. That may not be a term you're familiar with. No fooling around and absolutely no sex is allowed here."

"What are you gonna do about it? Send me back to Israel? And give Daddy back his two million?"

She was cheeky. A typical rich kid. Graham was fuming.

"That's enough, Talia. If you can't behave like a proper young lady, then maybe that's *exactly* what I'll do."

"You're...joking, right?"

"Far from it. All I have to do is say the word and Dad gets to own Sugarbush, while we continue running the farm. It will all pass away one day soon, anyway. And we take nothing with us when we go to heaven...it really makes very little difference whether the bank owns a big chunk of it, or I own it, or Dad owns it. But I'll tell you one thing, young lady...if you think you are going to outsmart me and everyone else you meet...think again. You may be real bright. I'll give you that. But you are very young, and you have much to learn. You would be well advised to take lessons from those around you that have lived longer and learned much in the process. For starters, you need to have some humility. You may be from great wealth and privilege, I'll give you that...but so far...I have not seen much class...though I'm sure your mother had it, and Lou definitely has it, as well. So either you're going to grow up a fine young lady in this house; or you're going to be branded as a loose woman. What's it going to be? What you do today and the choices you make now will affect your entire future."

"Okay, Graham...honey. She's crying now. I...I think maybe that's enough for now." Dana rose from her chair and came to where the child sat with her hands over her face, sobbing. "I'm sorry...Graham...I'm sorry Dana. I'm so sorry I disappointed you. I won't do it again." She put her hands over her face and continued sobbing.

Dana hugged her. "We forgive you, darling. Now let's ask God to forgive you."

"Okay." She hiccupped and stopped crying.

Dana said a brief prayer.

The child smiled. "I really am sorry. And it wasn't Zoltan's fault. It was all my idea."

"It's forgotten, honey. We'll move on. God forgives and

forgets, and so do we. It will never be brought up again. We'll put it behind us."

A big smile broke over her fact. She reached up and hugged Dana. "You and Graham are the best." She smiled. "I think I know why I did it. It was because I wanted attention...and I wanted to find out how much you and Graham really loved me..."

"Honey, it's all in the past. Let's just forget it."

"Okay."

But that night Talia was unable to sleep. She had lied to Graham and Dana. It had been Zoltan. He'd coaxed her into going to the barn and hiding in the haystack. She realized when she got there that he wanted more than kisses and petting. She'd lied to protect him, wanting to make sure that he would not be persona non grata at Sugarbush. Now she was in a dilemma. Should she fess up and take a chance that they would forgive Zoltan and give him another chance? Or should she leave well enough alone? She tossed and turned for hours, unable to sleep. Finally, she sat bolt upright in bed. Then the tears came. "I'm sorry, God. I'm sorry I lied. I'll confess to Dana and Graham tomorrow." Finally, emotionally spent, she fell into a restless sleep.

The next morning, she awakened, dreading what she knew she had to do. Why hadn't she told the truth to begin with? It would have been so much easier. But no, she had to lie. But the thing that scared her most was how strongly she felt about Zoltan. He was becoming her whole world. Everything came second to him. But she knew God was a jealous God. And he had to come first. She remembered that lesson from Sunday school.

She showered and dressed for school, hurrying downstairs to have breakfast. It was Violet's day to drive them. Somehow, she had to muster up the courage to tell Dana and Graham at breakfast. *Please God, give me the courage to confess my sin.*

Graham looked so handsome today, Talia thought. He

wore a light blue cowboy shirt, jeans and his usual tan cowboy boots. Dana looked cool, too. The vivid pink shirt she wore over jeans looked good, also. Dana's eyes sparkled with happiness. *She likely has early morning riding lessons or training lessons; maybe even jumping lessons. She'd finally gotten back to jumping. Talia knew the story about her brother's tragic death from horse jumping.*

Talia enjoyed scrambled eggs and hash browns for breakfast, along with everyone else. She glanced up at Dana and Graham a few times, trying to muster up the courage to apologize and fess up. . She opened her mouth to speak but no words would come. She lost her nerve.

Dana knew something was disturbing Talia. "Honey...what's wrong? You look so...upset."

Unbidden tears trickled down her cheeks. She dropped her head down. "I lied."

"Whatever do you mean, honey?"

"I told you...that it was my idea to...to go to the haystack in the barn. It wasn't. It was Zoltan's idea. And he pushed it. He sweet talked me into it. I defended him because...I didn't want him to lose visiting privileges at Sugarbush. So I...I covered for him." She dropped her head down and wept.

"Aw honey. You're forgiven. You're both forgiven. Let's just put it behind us."

Graham peered over at Talia. He was becoming very fond her, in spite of her failings. He felt fatherly protection toward her. "I'm proud of you, honey. ..the fact that you had the courage to tell the truth, despite the cost."

"So...like ...is...he...banned from Sugarbush?" She hiccupped.

"No. God has forgiven y'all; and we forgive you. Just forget it ever happened. We have."

Talia smiled. "I'll make you proud of me yet. You'll see."

"I do believe you, honey." Dana smiled. "Gotta go. First lesson starts in ten minutes."

"That's Violet honking. I gotta go, too." Talia grabbed hr jacket and school books and hurried out the door.

"The boys just ran outside to her car. We'll see you after school, honey. I won't be here; but Violet and Graham will be."

Chapter Twenty-Three

Danielle had finally met a man she really liked. She waited until the morning after meeting him to send him the text he requested. "Hi, Brandon, enjoyed meeting you. Danielle." She would let him lead the way. No way was she going to chat him up. If he's interested, he'll pursue her. Chasing men didn't work; and showing too much interest too soon could be a killer too. After all, she'd made a study of all this for her match making business.

Three long days dragged by. She kept her phone close by. But he hadn't called. *So much for the dream man.* She talked to the wall. "Oh fine. Now I've met a great guy and he hasn't even bothered to answer the text he requested I send." She sulked. "Next."

She put her feet up on the ottoman, made a pot of herb tea, found some chocolate cookies to go with it and turned on the TV. Her cell was buzzing. She grabbed it. A hospital name and number flashed on the screen. She answered it. "It's Brandon Scott. I've been in a car accident. I'm at the Cayman Islands Hospital. Any chance you could come visit me?"

"I'm on my way." She didn't have to think twice. She slipped into a favorite pair of slacks and a pink silky knit sweater and jeans. Slipped on white canvas shoes, hopped into the car and drove to the hospital. She rushed into emergency.

After determining that she was expected, a nurse led her

down a hallway to his room. He lay on the cot with his right leg propped up in a hoist. He looked good. A couple heavy bandages marred his handsome face, but she figured he'd soon be good as new. *Thank God he's okay.*

"How's this for a unique first date?" He grinned at her.

I'm in love, Danielle thought. She took in his handsome, rugged face. It was a face that had known life, a face that reflected wisdom, compassion...humor and strength. "What happened?"

"Car slammed into the side of my vehicle, just as I got in. An inebriated woman. My leg jammed against the dash board. It all happened so fast. The woman was charged with a DWI, so the nurse told me."

"So, what's a great guy like you doing single?"

"Who said I was single?"

Danielle's face dropped a mile.

"Just kiddin.' Of course I'm single. My wife...and I...we just never got along. Fought all the time. I never could figure out why I married her. But when she started playin' around that's when I filed for divorce. I've never looked back. Best thing I ever did. She gave me a real sweet daughter, anyway. God knows where my ex is now. She kind of disappeared. Guess we'll hear from her eventually. Brianna, our daughter, lives with Mom. She's twelve. Great kid."

"Where is she now?"

"She's with her grandma. She's fine. Takes the school bus to school every day. I see her as often as I can. She can't stay at my house, because I never know when I have to leave the house to go to a client's home and work with them."

"You're blessed to have your Mom."

"I sure am. So I see Brianna as often as I can. That means turning down work sometimes, if I've invited her over for dinner and a sleepover."

"Sounds like you're busy."

"I do pretty well. Most of my work is at the client's home. Often it's folks who run businesses out of their homes that I work with. I've been called a genius and an idiot." He chuckled. "The idiot comment occasionally get thrown at me after I've fixed the problem and the customer doesn't want to pay the bill."

"Human nature." She shook her head. "I guess when those clients call you next time...I bet you're booked solid."

"True." He grinned again. "It actually works out well for me; because the decent folks are the backbone of my business and the flighty types...I don't want them for clients, anyway." He winced. "Sharp pain."

"I'm sorry you have to go through all this. When will you be released?"

"I'll get the test results later today. That will determine if I have internal injuries. "I think God has healed me, anyway." He peered into her eyes.

"Why do you think that?"

"Because...other than your visit...and my Mom and Brianna's visits...I've been meditating on healing scriptures in Psalms and praying. God is the great healer. I put all my trust in him." His amber-flecked eyes peered at her. "I spend all my time worshipping and praising him. I'm expecting a break through."

She felt like he was looking right through her to her soul. Thrills and butterflies flitted around her stomach. *This beautiful relationship with this great guy seems too good to be true.*

An older nurse that looked burned out shuffled into the room. "Visit is over, ma'am."

She wanted to stay forever. That wasn't possible, of course. "Okay." She peered at Brandon. "Take care. Bye, bye."

He grinned at her, lifted his left hand and pointed his index finger playfully at her, as a parting gesture.

She wanted to rush over to him and throw herself into his big, strong arms and never let go. Instead, she smiled, taking a deep breath. "Bye for now. I'll be prayin' for you."

"You do that, honey." His face lit in a warm grin.

Her knees turned to water. "Sleep well."

The seasoned nurse gave them both a knowing look.

Danielle drove home on a cloud suddenly erupted in a song. *"I'm in love, I'm in love, I'm in love, with a wonderful guy."* She was lost in a starry gaze somewhere near heaven. She felt like she was floating on wings, surrounded by hundreds of angels cheering her on. Was she in a state of euphoria? Seemed that way. If he could make her feel this way after their second meeting... in a hospital, no less...how could he make her feel when they spent quality time together?

Danielle kept right on singing, hitting the high notes, lost in a lover's dream. That's when she heard it. A police siren. She glanced at the speedometer and realized she was seriously speeding. "Oh no." She slowed, pulling over like a good citizen, and then waited for the guillotine to drop.

An officer stood by her open window, a grave expression on his weathered face. "Do you know how fast you were going Ma'am?"

"No sir...I...I don't. I'm so sorry."

"I clocked you at over a hundred miles an hour. The speed limit along here is 80 as the signs indicate." He shot her a sour look and wrote up a ticket, handing it to her.

Though her spirits were somewhat dampened, she drove home wrapped in the memory of the sweet meeting with Brandon. God was in his heavens. Great and mighty things were about to happen. She remembered reading somewhere in the Bible that he stores up blessings for his children. She smiled, looking heavenward. "Lord, I feel your awesome touch. If I ever doubted your love for me, I'm sorry. After meeting this amazing man, I know that you are looking down from heaven and showering blessings on those that love you. *"I don't deserve it, but yet I'm blessed."* That song made famous by Tammy Faye Baker rang through her mind and heart.

After a whirlwind romance consisting of seeing each other almost every night, he proposed. Danielle was over the moon. The next morning, she put in a call to Dana. It was intercepted by Graham who gave her the cold shoulder. "Danielle, I'm happy for you. Best of luck. We'll pray that this marriage works out."

"Thanks. I appreciate that. I was thinking...maybe we'll fly out to Lexington and stop by for a visit. The twins must be so cute..."

"Danielle...this is not a good time. We've become a large family...a lot has happened since you left. I would need to speak to Dana first, but I'm sure she shares my view." Graham didn't trust a word out of her mouth.

"What are you talking about?" She had never known Graham to beat around the bush.

"Danielle, I think it's best that we go our separate ways. There have been all sorts of ugly rumors swirling around about you. We have four sons now and a student from Israel living with us for the next few years...maybe longer. We've moved on. .. started a new chapter in our lives."

"Which doesn't include me...I gather." She sighed. "I'm thrilled you have twin sons. I can't wait to see them. "She put a smile and joy in her voice as she spoke. "Hey, I'm the grandma, remember? And when you meet Brandon...woah... you're going to realize that God really likes me."

"Danielle. We're on overload right now. Look, I'll give it to you straight, Danielle. We're not in the mood to entertain you or meet your new man. There are folks out there who still believe that you had something to do with Dana's kidnapping. And sometimes I wonder myself."

"Well...you sure know how to bring my spirits down. I finally met my dream man, we're getting hitched, and I just wanted to share my happiness with y'all." She felt sour like the words she spat out.

"I appreciate that, Dana. Check out Ecclesiastes in the

Bible. The part where it says that there is a time for everything. Dana and I have talked about this at length. We need to move forward with our lives and go our separate ways."

Danielle was devastated. Dana was her daughter. And she had grandkids she wanted to bond with. He couldn't have been serious about cutting her off. And how had they found out that she was involved with Dana's kidnapping? She'd masterminded it to get cash, of course; but she couldn't fathom where the leak came from. She would continue to deny any involvement in the kidnapping, of course. "Graham, that is beyond outrageous. I *love* Dana, with all my heart."

"I'm not so sure, Danielle. I'm going to give it to you straight. You're jealous of her. Fiercely jealous. It's no secret that you set your cap for me. We don't trust you. Neither Dana nor I trust you, and that makes it pretty much impossible to have a relationship with you. We've talked it over for a long time. It's over, Danielle. We've taken a walk. Good luck with your new man and new life. Just remember one thing, Danielle. What goes around comes around. The Bible puts it another way "With the same measure that you mete withal, it shall be measured to you again." He paused for a moment. "Suffice to say, move on with your life. We've moved on with ours."

Danielle stared at her cell like it was a rare disease she didn't want to catch. Slowly she set it down as the full effect of what he said sunk in. She couldn't cry, couldn't deny the truth of his statement. He was protecting Dana from her. He saw her as a cobra. That night, sleep eluded her. It would be a lonely life without them. She'd been so busy with her new life and friends here that she'd put them on the back burner, thinking she would revive the relationship when she got around to it. Now it was too late. And it was over.

Three sleepless nights later, Danielle knew that she had to repent. Finally, she fell on her face before God Almighty.

That's when she got the idea about writing them a letter. She couldn't confess her crime in writing, that wouldn't be smart, but she could try to make amends that way. She scrapped the idea. Lame. She had a long, tearful talk with God. She hoped it wasn't too late to make amends; though she had no certainly of that. Remorse filled her soul. Was there a way back? *Lord, if there's a way back into their good graces, please reveal it to me. And, Lord...I'm sorry I took them for granted. I'm sorry I used them. I'm sorry for my wickedness."*

"Return to Me and I will return to you." That scripture flashed into her mind. Maybe there was hope.

Brandon healed up swiftly. After a whirlwind courtship, they tied the knot. She moved into his house, a modest two-story home he'd built himself. They settled into a routine. She worked the day shift with Flamingo Taxis, he did his computer consulting, working all hours. Evenings were spent relaxing, cooking together, listening to music, watching movies. Though, of course, some nights he worked, depending on clients' needs. They were compatible right from the start. Sure, she had to make some adjustments; and so did he. But generally, it was a match made in heaven. Until...his sweet daughter showed up.

Brandon had booked off for the weekend, posting that notice on his website. He'd invited Brianna for the weekend with a view to getting to know Danielle and spending some quality time with the two of them. He'd picked up steaks he would barbecue. Danielle would make corn-on-the-cob and a salad. "I picked up chocolate cheesecake for dessert." Danielle commented as she put it into the fridge.

Everything seemed to go well between Danielle and Brianna. The child was clever and precocious. The type of kid that accepted nothing she was told for gospel. She had to check it out for herself before drawing any conclusions. Steely eyes assessed Danielle. "How come you married my dad?" Her lips were clenched together.

Danielle reached over to the child, attempting to take her in her arms. But when the kid shrugged away, Danielle held her ground. "Because I love him...and I want to spend my life making him happy."

The kid's eyes had a steely gaze. "Like...why do you love him? There's lot of guys out there..."

Danielle leaned in close to Brianna. "I think God matched us up. Put us together. Do you believe in God?"

"I don't know. My real Mommy left...and never came back. Even though I prayed she would." Tears sprung to her eyes.

Danielle leaned over and hugged her. "Oh darling, I'm so sorry. She must have had lots of problems..."

"She said I was her only problem. She said I was a mistake. She never wanted kids. She said she hated being married...it was too...restrictive."

"I'm sorry all this happened to you, honey. But God always wants to turn our sorrow into joy. You know that, right?"

"I...I guess so. Maybe. If he's God...well maybe he *does* want us to be happy."

"Tell you what. From now on, we're going to believe that God will pour out his blessings and favor on us."

"Okay." She smiled.

Dinner was delightful, and Brianna was talkative and appeared to be quite happy. But as she was about to go, she started crying and hugging her Dad. "I don't wanna go back to grannie's house. I wanna stay here with you, Daddy..." She hugged him tight, tears trickling down her cheeks.

Danielle's heart broke. *That poor, sweet, suffering child. She missed her Daddy and Mommie. Lord, how can I help her?*

"Couldn't I stay here tonight?" She looked at her Dad with pleading eyes.

"Of course you can, honey. We just have to tell your

grannie that you're here, so she won't worry."

"I wish I could have you all to myself, Daddy." She looked at her dad, sadly, hugging him tightly.

"You mean you wish I hadn't married Danielle, don't you, honey?"

"I guess so." She sulked.

"Honey, a man needs a good woman in his life. Someday you'll understand. It didn't work out with your Mom and me, but that doesn't mean it won't work out with Danielle."

It hit her then. She's afraid to get attached to me. Afraid I might leave, too. "Brandon, if you could make yourself scarce for a while, I want to talk to Brianna...try to bond with her. Show her how wonderful life can be with a new step-mom on the scene."

"She's all yours. There's a football game on I want to catch, anyway." He vanished into the family room, leaving them in the living room to chat.

Danielle put her arms around the child. *Lord, you know how much I need this child. Especially after hearing the devastating news that I'm persona non grata with Graham, Dana and my grandkids.* Tears slid down her cheeks. *The twins must be so cute. Maybe I'll pray for a miraculous change of heart with Graham and Dana.* But could she ever live down the local scandal about her kidnapping her own daughter? *Lord, I know I need to dissolve the ruthless side of me. I need to start fresh. That's why I'm here. Please show me how I can reach Brianna.* It came to her in a flash. Love...that age old truth. *Love conquers all."* Brianna was perched on a bar stool at the kitchen island. Dana sat on the adjacent one. "Want me to make you a Mocha coffee?"

"That would be amazing." She leaned toward Dana, smiling.

"Provided there's chocolate and espresso in the cupboard, of course." Dana took that as a yes and went to work preparing two mugs of mocha coffee. "Brianna.... I'm sure your Mother loves you very much, despite her absence."

"How do you know if she loves me or not?"

"Because, my dear... when a woman gives birth, the love she feels for that baby...is powerful. It could move mountains. Your mom had problems...from what your Dad has told me, they were deep rooted... issues. She ran away rather than having to confront her issues and work through them. But I guess it was the best she could do at the time. Maybe the only way she thought she could survive emotionally. It's hard to understand, honey."

"I want my mommy back. I don't want *you* here. I want my Daddy all to myself. I don't want to share him with *you*." She ran from the kitchen into the family room to find him.

Danielle was crushed. Her world was falling apart; First the confrontation with Graham, now the clash with Brianna. It hit her then why Brianna's mom left. She'd been at the end of her emotional rope. She felt like she was reaching that point herself. Walking on eggs was hardly a healthy way to live.

Danielle drank her coffee and flicked on the TV in the kitchen and watched the news. Then flicked around and watched snippets of a few shows. Sooner or later, Brandon and Brianna would come and find her.

She was wrong. It was over an hour and they hadn't returned to the kitchen. Should she go check on them? Wait here? Go for a drive? Read a book in the living room? As she was mentally sorting through her options, Brandon loomed in the doorway, filling it with his large, male physique. His brooding eyes and half grin did things to her, despite her fear of him. "Hey, wanna join us? We're watchin' the game? Brianna just wanted some time alone with me."

"Sounds good." She felt relieved. She wasn't sure what to expect of him. She moved toward him. He clasped her hand. "She's okay, honey. Just...nervous and confused. She's just a kid. She'll be fine. And...she'll get used to you."

To Danielle's delight and surprise, Brianna cuddled up to her on the sofa, as they all sat together. Joy and hope swept through her.

But the next morning, Brianna ignored Danielle, focusing all her time and energy on her dad who was making French toast with fresh blueberries. It was Sunday morning and Danielle wanted to suggest church for all of them. Before she had a chance to do it, Brandon laid out his plans. "Hey, I got the day all planned out. We're going shopping for Brianna at the mall. Then I'll take the two of you to my favorite Italian café. You'll love it. Then back to the house. I rented a couple of movies from the library. Sound good?" He picked Brianna up and swung her around, playfully.

"Daddy. Daddy. You make me laugh." She squealed with delight.

Danielle winced. *Lord, I wanted to go to church and worship you today. But he's my hubby. I'm supposed to obey him. What do I do now?* She sipped her coffee and silently sought the Lord. She heard that still, small voice in her spirit. *Plan ahead. Put me first. I am a jealous God.* She knew then, that there were dark forces coming against their blissful union, and maybe if she didn't seek the creator with all her heart and mind and soul, this marriage, too, would crumble.

She knew breakfast would be ready any minute, so she began planning for quiet time with the Lord today, despite the busy schedule Brandon had lined up. *Lord, give me wisdom and sensitivity to handle the two of them.*

Breakfast was delicious. She adored men with culinary skills.

Brianna sat next to her dad, peering at him every second when she wasn't actually eating. "What time does the mall open Dad...like on Sunday?"

"11;00. A.m. One hour from now."

"Why is it an hour later on Sunday?" Brianna peered into her dad's eyes, continuing to ignore Danielle.

"Uh. Sunday is the Lord's Day. A lot of folks go to church. We used to take you there when you were young. Do you remember that?" Brandon peered at his daughter.

"No." She looked over at her father. "But I might like to go to church sometime. My friends all go."

"Okay. How about next Sunday, honey?"

She jumped off the kitchen bar stool and ran to her dad. "Cool. We'll do church next Sunday. Like...what time Dad?"

Brandon grinned. "Well, the early service starts at 9:00; late service 11:00. You pick."

"Early service." She smiled at her dad.

"Why?" Brandon was curious.

"Because...when I was little...I remember the Sunday school teacher saying that we should always put God before everything else. So...like...maybe we should start the day out that way."

"Okay, honey. We'll do it next Sunday. That way I can at least put a notice on my website that I'm not available Sunday morning. But I can't guarantee it will be every Sunday, because a lot of my clients are off on weekends and run a second business, sometimes they need my assistance for changes to their websites, etc. My clients and making a living come first. You *do* want me to keep this house don't you? That mortgage has to be paid every month, no matter what."

"Okay, Daddy." She was crestfallen. "But I really like church. I like it...because I feel close to God when I'm there." She smiled, tilting her head. "I can feel him smiling at me."

Danielle realized then that although Brandon had professed to be a believer, if he's admitting that he doesn't put God first, then she needed to have a talk with him. She'd learned that God was a jealous God and he wants first place in our lives. She'd had a rocky pathway to the peace with God she now possessed. She'd thought that serving God for Brandon would be a priority, but she'd just learned otherwise. A scripture flashed through her mind. *"I would that you were hot or cold, but because you are luke-warm, I will spew you out of my mouth." Maybe I jumped in too fast, like the last marriage. What was I thinking?* She silently spoke to the Lord. *I was lonely God. Maybe I jumped in too last. But now that I am married, maybe I can be a catalyst for Brandon to seek you with his whole heart. It's taken me a long time to realize that without you I am nothing and I have nothing. But with God, all things are possible.*

But when next Sunday loomed closer, Brandon announced that there was no way he could do church this Sunday.. He'd already had one of his best clients ask him to stop by Sunday morning to totally revamp his website and work with him on some tech issues.

Danielle sighed. They were having breakfast. It was Thursday morning. Brandon had informed her that he was driving out of the area to service a long-time client who had started a new business, working out of his home. Then he was headed for a meeting with the manager of a local real estate office, to revamp their website. She knew enough about the Word that she recognized this as spiritual warfare. "I'm glad business is flourishing, honey... but who gave you that success?"

"What do you mean? I've been working my tail off for decades to build my business."

"Think about the question." Danielle took a long sip from her mug of coffee, peering into his eyes.

He sighed. "I suppose you mean God. Well, yes… He has blessed me."

"Blessed you? You are nothing without him and neither am I." She shook her head. "And yet you don't have time to go to church, worship and praise Him and thank Him? Without Him, you are nothing. He created you fearfully and wonderfully...and he has great things in store for you. You haven't even scratched the surface yet. You think you're successful, but you haven't seen anything yet."

"What...are you talking about?"

"I'm saying that with God nothing is impossible. He wants us to live with great prosperity and joy; and yet all you want to talk about is chasing down new business on the Sabbath Day, even at the cost of worshipping the Almighty. Putting clients and their needs ahead of God is foolish. You see, honey, when that happens God cannot bless you because he is a jealous God and he demands first place in your life. By putting money before God, according to the Bible, you're actually worshipping mammon."

"Oh, Danielle, you're so fanatical. God understands my need to be on top of things financially and continue to build my business."

Danielle's dispirited gaze bore right through him. He stopped babbling. "You just don't get it, do you?"

"What's that supposed to mean?"

"If you are willing to put Him first, tithe, worship and serve him, *then* you will see an explosion of blessings chase you down. Instead of you chasing clients and bending over backwards to please them; they will be pursuing you."

"Is this some kind of dream philosophy? Of course it would be nice not to have to chase business and have it drop into my lap...but it's a tough, competitive marketplace out there. "

"I'm not suggesting anything to you that I have not personally tried myself. When I lived in Palm Beach, I returned to God with a whole heart...after heading down a lot of blind alleys...well that's when I saw the windows of heaven pour me out a blessing that I could hardly contain it."

Brandon was perched on a bar stool, his long legs straddled on either side. "So what was the deal? What went down?"

"All right, true confessions. I...did some time at a woman's correctional. After that, I had no livelihood, God started opening doors for me and before I knew it, I was running charities and raising huge sums of money." She glanced at him to assess his reaction." I did some things I'm not proud of. I've since repented and sought the Lord with my whole heart. Ultimately, I was issued a pardon by our president, Donald Trump. "

"Ah...now we hear about the skeletons from the past." He appraised her warily. "So...why aren't you still there? And how did you make a living while doing the charity gig?"

"I worked as a wine rep, promoting pricey wines to stores. I did some travelling with that job. My old friend Suzie Allen with whom I lived, introduced me to society dames. They liked me. I came up with some unique, creative ideas for their fund raisers. Before I knew it, I had become one of Palm Beach's most popular, high society fund raisers. My boss happily supplied the fine wines I was representing. Of course a lot of my new friends bought cases of it. By then, I already knew most of Palm Beach's top hostesses...so one thing led to another, and before I knew it, I was enmeshed. I spent all my spare time working on the charity events. It was a busy time."

"So why did you show up here? Sounds like you had a great life in Palm Beach."

"Wanderlust. Just can't seem to settle down. There's always somewhere new I want to see."

He nodded.

"Then...for personal reasons, I decided it was time for a complete change. That's when I showed up in the Cayman Islands."

"You still haven't answered my question. Specifically, financially...when and how did God bless you?"

"Look in the mirror."

"Me?"

"Yes, you. You told me I could run my own business out of the house. I intend to take you up on that. I just haven't decided yet what kind of business I'm going for."

"So...*I'm* your answer to prayer?"

"Yes, I have my own office, which you gave me...a good address. Now, all I have to do is figure out what kind of business I want to run."

"That's easy. I can help you there." Brandon grinned at her.

"Let's hear it." She was all ears. Her dream man was creative, too.

"Well, you've already done the research on matchmaking. You had a couple of bad actors throw you curve balls. Don't let that stand in your way. I'll be here to protect you. It so happens I'm a black belt in Karate." He demonstrated to amuse her.

"Let me think about it. If I don't come up with anything better; we'll do it."

"You're a character, Danielle. I think that's what I like about you. I mean how many women would have the guts to drive taxi? And how many women get to hobnob in high society and meet Palm Beach's elite, including the president?"

Danielle smiled. "God has been good to me."

"So what you're saying is that I haven't scratched the surface with God or his blessings. Is that the message?"

She chuckled. "Pretty much."

But that night, as they cuddled in front of the fireplace, sipping hot chocolate and smooching to the magnificent sounds of Beethoven's seventh symphony, he gave her a piece of his mind. "It's interesting, Danielle; that I have already accomplished a measure of success; while you've been jumping around like a jack rabbit, trying to find out what you want to do in life; and yet, you're the one trying to tell me exactly what *I* should do. Where do you get off at with that condescending mindset?"

His attitude and speech stopped her in her tracks. "Well, excuse me, Mr. Sensitive. I was just trying to make a good thing better. I wanted to inspire you to worship the God that has gifted you with a fine mind and entrepreneurial spirit."

She smiled, shakily. "I've come into a deeper walk with the Lord, and I see the hand of his blessing on my life...I just want the same for you, honey."

"You know what, Danielle? I was doing just fine until you came along insisting I have a problem… and you...and maybe God can solve it. I don't think so. I like things just the way they are. My motto is: If it ain't broke, don't fix it."

Danielle knew it was time to make nice. Slip into her feminine charm. She pulled him close to her on the sofa they shared. She gazed into his chocolate eyes, feeling her heart rate accelerate at his closeness. She inhaled the scent of his spicy after-shave and began to feel warm and fuzzy. *Lord, I'm so glad I'm married to this great guy. Thank you for sending him my way. You know I thrive on challenges. This marriage just might work out.* She took him by the hand and led him to their bedroom.

The next day she overslept. Upon reaching the kitchen, still in her white terry robe, she realized he'd already left for an appointment. She glanced around the kitchen, thinking he might have left a note to indicate when he would be returning. There was none. *Well, since he's designated an office in the house for me, I might as well make use of it.*

She climbed the staircase and went into her new office. Glancing around the stark room, she noted the old desk and a swivel chair. There was also a filing cabinet, which was dusty. Brandon had mentioned his former wife rarely used the office. She could turn it into an attractive, inviting workspace.

She headed back downstairs and made a couple of scrambled eggs and a piece of rye toast. She had breakfast and went back upstairs to see if she could get a vision for decorating the room and inspiration to proceed with a new business venture. She remembered her own lecture. "Put God first. Worship him in the first part of your day. Read the Bible first thing in the morning and pray. Then he will lead and bless and guide your day. *Sorry, Lord. I 'm a work-in-*

progress. She headed back down the stairs to the kitchen, grabbed her Bible from her Tote bag where she stored it. She kept it there so that when she waited for a call to pick up a passenger, she could sneak a few scripture verses in. Then, throughout the day, whether she was banking or working or whatever, she could snatch a few minutes to meditate on scriptures.

If his ex was so flakey, how come she had her own office and filing cabinet? Well, he said she was flighty, he didn't say she wasn't enterprising or clever. "She's a wacko," he'd said.

Her eyes locked onto a couple of cardboard boxes on the shelf in the closet. *Lord, I shouldn't do this. I should leave well enough alone. But some little quirk or hunch caused her to be curious. She wanted to see what was in the boxes.*

She remembered Brandon saying he wouldn't be home for lunch and would be working out of the area for most of the day. If she was ever going to get snoopy, now would be a good time. Better to get this out of the way and then she could focus on worshipping God and reading his word. *So much for her lecture about putting God first.*

She took down the first box, setting it on the desk. Dust particles flew from it. She began carefully riffling through papers. Suddenly, she stopped. Her blood ran cold. There was a copy of a document that looked official...and maybe interesting. She glanced through it, unable to stop herself. She'd always been a curious person. It was obviously a letter from his ex-wife's attorney. She'd cited abuse as the reason she sought divorce. With community property, her attorney told her that Brandon would be forced to refinance the house, so she would be able to walk away with cash, while he remained in the house. *That explains why he's working so hard. He's got a big mortgage. And every time she'd brought up finances, he changed the topic. The abuse issue had her attention. As she continued reading, she realized it was verbal and emotional abuse, not physical. Okay, Lord, I'm late starting my prayers, but I am doing them.* She carefully refolded the letter the way she'd found it and returned the box to the shelf.

An hour later, after praising God, praying and reading scriptures, she heard God's voice very clearly. *Be very careful. You do not know this man. If you had sought me with your whole heart, I would have warned you against him. But you did not. Listen very carefully in the next days, and I will tell you what to do and what not to do.* By this time she had morphed into shock. Ironic that the very lesson she sought to teach Brandon was the exact lesson that she herself needed to learn. She had jumped into the marriage without counselling, without fasting and lengthy prayer, without really getting to know him. And most importantly, without seeking God diligently to find out if marrying him would be wise. *When would she learn?*

Danielle showered, dressed, applied make up and was about to make more coffee, when she heard the glass door to the kitchen open, as Brandon appeared. Surprised, she glanced at him, realizing that he might have deliberately wanted to catch her off guard. If he'd come a few minutes earlier, she would be in big trouble. She masked her concern, always the actress. "Honey, you're home." She moved toward him, hugging him and planting a kiss on his lips.

He grinned, showing perfect white teeth and dimples she hadn't noticed before. "I am. What's for lunch?" He moved to the kitchen island, taking a seat.

"Lunch? Uh...let me take a look in the fridge and cupboard and... wait for inspiration to hit me." She breathed in the scent of his masculine cologne, peering into his dark, mysterious eyes. *I could never be afraid of you.* Still, she heard that still, small voice again. *Be careful. Be very, very careful.* Oh, oh.She spoke from where she stood at the fridge door. "Grilled cheese sandwiches with an amazing salad?"

"Sounds good, honey." He hung his light jacket on the

coat rack by the door. "I'll be in my office. Got a couple things I need to take care of right away. I'll be back in a few minutes."

Over lunch at the white granite counter in the sprawling kitchen area, she peered over at him. *He's too quiet.* Normally, he tended to be gregarious. "Everything going well, honey?"

"Of course. Why wouldn't it be?"

"Just checking."

His eyes narrowed. "You kinda get in my face a bit, you know." He became silent, his mood sullen.

Her heart skipped a beat. "Oh...sorry." They finished their lunch in silence.

His mood had suddenly shifted. Ironically it had occurred just after shed read the equivalent of a warning. It hit her then that his ex might have deliberately left the letter as a warning for his next girlfriend or wife.

Silence.

As Danielle stacked the dishes in the dishwasher, Brandon came up behind her. "Hey, gorgeous. I'm sure glad I married you. You've caused me to rethink my whole agenda."

She turned toward him, surprised. "Really? Like what, for example?"

"Well...I was bitter after the divorce; but now I see that it's the best thing that ever happened to me."

And the best thing that ever happened to your ex, according to her and her attorney. She smiled at him. "That bad, eh?"

"At times. Yes. Other times, she was as sweet as a lamb. But when she went on one of her tirades, throwing pots and pans at me, I had to duck and run for cover."

Danielle resisted the urge to laugh. *I guess there are two sides to every story.* "What do you think it was that finally drove the two of you apart?" She tried to act casual, as she busied herself in the kitchen, cleaning up after lunch, but actually, she wanted to get him talking about his former wife.

"Maybe when she admitted she married me for financial gain...not for love. Though, of course, she later denied that statement."

This gets more and more complicated. What do I do now, Lord? She heard the still, small voice. *Listen and learn. Okay. I can do that.* "Do you think she was in love with you, though?"

"That's a really good question, Danielle. And it deserves an honest answer. No."

"Wow. Must have been a rocky marriage."

His eyes were slits. He hesitated before speaking. "Very rocky."

"What drew you to her to begin with?"

He chuckled. "That's a really great question, too. And the answer is...I don't know. She cheated on me, ridiculed me, took my money...." He shook his head. "It's in the past. Let's not talk about it, honey."

Lord, everything he says is like the mirror opposite from the court documents. Who am I supposed to believe?

Be very careful.

Careful for what? She didn't know. The best she could do was to be a lady, be pleasant, cheerful, nice, accommodating, and avoid anything that might upset or annoy him. She'd walked on eggs before. She could do it again.

One week later.

They are about to go out to dinner and a movie. Brandon was irked that the sweater he wanted to wear was in the cleaners. They were hanging out in the family room watching Fox News, riveted to the latest natural disasters. He wore a black V neck cashmere sweater.

"I don't know why you bring your sweaters to the cleaners to begin with." Danielle shrugged.

"Because I don't have time to do them myself, obviously." He shot her a look which bordered on disdain.

Here it comes.

His eyes were shut. His teeth were clenched. Given the information in the court documents, she sensed he was fighting the onslaught of an attack of rage. How she knew that, she didn't know. But she just *knew.* "Mind if I look in your closet and see if there is another sweater you might prefer to wear?" She knew then, that God had sent her a warning signal when she'd stumbled on the court documents.

"Whatever you like." He shrugged but his mood had clearly darkened.

Danielle marched down to the master bedroom and into his walk-in closet. The upper shelves contained at least ten or more sweaters in various colors. They were nicely folded. She glanced through the sweaters, selecting a green turtleneck and a blue cashmere sweater. She pulled them out, taking a closer look at them. *Woah. This guy is seriously spoiled. The sweaters are obviously very expensive. Guess I'll take these two and see if His Majesty approves of either of them.*

She returned to the family room holding up the cashmere in her right hand, the green turtleneck in the other. "I like the blue cashmere. Does that work for you?"

"Oh. Yeah, those are nice. I forgot about them." He chuckled. "I'm usually so preoccupied, trying to solve other people's business problems, that I forget stuff on the home front."

"Understandable." She smiled, glad to be of help. *Would there be times when she'd have to walk on eggs? Time would tell.*

The next morning, he was in a sour mood. No matter what she did or said, it was wrong. Finally, she knew she needed to get out of the house. Her shift didn't start until 3:00, so she made an excuse that she had a couple things to take care of and drove off in the Pink Flamingo cab. She needed some space to cogitate on the court documents and the warning from God.

She got home shortly after 11:00. P.M. Brandon was watching TV in the family room, drinking a coke, his feet on the large ottoman. His earlier sour mood had darkened. Now, she was seriously concerned. He hadn't shaken off whatever was bugging him. "Is something wrong, Brandon? You seem…kind of down."

He sprung up from the sofa, his voice rising. "Yeah, something is wrong. Everything in wrong. I shouldn't have married you. You're no help at all…"

Danielle fell silent, waiting to see what he would say and do next. "What kind of help are you looking for?"

"Financial, of course. I thought you were a shrewd businesswoman. I thought you were going to reorganize my business and turn it into a multi-million-dollar enterprise; plus I thought you were going to launch a new business. You sold me a bill of goods…told me you hobnobbed in high society in Palm Beach…and all kinds of malarkey. Painted me a picture of some sort of financial whiz. Turns out you're livin' on your last dollars. What do I need you for?" He stood then, towering over her. He looked like a giant, with his large frame hovering over her. He was discontent, moody and snarky. What should she do? *Lord, give me wisdom, please.*

"Okay, so it's all about the money." *That was the only way to get and hold his attention; and the only way to appease him.* How soon could she have the marriage annulled? Regret, like a poisonous fluid coursed through her body. "In plain English; you thought I was wealthy. Is that it?"

"Well, ya. You told me you were from Palm Beach. I couldn't hear everything you said in the loud restaurant, but I assumed you'd bought the Flamingo Cab Company to give yourself a job...because you said you just got to town."

Danielle couldn't help laughing. "Where did you think I

hid the fleet of taxis?"

He lost it then. He rose from the sofa in a black rage and struck her. "You conned me. I should have known."

Be very careful. She heard the warning in her spirit and did not retaliate. *Help me to use my acting talent, Lord.* "I'm going to pour us some drinks. I'll be right back." Danielle hurried out of the family room and into the kitchen. Ever since the warning, she'd left her Tote bag with her car keys in the kitchen, ready for a fast escape. Instead of pouring them drinks, she hurried out the side door and raced to her pink cab. She opened the door and saw him then. He'd followed her to the car. "Where do you think you're going?" He glowered at her.

"To work, of course. I told you earlier." She was already in the taxi, her cell handy in case he got violent. She hadn't told him but said so anyway.

"You said you were pouring us some drinks. You lied. Why did you do that?"

"You said you wanted me to make money. I'm figured I better get to work. "

"Peanuts. That's what you make drivin' cab. We need to talk about you scrapping that job and getting' into something lucrative. I got a few ideas."

"Whatever you say, dear. You're the boss." She smiled "I love you, handsome."

That seemed to calm him down a bit, so she stayed on that tack. "I bet you can direct me into a lucrative business, with your brains and entrepreneurial spirit."

"What time you comin' home?"

"It will be around one. Want me to wake you?" She flashed him a sexy look.

Finally, he'd calmed down. "Yeah."

Danielle drove straight to the airport, parked her cab, went inside, bought a ticket for Louisville, Kentucky and boarded the aircraft. Pixie would pick up the cab. She'd left the keys in the secret place. She wanted out of the marriage.

Fast. She now realized he could blow up and go out of control at the least provocation. She'd jumped into the marriage; she'd jump out. *If only I had sought God's wisdom to begin with. Thank-you Lord, for leading me to the correspondence from his ex.*

Chapter Twenty-Four

Graham, Dana and the rest of the family thrived. Everything was going smoothly, until Zoltan again asked if he could go to a movie with Talia. He said Lila would accompany them as an escort.

Graham asked Talia and Zoltan a few questions and then gave them a curfew. "Enjoy the movie. I'll expect Talia home around 9:30." He peered over at Zoltan. "So you're sure Lila won't mind driving Talia home?"

"She's good with it."

But that night they didn't return home at 9:30 after the movie. By 10:00 Graham was livid. "I'm calling to find out why Talia isn't home, honey." Graham peered over at Dana who was nursing one of the twins in the nursery. "No answer on her cell. Okay, she wants to be this way; we'll ground her when she finally gets home."

By 3:00 a.m. there was still no word from Talia. Unable to reach her by phone, Graham alerted the sheriff. He told him what he already knew, that she would not be considered missing until 24 hours. Graham and Dana couldn't sleep. Instead, they sat up reading scriptures and praying.

"What could have happened to Talia?" Finally, when daylight was breaking, Talia slipped into the house and saw them in the kitchen praying and drinking coffee. She moved slowly toward them, her face downcast. She'd been sobbing. "Hi."

Graham took a deep breath. One look at her told the story.

Dana embraced Talia, holding her close. "Oh darling, I'm so sorry…" She knew Talia had been violated. She was in bad shape. She'd obviously been raped and beaten. She shook as she sobbed, covering her face with her hands.

Horror struck, Graham and Dana scrutinized her. Soon he folded her into his arms and held her while she sobbed. "Honey, what happened?"

Talia continued sobbing.

Dana looked on, sadly. "I think we both know, Graham."

She continued sobbing. Finally, she spat out the words. "Zoltan…raped me…and then beat me up."

It was Dana's turn. She wrapped her arms around the child, soothing her, stroking her hair. "You'll be all right, honey. Thank God you're home." She sighed, as a few stray tears made their way down her cheeks. "I had a bad feeling about him right from the start. Didn't you, Graham?"

He nodded. "Yeah, I did. But then when he played nice, I thought maybe we were being too hard on him. Turns out we read him right in the first place. He betrayed us."

"Don't tell Daddy. He'll be so livid…I don't know what he might do."

"We won't say anything, dear. Don't worry. No need to upset him. It's over. You're safe now. Lesson learned. We'll move on from here."

Talia clung to Dana for the longest time. An idea sprung to Dana's mind. "Tell you what. How about I come and sleep in your bed with you for a while until I'm sure you're fast asleep. You've been traumatized and we wat to give you all the comfort and support we can."

Talia's face lit up. She flashed Dana a big smile. "Oh yes. I would *really* like that. Can we do that?" Then her countenance darkened. "What about Graham?"

"He'll survive. It's probably good for him to do without me for a few hours." She smiled. "We stayed up all night, but we'll probably just sleep a few hours so our systems don't get out of whack. You deserve some extra comfort after all you've been through tonight. I'm cancelling my lessons and driving you to see my doctor as soon as you get up. She'll fit us in. I'll push to get you in for tests as an emergency."

Tears tumbled down Talia's cheeks. She pressed her lips together, nervously.

"The aftermath of a trauma like this can be devastating." She peered at Talia. "Who drove you home?"

"Lila did. She yakked on and on, assuring me it would never happen again. She dropped Zoltan off at her house and then she drove me here. She didn't say much, but I had the awful feeling that it wasn't the first time he misbehaved on her watch."

"We'll talk more tomorrow. Right now, honey, I'm going to run you a hot bath upstairs and bring you some hot chocolate with marsh mellows in it. She took Talia's hand. "Graham's in the bedroom, I'll just tell him what I'm doing and be right back to make the hot chocolate."

Six hours later, Dana woke Talia to tell her they would be driving to see her doctor. "Get dressed, honey. You'll love my doctor. She'll make sure you're okay."

The ground line in the kitchen rang. She moved to the counter where the phone sat, glancing at the call display. LOU STEIN. *How interesting that he's calling when Talia has just survived a trauma.* Maybe he sensed she'd been in trouble. She'd always believed in mental telepathy. She answered the phone. "Hey, Lou. What's going on? Where are you?"

"I'm in New York and I'll be checking into the Hilton in Lexington on Friday. I have a meeting there. And I'm hoping to take you and Graham, as well as Talia for dinner."

Dana took a deep breath. *What interesting timing.* Her mind raced. She would say nothing about the trauma before she prayed and consulted with Graham. "Great. Call us when you get here, if you would."

"Will do." He signed off.

Talia would be thrilled to learn her dad was coming to town. Though maybe he'd already contacted her.

Dr. Sorenson reassured Talia that she was going to be fine. She ran some routine tests and examined her. Back in her office, she said she had no cause for concern, but the tests would verify that.

As Dana drove Talia back to Sugarbush, a peace and joy swept over her. *Lord, thank-you for giving me a daughter. I didn't even know how much I wanted one until Talia showed up in my life.*

Twenty-four hours later, Dana received a call from her doctor that the tests all came back negative. She did not have V.D. That was a relief. The pregnancy tests would have to wait until later.

Dinner with Ambassador Louis Stein was fascinating. He doted on Talia.

Dana basked in the joy of their beautiful relationship. He was a man of very few words. Graham had told her that it was the nature of the beast. Diplomats were notoriously close-mouthed and every word out of their mouths was calculated and assessed before it was spoken. Dana found the man fascinating.

Talia was a perfect young lady with impeccable manners. The evening was brief. They all hugged in the lobby as they waited for Graham's jeep to be brought around to the front door.

On the ride home, Talia was very quiet.

"What's going on, honey?" Dana turned to glance at Talia in the back seat, sensing something was wrong.

Talia was gently sobbing. "I miss Daddy... so much. You... heard... us speaking in French. Well...like he wants me to meet him in New York for a weekend. He's going to let me know what his schedule is..." She smiled big.

Dana turned around in time to see her big smile. *Lord, you are a great and mighty God. And you are so faithful. Satan tried to bring Talia down, but God has inspired her Dad to make time for her, despite his busy schedule, and You protected her body from disease. She was reminded of a scripture. "And if they drink any deadly thing, it shall not harm them." Yes, those persons who love you and follow you are supernaturally protected.*

Violet suddenly announced she was going on vacation. She would find her own replacement to cover for her. Graham and Dana approved of a Mexican couple that would live in temporarily, cook and clean, etc. Violet was heading to New York at the same time that Talia was travelling there. She had worked there decades ago and had always wanted to return for a visit. She offered to accompany Talia.

Danielle had taken the first available flight she could get. It was headed for New York City. Her old stomping ground. She was glad she'd upped her limit on her credit card. New York would be pricey but she'd only stay a few days and move on. She'd always wanted to see some Broadway shows. Visiting The Great White Way was high on her bucket list. Now was as good a time as any to do that.

As the jet touched down at La Guardia, she breathed a sigh of relief. She knew she'd done the right think abandoning the marriage. She knew God would not condone marital abuse. She would pray tht he got the help he needed.

Stricken with wanderlust, she wondered if she would ever be able to settle down. Sometimes she thought that restlessness was because she had never given birth, though of course she didn't know for sure.

Danielle excitedly disembarked, soon checking into the Sheraton hotel on Avenue of the Stars. It was close to the Broadway shows and centrally located. She peered out of her tenth story window, joyfully watching masses of people rushing to and fro. They hurried down the streets, many pedestrians jay walking amongst stalled vehicles; mostly cabs and limos. *New York. I love it.*

Violet loved playing grandma to Talia. They checked into the Hilton at Ambassador Lou Stein's insistence. He said security was excellent there. When he'd learned Violet had offered to chaperone his daughter, he was delighted. He'd texted Talia, telling her to sign their room number for their meals.

Danielle walked down Broadway, sandwiched among throngs of tourists mingled with New Yorkers, hurrying to their destinations. She walked swiftly to the box office and stood in line in the hope of snagging one ticket for any Broadway show for tonight. The line was very long. Then she realized she could likely get last minute tickets on her I-phone. Sure enough, Today Tix App offered that. She got a discounted ticket for $60. On a rush seat for the new musical "Waitress." She could hardly wait.

She was very lucky to snag a single ticket in the back of the theatre for the hot, new musical."

Back in her hotel room, she relaxed, kicking back briefly on her luxurious bed and clicking on the T.V. The news reported continuing disasters, more hurricanes and more earthquakes. *Jesus is about to return. We're living in the last days. I better get my act together and help others see the light before it is eternally too late. She thought of Noah and the Ark. He'd warned all the people of the coming flood that would take their lives. He told them to repent, but no one would listen to him. Instead, they ridiculed him. Then, one day, the rains came and the area flooded. They all knocked frantically on the door of the arc. But God had shut the door. It was too late. Noah was greatly saddened as he heard their frantic pounding on his door. The arc was shut, and God judged the wicked people. None of them survived.* She clicked off the TV. Time to shower, dress and go.

Soon she was ready and headed downstairs where the doorman whistled, hailing a taxi. Sometime later, she jumped in the back seat, excitedly heading for Sardi's and the theatre.

Sardi's pulsed with high energy. She recognized a few famous faces. Lucky to get a seat at the bar, she ordered fried oysters on the half shell and a glass of the house white. The famous theatre hangout buzzed with energy and excitement. She recognized many celebrities coming and going from the famous restaurant.

She thought she was seeing things when she spotted a woman looking identical to Violet, having dinner with a teenager. *I better get some sleep tonight. I'm seeing things. She kept peering toward their table, until she could stand it no longer. Either Violet had a twin or that was her. Never a wilting Lily, she told the bartender to keep an eye on her drink, she wanted to say hello to a friend.*

Violet and Talia were engrossed in conversation and didn't notice her standing over their table.

Danielle smiled. "Fancy meeting you here Violet. You certainly get around." She smiled at her. "Who is the pretty, young lady with you?"

Violet was stunned but quickly recovered. "Well, well, well. *You* certainly get around. Do you live here now?" Violet knew Danielle was moving around a lot.

"I could say the same for you, Violet. What are you doing in New York? Do introduce me to your young friend."

Violet made quick introductions. "What show are you going to see?" Violet knew Danielle was a theatre buff. I snagged a single seat in the back of the theatre for the new musical *I'm Not Looking Back.*"

Violet smiled. "We might as well share a taxi, since that's where we're headed, also. We've been warned taxis are as rare as hen's teeth." She glanced at her watch. "Maybe we better pay our bill and try our luck. If not, maybe we can all walk together. It's not far."

They couldn't find each other during intermission, but when the curtain went down and the resounding noise of enthusiastic clapping filled the theatre, Danielle caught a glimpse of them, hurrying down the crowded isle.

A long row of limos were lined up outside the theatre. Danielle knew from her friends in Palm Beach that frequented New York; that limos were the only way of being assured of a ride. Masses of tourist typically tried hailing taxis. Getting one was close to impossible once the curtains came down on the Broadway shows

Danielle was stunned when she spotted Violet and a pretty young woman step into the rear of the consular vehicle. She thought she was seeing things. She was tempted to try to horn her way in, but thought better of it. Instead, she watched, fascinated as the consular vehicle pulled away from the curb. *Who would have thought Violet had connections like this?*

Still, Danielle was part of the masses of theatre-goers waiting for their limos or taxis. She'd been told it was nearly impossible to snag a taxi after a show.

She could hardly help noticing that the first two luxury cars at the head of the row of limos had government markings which read *Diplomats and Consular offices. In the shaded rear window, she could barely discern the outline of a gentleman.* The chauffeur was at the wheel.

A doorman from the theatre held open the back door of the car. As Danielle stood waiting for the limo she'd booked, she was stunned to spot Violet and Talia step into the back of the official car.

Danielle called Violet at the Hilton the next day. "I had no idea you knew people in such high places. I'm impressed."

"It has nothing to do with me. A young woman named Talia now lives at Sugarbush. Her dad is ambassador to Israel for the United Nations. We're here to meet with him. I'm her...travel companion. Sorry, I have to run."

Danielle called Violet the next day to invite her for lunch. They met at an Italian place Danielle picked out from the small glossy brochure on the desk in her room. She'd have to take two jobs to pay off her Visa bill when she got settled into her new place.

Over lunch, she confessed her deep desire to reconcile with Dana and Graham. Violet listened but didn't say much and didn't make any promises. Seeing her lack of success, Danielle pushed for another meeting. "I'd love to see that delightful young lady...Talia, again. Any chance of that?"

Violet was always fair; and as much as possible, gave people the benefit of the doubt. "I'll suggest it. I can't make any promises."

Over afternoon tea at the Hilton, she got to know the sweet, brilliant Talia. The girl was special. *Really special.* Danielle was impressed that Dana, Graham and her father trusted Violet to be her chaperone. She realized, now, that Violet was a special, shrewd woman. God must have sent her to Sugarbush where she was needed.

Talia had heard snippets of conversation with Dana and Graham and knew that Danielle was persona non grata at Sugarbush. She'd heard them talking about their decision to cut Danielle off from further visits and communication. It upset her. Having been brought up with an Ambassador for a father, she'd learned the power of diplomacy firsthand. Her instincts were to play liaison and get the relationship patched up. Whatever happened in the past was over. She believed in reconciliation. Somehow, maybe by osmosis, she'd gleaned much from her dad. It was time to put that lesson into practice. She didn't know if she had that sort of influence, but she was willing to try. She didn't worry, though. She knew that when she was weak He was strong. She shot up a prayer to God Almighty. *Lord, I'd like to help Danielle become restored to her daughter and Graham. Please show me how I can do it.*

When Talia and Violet returned to Sugarbush, they recounted their fantastic trip, including the unlikely meeting with Danielle.

Violet never knew what Talia said. All she knew was that she should prepare Danielle's room. Danielle was coming to Sugarbush alone. She'd left her new husband.

Christmas was only a few weeks away. Danielle flew out of La Guardia to Lexington airport, rented a car and was soon on her way to Sugarbush.to spend Christmas with Dana, Graham and her grandkids.

Danielle stunned everyone at the dinner table by making a full confession. Yes, she had been instrumental in Dana's kidnapping. She was very sorry and she believed with all her heart, that God had not blessed her because of her wickedness. Though she'd repented in tears many times, she had never humbly approached Dana before, begging for forgiveness and mercy.

After Dana and Graham recovered from their shock and anger, they both knew what they had to do: Embrace her, love her and reconcile. Dana praised the Almighty for sending Talia into their lives. She had not only been the catalyst responsible for their two-million-dollar windfall; but she had also been the liaison for the most unlikely reconciliation imaginable; Danielle's confession and Graham and Dana's total forgiveness.

Danielle was so overwhelmed, that all she could do was praise Jesus over and over for the miracle.

Danielle moved into the old mansion at Sugarbush to help Violet with the cooking and housework and her grandkids. She never heard from Brandon again. She hadn't asked for anything when she'd fled. She'd just wanted out. She knew she'd jumped in too fast. *Jump in. Jump out.* She wasn't going to stay around to find out if her hunch about him was true. Somewhere in her gut, the letter she'd read had clicked in and she believed it was warning from God. She prayed daily that he would get the help he needed, and that God would do a miracle in his life. But she knew her place was to help Dana with the grandkids and the work it took to keep the great, old house they all cherished, running smoothly.

Talia went to the University of Kentucky, majoring in International affairs. She hoped to follow in her father's footsteps. Lou Stein married his fiancé and invited Talia to come and live with them in Tel Aviv as soon as his work as ambassador was completed.

The End

Don't miss the first two books Kentucky Cowboy and Kentucky Dreams

Or

Angel in Shining Armor

Love Found in Manhattan

Marlene Worrall is an actor/ speaker as well as a screenwriter/author. Marlene has adapted two novels for the screen, including her debut novel Angel in Shining Armor. Her memoir On Fire for God will soon be released. She enjoys penning stories that show God's love and forgiveness.

Made in the USA
Middletown, DE
11 April 2019